Rosy Thornton is a Fellow and Tutor of Emmanuel College, Cambridge and a lecturer in Law at the University of Cambridge, with specialisms in housing law, charitable trusts and feminist legal studies. She has published five novels, including *Ninepins* (Sandstone Press, 2012) and this is her first short story collection. She divides her time between Cambridge and the Suffolk sandlings.

By the same author

More than Love Letters
Hearts and Minds
Crossed Wires
The Tapestry of Love
Ninepins

SANDLANDS

ROSY THORNTON

SANDSTONEPRESS
HIGHLAND | SCOTLAND

First published in Great Britain
Sandstone Press Ltd
Dochcarty Road
Dingwall
Ross-shire
IV15 9UG
Scotland.

www.sandstonepress.com

The publisher acknowledges support from Creative Scotland towards
publication of this volume.

ISBN: 978-1-910985-04-5
ISBNe: 978-1-910985-05-2

Cover design by Antigone Konstantinidou, London.
Typeset by Iolaire Typesetting, Newtonmore.
Printed and bound by Totem, Poland

*In fondest memory of John Thornton (1935–2014),
who loved the Suffolk countryside.*

ACKNOWLEDGEMENTS

Four people read these stories in draft and encouraged me with the project: Victoria Best, Julia Chellel, Robert Dudley and of course Mike Gross. Louise Fryer ran her usual eagle eye over the text. My editor, Moira Forsyth, believed in me and gave me the benefit of her patience, precision and insight. I trust they all know how very grateful I am.

CONTENTS

THE WHITE DOE

The first visitation occurred in January, very early one morning.

They came from the Seven-acre, which still bristled with the ruined stalks of last year's barley, up the grass bank and through the patch of scrubby fruit trees that Fran's mother had referred to as 'the orchard', before joining the track beyond the cottage and heading out to cross the road and regain the woods. In summer, the deer rarely ventured out beyond the cover of the woodland, sticking to the secret, shady places to raise their dappled young. But in the winter months, hard ground and sparse fodder forced them out into wider orbits, crossing field and farmland along well-trodden pathways – the same old ways followed, no doubt, by their mothers and grandmothers.

At the top of the bank, each animal in turn crested the ridge with an identical movement, half lurch and half leap, head lowered and withers high. Five of them, six, eight, dark shapes on a pale canvas, and then there she was towards the back, not much more than a gap in the line, a movement, a reflection. There was a low mist, and in the bleached half-light of the winter predawn

1

she was almost invisible, white upon white. Fran's angle of vision also had a strange foreshortening effect, from where she leant with thighs hugged to the radiator at her bedroom window while she psyched herself to move and head along the ice-cold landing. Through the steamed-up glass the doe, that first time, appeared insubstantial, even ethereal. For a full minute after the deer had gone Fran stood stock-still and almost unbreathing, before a shifting behind her from the bed told her Mark was awake.

His eyes were screwed up, swollen with sleep. 'What is it? You look like you've seen a ghost.'

There was no wonder they were the stuff of mythology, she said to him later, over supper. The aberrant and anomalous, endowed by uncomprehending humans with magical meaning.

'Isn't there one in the *Morte d'Arthur*?' He broke off more bread, refilled his own wine glass, then hers. 'I remember it vaguely from school. Gawain gets sent off to hunt for it or something. One of those quests they were always having.'

'Yes, but that was a stag, I think. The white hart – like the pubs. A hart is a male deer, isn't it? Mine was a doe.'

His attention, however, had shifted to more empirical ground. 'We should look it up. See how uncommon it is. I wonder if it's an albinism thing, or some other genetic quirk. Probably a recessive gene...'

Fran's mother would have shared her curiosity. Ever the hoarder of washhouse tales, both earthly and supernatural, she was also the self-appointed chronicler of family folklore. Birthing stories were her favourite – a grisly pleasure quite at odds with her otherwise mild, fastidious nature. There was Fran's cousin Tom, who, born in the days before rhesus immunoglobulin treatment, had to be snatched from his waiting mother's arms and, according to the established account, his infant blood drained out and replaced in its entirety. But for this, Aunt Pamela's antibodies would have cannibalised her child.

Then there was Fran herself, a breech presentation whose head stayed stubbornly lodged. When with the aid of forceps she finally emerged, the doctor and midwife could not suppress the recoil of horror at the monster they had delivered – a monster with a second head. What they saw, of course, was no such thing, but a ball of superfluous cartilage and soft tissue attached by a strand of skin: a simple birth defect, removed with a snip to leave only a tiny nubbin close to her left ear.

'I wanted to call her Miranda,' her mother would relate to anyone who'd listen. 'My own little marvel. And the doctor said, for a moment back there we thought that Hecate might be nearer the mark.' Then her grin would soften to a reminiscent smile. 'It was her dad who insisted on Frances.'

There was no chance of a similar shock with the birth of her own daughter twenty-eight years later. By the time of Fran's confinement, obstetric ultrasound ensured that the image of her incipient daughter had been imprinted on her heart from twelve weeks' gestation. In any case, there was no story to be told there: just the routine misery of twenty-four hours' grinding contractions followed in the end by the caesarean she had opted against a lifetime earlier, so that when Mark leaned to lay Libby on her breast – her heart-blood, her life's consuming joy – she was almost too exhausted to greet her.

The appearance of the white deer, Fran discovered, was sometimes a divine manifestation. In eighth-century

3

Ardennes, Saint Hubert rode out to hunt on the morning of Good Friday when he should have been at prayer, only to encounter an admonitory apparition – the Holy Spirit in cervine form, which warned him back to the path of piety. But it was a white stag in that story, too. The haloed creatures portrayed on the Internet seemed all to be crowned with majestic antlers.

For the Lenape people along the banks of the Delaware River the Great White Deer was a spirit to be venerated, even though this lesson was one destined to be learned over and over by the young men. I'll be the one, would brag the youths of each successive generation, I'll be the one to slay the Great White Deer and carry home his pelt. It was the women of the Lenape who understood the truth: that the creature was their talisman and never to be harmed. Mothers would follow their sons out on the hunt, and wives their husbands, and when they saw the White Deer would seize their arrows from them, and stay their hands upon the bow. Always *his* pelt, though. The Great White Deer was a buck.

Fran found only one tale in which the animal was female, and it was this one that particularly haunted her. Its source was an old French folk song, the lament of the *blanche biche*: the white hind, or doe. She recalled having heard it many years earlier at university, on a cassette tape belonging to an exchange student over from the Sorbonne. The ballad tells of a young nobleman by the name Renaud, who nightly hunts for deer for the table with his dogs. His sister, the fair Marguerite, dares tell no one that she is under an enchantment, compelled by night to roam the forest in the form of a white doe. Going to her mother, she implores her to tell Renaud that he must not shoot the white doe. In spite of this, the brother and his huntsmen are drawn to the mysterious creature, and

4

at the third blast of Renaud's copper horn, she is brought down. While in the kitchens the white doe is quartered for the spit, the cook marvelling at the fairness of her skin, the company are all seated at breakfast but for gentle, blonde Marguerite, who is nowhere to be found. As the search party reassembles, empty-handed, a voice is heard to echo from the castle walls. *My head is on the serving dish, but my heart is cleft in two, my blood smears the kitchen and my bones lie charring on the black coals.*

There were more sightings after the first. Several times she glimpsed the herd in the woods, away to the left of the path. Twice they moved almost in step with Fran but along a parallel ride, separated from her by a band of silver birches; on another morning they had gathered to graze in a small open area, cleared in the autumn by volunteer coppicers. Always it was the white doe that was visible before her sisters, whose coats bore the same muted grey-brown hues as the winter woodland.

February brought an iron freeze that silenced nature's soundtrack and drew all evidence of life to a standstill. The mercury sank below zero and stuck there, night and day, for the best part of a fortnight. It was too cold for snow. At the forest margins, the leaves stood crisp and edged in white, like bereavement cards in negative; deeper in, the frost was colourless but its grip no less complete. The sand of the path was set to a crust which hardly yielded under the weight of Fran's boots, the patterns of past patterings and scurryings preserved there in a strange suspended animation. Of the deer there was no sign.

When, with the thaw, they made their reappearance it was quite sudden and at unexpectedly close quarters, as Fran was walking early on the road to the village. First one then another, they erupted from a field entrance barely five yards in front of her, their hooves striking an alarming clatter from the metalled surface; she stopped where she stood and waited for the whole string to follow, nine of them in all, then watched as they crossed the road at an angle away from her before shouldering through a gap in the hedge at the other side. It was curious how ungainly they appeared at this unaccustomed proximity; no longer the graceful spectres of the forest glade, they seemed clumsy, earthbound, heavily bovine. And the white doe was no pale ghost but specked and spattered with mud, the fur of her belly matted and yellowing.

She's solid, thought Fran, with a pang that was almost disappointment. Fleshly; a thing of the flesh. They used to call meat 'flesh', didn't they, back in those less queasy days? *Bring me flesh and bring me wine.* For an instant Fran caught the flash of Renaud's hunting knife in the firelight of the castle kitchen. When she closed her eyes she saw the blade as it sliced through hide to part the tender tissue beneath – dividing sinew, jarring against bone – and Renaud's great wooden table, slick and darkly stained.

Yes, her mother would have been the one to tell. But it was six months now since the funeral and the cramped gathering back at the cottage, with too much turmeric in the coronation chicken and not enough chairs for the elderly to sit down. And then there was the bleak task of sifting through her things. Fran had cleared the bureau and one wardrobe before losing courage, then boxed and bagged the remainder without examination and moved them to the attic here, where their weight pressed down from above, heavy on her conscience and her heart. For once in her life she felt the loneliness of being an only child.

Libby would have lent a hand, but she had to get back to New York. 'Let me help,' Mark had offered, and meant it. He would be bracing, she knew, robustly practical, piling black sacks for the tip. And she would be grateful for it – but not just yet.

Friends were coming for supper and Mark was thumbing his Fearnley-Whittingstall.

'What is it, again, that Jo won't eat?'

Fran couldn't remember. 'Prawns?' she hazarded. Something with shells, or maybe tentacles. 'Squid?'

'And is veal still blackballed, now they've stopped with the crates? There's a recipe here where you cook it slowly in milk with sage and lemon peel, and the lemon makes it thicken and clot. Mind you, it's a bit near the knuckle – boiled in its own mother's milk. Like that Mexican thing, or is it Filipino, where you serve the unlaid hen's eggs inside the mother hen. It's all enough to make you want to go kosher.'

Fran laughed. 'Just as long as it's not venison,' she said. 'I don't think I could stomach that just at the moment. Let's not have venison for a while.'

During dessert the conversation began to fragment, crazing like a shattered mirror into a kaleidoscope of jagged, disconnected shapes – a sure forewarning of one of her migraines. Mark somewhere in the far distance, telling an anecdote she had heard ten times before, about the first time she'd brought him home for tea. 'Fran's mother was like a vixen with her cub. She wax-polished the shoes I'd left by the door. Her version of scent-marking.' Then Jo, drifting in and out of focus with some medical folk tale from the Internet of vanishing twins: of fetuses, dead *in utero*, reabsorbed by their surviving

7

sibling. Jo's husband, Lucas, with a sudden flare of laughter, which appeared to Fran as vivid purple, shot through with scarlet. And Mark again, suddenly close at hand and abnormally amplified, asking her if she was all right.

The migraine took hold in earnest later that night after their guests had gone home. These episodes had been with her for as long as she could remember, but were worse since her mother's death. They began always in the same way, with a faint, unfocused tingling below her left temple, close to the joint of the jaw. The tingle would gather and locate itself into the first sharp pinprick of pain, bright as a point of light, experienced almost visually in her crackling nerve endings. Sometimes, just occasionally, she could halt its progress if she massaged the side of her head, tracing the hairline slowly with bunched fingertips, up from jaw to brow and back again, up and down, pausing only to linger now and then over the vestigial protrusion of cartilage. More often, the pain splintered and blossomed and spread until it exploded in a starburst of colour, depriving her of sight and filling her head with searing white fire, so that all she could do was retreat to a curtained room to lie down and wait for it to pass.

'She's a martyr to her headaches, poor thing,' her mother used to say. 'Always has been.' When Fran was small she would sit by the bed and make her close her eyes, laying a wet flannel across her lowered lids. Cold water would find its way in runnels down the sides of her ears, dampening her hair and soaking the pillow. But heat and cold were topsy-turvy, indistinguishable one from the other, as in the dislocation of a fever.

'Mum,' Fran murmured now, though she knew that the figure by the shrouded lamp was really Mark.

8

Allez, ma mère, allez bien promptement lui dire... Go, my mother, go at once and tell him, to call off his dogs until tomorrow at noonday.

But still she was brought down; at the third blast of his copper horn, she fell.

Some days later Fran was in the attic, hunting out some old jackets of Mark's for the church jumble. Not that she was a congregant herself these days; recently with greater distance the mysteries of the broken flesh seemed morbid to her: grotesque, the ritual sharing of the body and the blood. But the rector was young, female and highly persuasive. Pushed low under the eaves along one side was the line of boxes from the clear-out at her mother's. Just a quick start on one or two while I'm up here, is what she told herself. Little by little: it might be more painless that way.

The nearest box, which had once held twenty-four packs of Cadbury's chocolate fingers, surprised her with its weight when she dragged it towards her. Books, was it, from the sitting room bookcase or the many piles beside the bed? Only six months, but the packing was a distant fog. When she slit the parcel tape with her fingernails and raised the flap, she saw that it was filled with assorted fat brown envelopes, the mainstay of her parents' filing system. The top one disgorged nothing of greater interest than a decade's worth of insurance documents: car, vehicle breakdown, home and contents. The next looked like old bank statements. But the one beneath that was bleached with age, soft as tissue and worn at the corners – altogether more promising.

The first thing to slide out when she tilted it towards her was a small index card, printed across the top with the name and crest of the Ipswich Maternity Hospital,

9

pale pink ruled in grey, filled in by hand with a blue-black fountain pen. Pink for a girl: it must have been how they catalogued them then. It bore her own name, Frances Ann, together with the date and time of delivery and her weight at birth: 6 lb 12 oz. Babies were so small, so fragile. Libby had been 7 lb 9 oz.

Attached to the card by a paper clip, which left behind a double rust-edged groove when she pushed it aside with her thumb, was a small passport-sized print – her first 'official' photograph. Staring down into her own infant eyes, Fran was struck, in the angle of the brows, the familiar lines of nose and mouth, by something she must always have known but had never really seen before, or never this clearly. Her own asymmetry; her own essential incompleteness.

The final encounter came towards the end of March. A long-delayed spring had finally crept in and taken the woods unawares. The carpet of moss bordering the path had brightened in a matter of days from khaki to emerald, and the creak of timber in the wind had given way to birdsong. The early warblers would be returning soon; last year it was not yet April when Fran heard her first chiffchaff. The tired winter celandines would be smothered by swathes of wood sorrel and pink purslane.

Everywhere buds fattened, but for now both canopy and scrub were still as sparse as January, letting through broad shards of sunlight to warm the forest floor. It left the deer with little chance of camouflage and she saw them straight away, clustered in the coppiced clearing. For a moment, just long enough for anxiety, she thought the white doe was not with them, but then the group shifted and she became visible, standing slightly apart from the others, away to the rear. Her head was raised and turned in Fran's direction, her ears alert with communion – or warning.

The pain arrived from nowhere, a sledgehammer blow. No migraine had ever come like this before, detonating all at once in an intensity of brilliant light, which arced and leapt in tongues of flame from its source at the left side of her head. Every nerve receptor, every synapse was on fire. She clenched her eyes tight closed and clamped her hand hard over her ear but nothing could shut out the pain, the unbearable, all-consuming pain.

Nor could it hide the slash of the hunter's knife, the slice of the surgeon's scalpel, which parted flesh, which severed, divided. She felt its full force, the fatal blow: the final cutting away. *My heart is cleft in two.* Then she sank to her knees, there on the path among the trodden, rotted leaves, and doubled over, both hands clawing to bury themselves in the crumbling mould. Earth to earth. *My bones lie charring on the black coals.*

And slowly, slowly, as pain released its grip, so her tears at last began to fall, tumbling to join the moisture of the dark soil, while away in the trees, half hidden now, the white doe lowered her head, exhaled a soft, sweet breath, and nosed with her muzzle at a clump of coppiced twigs in search of the first green hazel shoots.

HIGH HOUSE

Folks who aren't from hereabouts – seedypuffs, as my old neighbour Kezzie Hollock calls them, blown through on the wind like dandelion down – always make out that Suffolk's flat. Well, it might be true of some parts, over westwards past Bury or up there in the Breck. But my Suffolk's not flat at all. There's no field I know without some kind of a rise to it, a top hedge and a bottom.

You only have to think for a minute to know there's nothing flat about us round here. There's not a lane you can take when you walk out from the village that doesn't have a climb in it here and there – enough to notice on a warm day when you've got to my age and have a bag to carry – and between the climbs there's always a dip. There's the valley itself, of course, where the land slopes down to the Alde. But even to the south and east, away from the river, there are places that lie low, stubborn places where sand collects in summer and where the water backs up murky brown in the mornings after a night of rain. Oh, yes, you'll need your wellies on, whichever road you're taking, if it's come down heavy overnight.

It's why I like to be out and walking, even though I'm on my feet all day with the hoover, at my various houses.

Not the puddles, I mean; I could do without them. No, it's the ups and downs I like. Always a new view round every corner. Not what you'd call a view, of course, if you went on those coach tours like Mrs Fitzpatrick does with the Air Vice-Marshal, and shows her slides at the Mothers' Union: Switzerland or the Italian lakes. But still, there's always something to look at that's not just flat to the sky; when I stay with my sister Barbara up near Lynn it fairly drives me crazy, all those miles and nothing to see. It might not be the Matterhorn but to my thinking you could go a long way and not see anything as pretty as the bit of a sweep below the road to Snape: the river winding through the flood-meadows between its stands of reeds, and often as not half a dozen wild geese, grazing alongside the cattle.

The village itself is a cheerful sight, too, on its little hill that's more of a hummock, with High House sticking out at the top. I say 'the village' but ours is a village with no proper middle; if seedypuffs stop in their cars and want to know, 'Where's Blaxhall?' I never know quite what to tell them. There's Stone Common and Mill Common and Workhouse Common, and the row of flint cottages on the road down to Parmenters. Then there's St Peter's with the rectory, the Yews and Church Cottage, and another cluster by the village hall, not to mention all the outlying farms. But when I picture 'the village' it's the houses between the pub and the old school that I have in mind: the nearest we have to a street. They're on both sides of the road there for a short way, before you come to the allotments, and added to that there's the stretch along the lower road from the pub to where the post office used to be. There must be twenty or thirty homes in all in that small patch. Whichever way I'm coming at it, that's the view I think of as Blaxhall, with the L-shaped red roof

13

of the Ship Inn at the bottom and at the top that double oblong of High House with its barn at the side.

'You can't miss it.' That's what Mr Napish always says to people, with that sudden awkward laugh of his that he smothers in his beard so fast, you can't quite be sure if it wasn't just a cough. It's what he said to me, that first time on the telephone when I rang about his advert. 'I'm at High House,' he said. 'You can't miss it.' Though in my case, of course, I knew the place already, as I pointed out: I've lived in Blaxhall more than sixty years, I told him. 'Well, if you ever forget,' he said, 'you'll be all right. Just look upwards and there it is.'

He's not one of the snooty ones, isn't Mr Napish. He might be hesitant until he gets to know you, but he's never been standoffish. It must be two years now since I've been doing for him, and he'll tell me anything. He talks about all sorts. And he always makes me coffee, every time. Not like some I could mention: there's one or two who'll put the kettle on and make a cuppa for themselves and it's like I'm not there, even though I'm right beside them polishing the taps. I'd rather get on by myself in an empty house than work round some of them – and it might as well be empty for all they speak to me. But Mr Napish makes a pot of coffee every morning sharp at eleven o'clock. It's one of those smart Italian chrome contraptions that heats on the gas, and he's liberal with the coffee measure, too. I've never liked to tell him that I like my Mellow Bird's. The first time, I took a sip and started on the kitchen worktops, but he wouldn't be having that. 'No, no,' he said, 'it's break time. Elevenses. Come and sit down,' and he opened a packet of garibaldi.

I know a lot of retired folks who like to keep busy, to keep a structure to their day, and Mr Napish is one of them. He's often reading, in his study or at the kitchen table, from one of his mountains of books, or else he's out in that barn. I'm not sure what it is he does out there; he must have some sort of a workshop, the hours he spends. I dare say he's tinkering, the way men like to do. But rain or shine, inside or out, he stops what he's doing on the dot of eleven and puts on his pot of coffee.

It was over our elevenses one day that he told me about High House, and how it came to be there. He was quite an important man who had it built, and the barn as well, back in Victorian times. An engineer, it seems, who designed the sluice gate by the bridge at Snape, and others like it all up and down the coast. I never thought much about those sluices before I met Mr Napish. 'They're what keeps your feet dry,' he said, with that swallowed-up laugh in his beard. Without them, he told me, salt water from the estuary would run in and flood the valley on every high tide, and not only the Alde either, but the Deben and the Blyth, and Butley Creek, and Minsmere Old River and the New Cut. 'Half the coast would be under water.'

'I wonder if that's why he built his house up here,' I said, 'on the highest piece of ground for miles around? To keep his feet dry?' But Mr Napish didn't laugh this time; he just nodded gravely and said nothing.

This week it seems to have done nothing but rain. I set off on Tuesday to walk to the rectory to tidy round for Mrs Jackaman before her prayer group meeting in the afternoon. I can never bring myself to call her Kimberley, however much she tries to make me. It's Reverend if she's in her dog collar, or Mrs Jackaman in her pyjamas – and I had to double back and go right round by Stone Common. The road past Bellpit Field was flooded as it often is, but the lane up from the level crossing was also awash. Not just a short stretch like sometimes, that you can squeeze past by hugging the hedge on one side, but a great expanse of water, dark and swirling with a scum of white on it like you get on the sea, complete with little breakers whipped up by the wind. It looked deep, as well, deeper than the tops of my wellies. To get around it you'd have had to clamber across the ditch a good way back and tramp three sides of Willett's meadow in a long detour, and even then you'd be half drowned in mud. Mr Willett's poor cows were huddled together in the far top corner looking forlorn, on the only patch of grass that was clear of the mire. I didn't risk it; I couldn't be dripping on the rectory carpet.

'At least I know I can always get to you,' I told Mr Napish the next morning. 'You'll always be high and dry up here.'

That's when he told me about the coastal floods of 1953. Not that they were caused by the rain, or not by the rain alone. It was a lot of factors, he said, all coming together at once. A *concatenation of circumstances*, he called it; he does use some lovely words. Extra high spring tides struck land already saturated by the winter's rainfall and then, on the final night of January, a northerly gale blew in off the sea, driving the swell before it and raising the water to a great surge fully eighteen feet above its normal tideline. At Felixstowe, he told me, thirty-eight people died.

He knows all about it, Mr Napish, because it's what he did for a job, before he retired. An engineer, he was – just like the man who built his house. He worked for some government agency or other, based up in Lowestoft, and his job was to stop the flooding. 'Maintaining the coastal defences' is how he put it, and I said he made it sound like the pillboxes, in the war. That made him laugh. 'It was the sea we were trying to keep at bay,' he said, 'not the Germans. Mind you, it was always going to be a hopeless task. We were like so many King Canutes. It was only ever a matter of time.'

Nor was it just around these parts either, the flooding in '53. The whole of the east coast was hit, from Scotland down to Kent. Across the water, too, on the opposite shore They had it even worse over there, in fact. *Watersnoodramp* was the word the Dutch used for it – Mr Napish wrote it down for me so I could remember it – and two thousand of them drowned, poor souls.

I laid down my coffee cup and stared at him. 'So many?'

'They didn't have the forecasting we have today,' he said. 'The storm surge came with little warning, so people were unprepared. It's different now. We know it's coming. We can take precautions.'

From what I read the next day in the parish magazine, they're taking them already. Every village, it said, must have a designated Emergency Planning Co-ordinator. For Blaxhall the job belongs to Raymond Ketch, the publican at the Ship. He's got the right face for it, at least, has Raymond. Never mind 'Cheer up, it might not happen' – he always looks as if it just has. I had a giggle with Kezzie Hollock when we read about it.

'Is that the emergency plan, then? Get everyone into the pub? Or do those pen-pushers think it's an actual ship?'

'Ha! We'll all hole up in the bar until it's over, and drink to forget our troubles.'

Mr Napish didn't laugh when I told him the story. 'The drowning of sorrows,' he said, and I didn't know if he was joking or not. You can never tell, with a beard.

For all he's a talker once he gets going, it's nearly always about things. That's often how it is with men, I find.

17

It'll be more likely the new rail timetable or Japanese knotweed than their chilblains or the grandchildren. I asked him once how he found retirement and all he said was, he'd been glad to stop shaving. So he must have been retired a while, by the quantity of growth. It makes me think of that Limerick my old dad used to recite to me. 'There was an old man with a beard, who said, "It is just as I feared...".' I shouldn't be the least surprised to find there were larks in there.

He's not one for family photographs either – not like some of my houses, where I'm dusting nephews and cousins enough for Queen Victoria. No... I'd call him a private man, and perhaps a lonely one, too, though he never seems exactly what you'd call sad. He's a widower – he's shared that much – with three sons, all married and moved away. So now he has just his cats for company. They're great fluffy cushions of cats, both of them: pale orange Persians with snub noses and a complaining tone of voice. Enlil is the tom, and Ninlil his lady friend. Daft pair of names, to my thinking, but they're daft-looking cats, and he had a sort of reason for it. 'Enlil and Ninlil were the creation gods in Sumerian myth,' he said.

'Sumerian? But I thought your cats were Persian.'

'Sumeria – southern Mesopotamia – was on the Persian Gulf.' He showed me in the atlas. 'This area here – in modern day Iraq.' He could have been a teacher if he hadn't been an engineer.

They hate the wet, those cats – another pair who like to keep their feet dry. We had another soak last night and there were puddles standing even up here this morning, on the front lawn at High House. There was Ninlil as I came up the path, picking her way across the grass with a distasteful shake of the paw at every step. She looked up when she saw me and gave me a glare of deepest umbrage, as if it were her own best carpet and I'd knocked a bucket of bleach across it.

'Hello, Puss,' I said, but she turned her head away. Neither of them answers to Puss.

Mr Napish was at the kitchen table looking at a map. He loves his maps; he has them on his bookshelves by the dozen. This one was a map of England with patches round the edges coloured blue, like the sea but one shade lighter.

I stopped a minute and leaned to take a look. 'What's this of, then?'

It was only politeness really, but his answer had me intrigued: 'It's a map of the future.'

I put down my Mr Muscle. 'What do you mean?'

It was a map, he explained, of what the coast will look like if the sea level rises the way the scientists think it might. And very strange it'll be, too. Barbara will have to move house, for a start: King's Lynn will be swallowed by the Wash along with half of Cambridgeshire and Lincolnshire, and the Norfolk coast up past Hunstanton. We'll be on a little island here, according to this map. The Deben and the Alde will join round behind us to cut us off from the west, with Aldeburgh to the north completely under water and Woodbridge to the south a seaport.

'So this will be with the global warming, then?' I asked him. 'Melting all that Arctic ice?' But it turns out it's not so simple.

'Temperatures are rising, certainly,' he said, 'because of our burning fossil fuels. The polar ice caps have begun to melt. But that's not the only factor.' It's another of those concatenations of his, it seems. There's something in the feel of the word that makes it right for upheaval on this biblical scale, this invasion by the sea. A conquest and a cataclysm. 'There's more to climate change as well. Erratic rainfall patterns, more frequent storms.'

He's right there. They were saying on the radio only this week that it's been the rainiest November since measurements began, and it seems like it's always some new record or other, these days. The hottest, the coldest, the windiest, the wettest.

The strangest thing he mentioned was one that was new on me, a thing he called 'continental tilt'. I'm not sure if I quite understood it, but apparently the land is still moving from back when the North Sea formed and divided us off from Holland, all those millions of years ago. Scotland is slowly rising further from the sea, while down here in East Anglia we are tipping into it, a little more each year. Two millimetres, he reckoned, which might not sound a lot but it was enough to make me feel slightly giddy, the whole idea. I sat down on the chair next to his.

'Dredging,' he said, as well.

'I beg your pardon?'

'All the offshore dredging there has been, clearing shipping lanes and taking sand and gravel for construction. It gradually undermines and destablises the coastline. It means that when storms wash away the sand and shingle from the beaches it settles and stays to fill the voids instead of being washed back up by the next onshore gale.'

Like at Dunwich and up at Covehithe, I thought, where the sandy cliffs are disappearing by feet and inches. But that's been going on for centuries, before the modern dredgers. I asked him, and he nodded, frowning. 'It's the scale of things that's different,' he said. 'The pace of change.'

The giddiness came back. I think it was the way he spoke the words, and all that pale blue on the map, but I had a sudden image of us running towards the cliffs ourselves, of toppling over them in a tumble of sand, of being swallowed by the waves.

And that's another problem, he told me: the sand. We have no hard rock here in Suffolk. The coast is all shingle beaches, soft sandy cliffs and dunes, and low salt marshes lying open to the sea. For most of its length there's not even a sea wall. 'The old wooden groynes are being eroded, too, or covered by the rising sea.'

'Couldn't they build some more?' I hoped the question wouldn't offend him: it had been his job, after all. But he didn't look offended, only a bit preoccupied, as if his thoughts had strayed elsewhere. And then he laughed – his sudden laugh, quickly smothered. 'The battle is lost,' he said. 'The policy's one of "managed retreat".' And I remembered King Canute.

'There's one thing about the sand round here, though,' I said presently, to break the silence as much as anything. 'It means when it does rain the water drains away again quickly.' It's true in my own garden: you go out after a shower and there are puddles all over and an hour later they're gone. Or you can come in with what looks like mud all over your wellies and stand them on the mat; as soon as they're dry it just falls off them. They're clean again without a wipe, and there's just a pile of fine grey sand to sweep up.

It's different with the roads and fields, though, those places where it floods. I'd come by one of them again that morning on the way to High House, on the lane that leads down to the level crossing. There was water standing right across the road and into the entrance to Joe Wakeling's big beet field. To get past I had to scramble through a gap in the hedge and pick my way round in a wide circle through the beet tops. Even then I was hopping from ridge to ridge across furrows half full of cold, black liquid. Kezzie Hollock claims it's the big machines they have nowadays, the harvesters and loaders and those great wide tractors that crush you into the bank if you meet them on our narrow lanes. She reckons they're too heavy, so they compress the soil and wreck the drainage, and too wide, so they flatten out the grips and gullies all along the verges. I asked Mr Napish what he thought to Kezzie's theory, and he stroked his beard and seemed to be giving it consideration. But I think he was actually miles away. His eyes were back on his map, and he just said vaguely, 'Perhaps.'

When I was doing the dining room later on and I looked out of the French windows, I was surprised to see that the lawn had barely drained at all. The cat was gone but the puddles were still there.

Mr Napish was right twice over. He was right we were due for another tidal surge, like the one in '53. But also that this time we couldn't say we hadn't been warned.

They were talking about it on the radio for days beforehand. The news is all about the weather these days, and the weather's like the news. They were saying how high the water was likely to reach, and where the weakest spots were that were most at risk, and all the damage to expect. Not that there was all that much you could do, it seemed to me, if you lived along the seafront or somewhere low down near the river or the marshes. Except to get out before the flood came, and that's what they had to do, poor souls, knowing they'd be coming back to a scene of ruin. It's the smell that's the worst, according to a lady in the paper shop at Snape this morning, who's staying with her brother up the hill. 'I can't go back to that terrible stench,' she said. The drains started flowing in the wrong direction, she said, even before the tidewater reached them. Just imagine it, raw sewage bubbling out of all the sinks and basins. And she hadn't had time to take up her carpets.

The winds had already got up the day before, and by the morning of the surge it was blowing a rare old gale, in confirmation of the forecasts. They knew exactly when high tide was due, of course, which was good in a way but also terrible, like a bomb ticking down against you. It's why no lives were lost, some man said on the radio, and that is true, but only if it's human lives you're meaning. I stood and looked down across the valley the next day when the tide had ebbed a bit, though there was still more water to see than fields, and there were sorry grey humps of feathers which had been wild geese, left washed up like litter on a beach. You'd wonder why they didn't fly away to higher ground and safety, but maybe the waters rose too quickly and their wing feathers became saturated, or they were disorientated in the darkness by the strange, altered landscape.

There was the saddest story in the local newspaper, about the pub at the bottom of the hill between the Maltings and Snape village. The landlady was fattening turkeys for the Christmas menu, with its being December. They keep their own animals for organic meat: Gloucester Old Spot pigs and a few sheep and goats as well as the turkeys. Anyway, the police came round in the afternoon to tell them to evacuate. High tide was due for ten at night and they wanted them out by six at the latest to be on the safe side; it was already well past lunchtime when they heard the van with the loudhailer on top, instructing them to pack up and go. So of course they forgot about salvaging their belongings or trying to protect the fittings in the bar, they were so concerned for the livestock. They managed to find a nearby farmer with some empty sties and some transport to move the pigs, and the sheep and goats were taken by a neighbour with an empty field – but this took up the whole afternoon. It came to half past five and the policeman was insisting they really must be leaving soon, and there were still the turkeys in the barn. So the landlord dragged some straw bales in there and stacked them up to give the birds a place to roost that would be out of harm's way, and they shut the door and left them. When they came back three days later once water levels allowed, every one had drowned. The bales had disintegrated in the swirling tide, leaving the turkeys no place to escape. Forty birds, and not one left alive.

'I couldn't stop crying,' the landlady was quoted as saying, as she described the scene of desolation that they found. Which some might think odd, when the turkeys were all to have their necks wrung for the table within a few short weeks, but I didn't find it odd at all. I completely understood.

There was one more victim of the big storm surge, another unlucky refugee to add to the hundreds of people who still can't go back to their homes. I found him – Mr Napish says he's definitely a 'him' – by the side of the road that leads down to the Alde at Langham Bridge. I thought at first it was a sodden sandbag lying there in the long grass, because the farmer down there had brought in piles of sandbags to try to protect his house and outbuildings, and a lot of them had been washed away. It was sort of humped and the right kind of colour, a dark, musty grey which must have been the river mud, because when I came nearer I could see that on one side there was a lighter patch, more of a reddish-brown, and that's when I knew what I was looking at: a dead fox. Except that he wasn't dead. I've no idea what made me go and take a closer look. I'm not squeamish about dead animals – I'm not some seedypuff who's never skinned a rabbit – but there's no reason, is there, to go peering. It's

24

a feeling about dignity, I suppose; I shouldn't want folks staring at me when I'm 'a corpus' as my dad used to say. But for some reason, as I say, I was curious, and when I leant down the thing gave a sort of shuddery twitch, like sometimes when you are just falling asleep. It lay still then and I thought maybe I'd imagined it, but when I watched carefully I could just make out the tiniest movement across the middle of the hump, the barely noticeable rise and fall of the ribs. He was breathing.

Goodness knows the diseases you can catch from a fox, let alone the ticks and fleas, and this one wasn't just filthy, he was dripping wet like a mop in a bucket, but I couldn't leave him there. I think it was with my thinking he was dead, and then his not being; I couldn't just let him die after that. As I picked him up, though, and he didn't struggle or snap but just flopped there all limp while I wrapped him in my long Fair Isle scarf, I didn't give much for his chances, either way. That scarf is for the dustbin now, too, and it took me an age to knit.

It was Mr Napish I thought of, right away. I suppose it's with his having been a scientist, even the wrong sort – and who else was there to ask? Folks with livestock know about animals, but they can't abide foxes! My arms were aching by the time I reached High House, and the mud and water had soaked right through the Fair Isle and stained all up the front of my coat, and the fox still hadn't stirred so I wondered if it was too late anyway and the whole thing had been a wild goose chase, if that's not an ill-fitted phrase. But Mr Napish didn't seem to think so. He didn't bat an eyelid, which I knew he wouldn't – nothing seems to get him in a fluster.

'Ah, Plathubis, bringer of rain' was the first thing he said, which struck me as rather peculiar, but he took my bundle from me and carried it to the Aga, where he opened the warming oven and laid it gently inside. Then he turned to me and gave a slow nod of the head. 'Leave him with me,' he said.

The river is still in high flood, even after more than two weeks now. Mrs Jackaman kindly gave me a lift to the shops at Saxmundham in her big old estate car on Monday after I'd finished doing round for her at the rectory; she said she needed to pop into Tesco herself. As you come down Langham Lane it's like another world, a world all turned to water. You can't tell what's river and what's land. On a day like today, with the sun on it, there's just one smooth, flat surface like mirrored glass. If it weren't for the line of trees on one side and the fence posts on the other you wouldn't know where the road goes at all. At least the crest of the bridge is visible now, just clear of the water, where a week ago it was submerged. 'Something to set a course for,' Mrs Jackaman said gaily.

Even so, I'm glad it wasn't me driving. There was something unnerving about striking out into all that expanse of silver without knowing what was underneath. A pair of ducks drifted alongside: life returning, I thought. We set them bobbing as we went by; we were leaving a wake behind us like a boat.

Against the odds, my fox is still with us, and appears to be on the mend. It has to be said, Mr Napish has worked miracles with him. He's still rather groggy and listless, but I dare say it's just as well or he'd have your fingers off. But with all the mud cleaned off him and his fur dried out you can see his proper colours, which are a rich orangey-red on top and soft, pale grey underneath, except it isn't really grey at all when you look closely but white with a sort of darker down showing through at the roots; and his coat's not straggly either but in pretty good condition, considering. Mr Napish thinks he's a young one, maybe this year's cub. He's winter-thin, though: when he stretches you can see the outline of each rib. 'We'll soon do something about that,' Mr Napish says. He's giving him prime minced beef with Ready Brek and warm water mixed in. And he's made him a box to sleep in, closed in except at one end – 'So that he feels secure but not trapped,' he explained. It's a lovely piece of work is that box. It turns out Mr Napish is quite a woodworker. That's what he does in that barn of his: he builds things out of wood. I suppose it fits, with his having been an engineer. 'What kind of things do you make?' I wanted to know, but he didn't give me much of an answer. He just gazed towards the window absently and rubbed his beard. 'Whatever's required.'

He's filled the box with clean, dry leaves and it looks extremely cosy. Enlil and Ninlil, I've noticed, give it a wide berth; they stalk past at the far side of the kitchen, the tips of their tails twitching. This morning the fox was asleep, his eyes two tight black slits, although his whiskers flickered when I moved close by with my duster. And when I looked again his eyes were open and fixed on me without blinking, a hard, glassy orange the same colour as his coat.

'Tough little fellow, isn't he?' I said when we sat down to our elevenses. 'To have come through all that and survived.'

'This time,' said Mr Napish.

It's one of his pet themes, and not a very cheerful one, I must say. Just because we've had one tidal flood doesn't mean that's an end to it; there'll be more to come, he insists, and worse. When he worked in coastal defence, he told me, they used to call it *The Big One*, like they do in that place where they get all the earthquakes – Japan, did he say, or California?

I must have been looking a bit cast down because he caught my eye, then, and seemed to soften. 'There's certainly some spirit in him. Animals have a tenacious instinct for life. There will always be those that survive.'

Well, that's Christmas and the New Year come and gone, and still no sign of any winter weather. Nothing I'd think of as winter, anyway: you expect it to be sparkling cold at Christmas, don't you? No snow, no ice, and scarcely a frost to speak of so far, though we're well into January. Instead, it's been unseasonably mild with week after week of leaden skies. So dampening to the spirits when it's grey at this time of year, I always think. The days are short enough anyway, and when it's dull and overcast it feels as if the sun's never properly got up at all. I need the lights on to see what I'm dusting, even at midday.

And rain – it seems to have been non-stop. I can hardly remember a morning when I haven't woken up to the sound of water splattering down from the corner of the outhouse roof and onto the coal bunker. I must remember to get that gutter fixed. There's water standing round the lanes in places where I've never known them flood before, and all the fields are waterlogged. They were talking about it on the radio: how usually you'd think of rain in January as good for the winter wheat, but how this year the soil's so wet that the plants are starved of oxygen. One farmer said that half his crop had rotted.

It's a trial for the livestock, too. Mr Willett's cows are gone from his big meadow. I heard he's having to pay for grazing for them over Framlingham way because he's no fields here that aren't half under water. And I saw Joe Wakeling's daughter's donkey the morning after a recent storm with filth up to its hocks, marooned on a tiny island of grass in its submerged paddock. The poor thing was too scared, Joe said, for them to lead it through the water and bring it under cover. They just had to leave it there to take its chances, and now it's lame with the mud fever – and little wonder, poor creature.

The tidewater along the Alde has fallen back some way at least since the night of the surge, but it's left behind a patchwork of small lakes and cut-offs. In places the river is still far wider than it should be, while in others, where it's back between its banks, it's swollen and churning like a pan on the boil and nothing like its familiar, lazy green self. The fields that have re-emerged from the departing flood are in a sorry state, the turf silted a greasy grey and littered with broken reeds and branches. Clearing up the mess will be the least of it, according to Mr Napish. The real problem, apparently, is the salt. The water from down below the sluice that came flooding upstream was saline. It was estuary water: seawater, more or less. The ground that it covered was standing feet deep in brine, and the salt will have soaked down into the soil. It will be there long after the water has drained away, he says, contaminating the land and leaving it toxic to cattle and infertile for crops. It could be barren for decades. Such an odd, almost eerie notion: an invisible poison, and it's something as ordinary as salt.

There was a rare break in the weather after breakfast today when I walked up the hill to High House. There was a bit of a wind and the clouds were less like a military blanket; they had risen and were shifting so you could see shapes and colours in them, and at least the rain had stopped.

I'd called hello and was pulling off my wellies in the hallway when Mr Napish appeared from the kitchen. 'No, keep them on,' he said, 'and come with me.'

He led me across the patch of lawn to the side of the

house and over to the barn. I'd never been this close to it before, let alone inside. It's a great, tall hulk of a thing, not made of wood like most barns hereabouts but brick like the house. It must have cost him a pretty penny, that Victorian engineer. Goodness knows what he'd be wanting with it, unless he farmed as well as building sluices. You could fit half the village in it.

There were heavy double doors, the old-fashioned kind, high and wide enough for a big farm wagon. He slipped the bolt and dragged one of them open. It was evidently quite a weight; he had to put his shoulder to it. Inside it was pitch black, and even when he'd felt for the switch and flicked it on, only one patch near the door was properly lit up, with a big workbench and a stack of timbers leaning against the wall. The rest of the barn was looming shadows.

'Over here.' He led me to the bench, which was arrayed behind with saws and planes and chisels and allsorts, hanging neatly on rows of hooks. But he was pointing underneath, beside a stack of those extra-large catering tins: chopped ham and marmalade and Heinz beans. Empty ones, I can only imagine, and used to keep his nails and screws in. It wasn't the cans he was pointing at; it was something next to them, beside a pile of shavings. The box with my fox in it.

'Oh, how is he?' No longer needing to be inside by the Aga, at any rate, which had to be a good sign. I stepped nearer to take a look, and saw that there was a second compartment now, built on behind the first. It was also roofed in at one end, while at the open end I could just make out the tip of a whiskery orange snout. Another poor washed-up soul. I wondered where he'd found it.

'This one's a vixen,' he said. 'She'll be a mate for him.'

He showed me something else as well. High up above

the workbench, above where the bulb shone, there was a small hole in the brickwork which sent a pale, round shaft of daylight slanting in from outside, lighting up in a haze of circling dust a sort of wire mesh cage. In it were pressed together on a dowel perch a pair of birds – what looked like pigeons, or in fact more likely those collared doves. One of them, I noticed, had half a leg missing on one side. Not just the foxes, then.

My eyes must have been adjusting to the darkness because I could also make out more clearly what I had taken at first for some kind of partition, maybe a part of an animal stall. It towered up through the gloom, a smooth, sheer wall of wood. But now I saw that there was an unusual curved shape about it, and the more I peered the more it held my attention, until I realised what I was looking at. It was the hull of a boat – a big boat.

Mr Napish was looking towards me, but his back was against the light and I couldn't make out his expression.

'Well, standing here and chatting,' I said, the way my old dad used to, 'won't buy the old lady a new hat. I'd better go and make a start on that hoovering.'

When I stepped out from the barn I saw that the sky had grown darker over the valley. It was beginning to rain again.

RINGING NIGHT

Thursday night was ringing night. It always had been, for as long as Jack could remember. With Dad away for long spells when she was small, and Mum working late, Jack was often left in the charge of her namesake, old Jack from next door. If it was a Thursday then she knew she mustn't dawdle over tea or daydream in the bath if she wanted time left for a story, since old Jack was a ringer and had to be at the church for seven o'clock. The day and the time had never varied since.

Jack had made a careful study of the signboards in the ringing chamber, and the peals documented there as having been rung at St Peter's over the past century or more had all taken place on a Thursday. She had consulted an old almanac she found in Leiston town library, one day after school. *A Course of Kent Treble Bob Major, 27th September 1894*: that was a Thursday. The man on the tenor that day was one Geo. Woolnough, great-grandfather of the present tower captain. *A Peal of Grandsire Triples, 22nd June 1911, Sounded in Celebration of the Coronation of His Majesty King George V*: also a Thursday, though it seemed a piece of luck that the coronation should fall on St Peter's practice night. Jack's favourite of all was a notice near the cobwebbed ladder that led up to the bell loft, the lettering hand-painted, black on peeling white. It recorded only a simple *Course of Plain Bob Major*, conducted one Thursday in April 1986, but the ringers' names that night included that of *Jack Deeks, 4th*.

Babysitter, neighbour and teller of bedtime tales: it was partly in his honour that she had shed Jacqueline or Jacqui in favour of Jack at the age of nine, along with pigtails and all things pink. On Thursdays after he'd gone and Mum had tucked in the covers, still in her starchy blue tunic and smelling of antibacterial gel, Jack used to lie cocooned and wait for the bells to start, flowering in the darkness like distant bursting fireworks. She learned to tease from the merging resonance the individual chimes, and she hugged close the sound of the number four bell, knowing who it was that made it speak.

When Jack senior hung up his rope, it made sense for Jack junior to take it over, replacing him on the fourth. *Linguis hominum loquar et angelorum* read the legend encircling the bell's waist – with the tongues of men and of angels – and, around the shoulder, *Jacobus Guernerus me fecit*. So it truly was, as she always thought of it, Jack's bell.

They weren't up to adding a new peal to the display boards these days, not even a plain hunt. Danny and Liam from school had both begun at the same time as Jack in a mini drafting spree. There'd been some attrition among the core of older ringers, with old Jack's retirement following hard on that of Mrs Cattermole when she had her first hip done, and the death of old Harry Housego, who'd been pulling the treble since his return from a German prison camp in 1946. The three raw fifteen-year-old recruits were knocked into shape by Willie Woolnough and the other

33

old stagers, Walter Gosling and Olive Fisk, and they'd all kept with it for the three years since. But they still stuck to rounds or a few call changes, less now on account of the young novices than of Walter's lumbago.

Jack was the first one there tonight, and opened up. She had a key: iron, black and weighty, hand forged by the village farrier. It was hardly a thing you could get cut in Timpson's. There were only four in all – the rector had one, and Willie of course, and the spare was kept by the Air Vice-Marshal at the Yews – but this one had been old Jack's and she was allowed to keep it. Through grooves worn smooth by centuries, it slid to unlock the low-arched corner door of heavy oak that led up a flight of spiral stairs to the ringing chamber. She'd barely let herself up there and switched on the lights than there was a huffing on the stone staircase and Olive Fisk appeared.

'Still hot out.' The collar of Olive's apricot nylon blouse was damply tight. She wore the same fitted skirt and stout shoes in July as in January; no wonder her face powder looked streaky.

'Baking,' agreed Jack, although the air was always cool within the encasing stonework of the tower. She moved to unloop the nearest bellrope from its hook up on the wall.

More footsteps on the stairs, and two voices, baritone and bass, announced the arrival of Walter and Willie. Soon all the ropes were unhooked, uncoiled and in position. They didn't bother to ring the bells down between times at St Peter's, but left them set against their stays. It wasn't as if anyone ever came up here except the ringers, and it saved the time and trouble of ringing them up. It was a pretty impressive ring of six for a small parish church. The tenor, Walter Gosling's bell, weighed in at a stately twenty-two hundredweight. Jack's fourth was a big bell, too: nearly sixteen hundredweight but, beautifully balanced, she handled like a dream. Close to and in motion, they were a startling sight. Old Jack had once taken her up the ladder to the bell loft to watch them swing in their massive wooden frame, the great oak timbers creaking and shifting with the swish and swoop of metal. Crazily clamorous she had found them, even through her earplugs, flinging their sound wide open-mouthed, like raucous laughter or the bellowing of pain.

Now, while they waited for the two boys, the captain nodded towards Jack's rope. 'Turn her over,' he said, 'and hurry along those dally-dawdlers.'

The measured, tolling note sounded out from high above them, beyond the wooden roof and the empty stretch of tower beyond, distant and detached, its timing strangely disconnected from the rise and fall of her sally. Jack found her rhythm easily, feeling the movement of her bell, taking her up almost to the balance on each pull and holding up just a fraction on the handstroke as Willie had taught her.

Unsmiling, he nodded his approval. 'And stand.'

1649, according to the inscription, was the year when that first Jack or Jacob Warrener had cast the fourth, making her the oldest of St Peter's bells. That meant she was made not in the foundry in Bury St Edmunds nor yet at Whitechapel as her younger sisters were but, according to local belief, in a meadow adjoining the churchyard, which still bore the name of Bellpit Field. The field had been old Jack's, like the bell, and he'd told her many times the tale of the casting; the best of his bedtime stories had not come out of books. The digging of the pit and the gathering of straw and brushwood for the fire; the clay and horse dung shaped to cover the core and outer cope, then baked to form the mould and laid within the pit; the heating of copper and tin to a liquid red-gold, a sparking lava flow of fire as it tipped to fill the mould: every detail of old Jack's account felt so fresh and first-hand, it was hard not to think that he'd been there. Like the bell, he had been born here in the village – not in the hospital in Ipswich like Jack herself, as she thought all babies were supposed to be. She sometimes imagined him hauled like the bell from the depths of Bellpit Field, coughing the sandy soil from his infant lungs.

Jack had done the Civil War this year for A-level History, and was struck by the bell's date. Odd to think that while the King stood trial for his life at Westminster Hall, craftsmen in a Suffolk field went calmly on with their appointed task, making bells to call the impervious faithful of the fledgling Commonwealth to prayer. Strange how – give or take a few witches – things must have gone on much the same. Jack's bell, she supposed, would have rung for the execution and again for the Restoration, as for the changing Christian seasons, the births and marriages and deaths of the parish, the old year and the new, for more than three centuries since.

The field was no longer old Jack's as it had once been, along with Silly Hill and all the land beyond the church and down towards Stone Common, but had been sold as a lot to the Bradcocks, who worked it with their farm at Campsea Ashe. He'd been forced to retire from both bellrope and farming, first by arthritis in his shoulder and then by something more invasive and deeper in. After more than three years now he'd admit it was his kidneys, but still never called it cancer.

It was three minutes past seven when Danny came jogging up the stairs and almost five past when Liam eventually

36

appeared, his apology shrivelling under Willie's glittery stare.

'Right.' The tower captain moved to his rope, and they all followed suit. 'We'll start in rounds, and let's have no lumping. Make it good and even for his nibs.'

His nibs was Air Vice-Marshal Fitzpatrick, the church's nearest neighbour at the Yews, and who owned Church Cottage too. No campanologist himself, he was still a fierce critic of the art.

Jack eased her bell up to the balance. The fourth was set very shallow, and it only took a nudge to free headstock and stay from the wooden slider.

'Look to,' said Willie. 'Treble's going – she's gone.'

It was quite good, tonight. Liam, who had a tendency to let his number three bell get on top of Jack's, kept things tolerably even, and by the final few rounds, before Willie told them, 'That's all,' and signalled for them to set, their spacing was pretty well perfect.

'Not bad,' he said – high praise indeed from Willie Woolnough.

Old Jack had kept a dairy herd but never a dog, so he brought in the cows for milking with his Land Rover. Never a collie, that is. He had only old Fern, a spaniel and a stickler for demarcation: a flusher of pheasant, not a rounder-up of stock. She bestrode the passenger seat with front paws on the dashboard and watched operations with the fervent pleasure of a sports fan. When Jack was small, the old man had let her steer the Land Rover, cresting the ancient ridges and furrows like a galleon in full sail. Perched on his bony lap, her legs in any case too short to reach the pedals, she threw the wheel now left now right to head off any beast which broke from the pack, stiff-gaited, a parody of stupid, roll-eyed terror.

37

There was no money these days in dairying, according to Mr Bradcock, unless on an industrial scale. After four human generations and many more bovine ones, the Deeks herd had been broken up and sent for auction, while Bellpit Field was ploughed and put to barley.

'People still want beer,' Mr Bradcock said.

There was no Deeks to take over in any case. Old Jack had had no children of his own, which Mum always said was a crying shame. His wife, Mary, had contracted an infection delivering their only, stillborn, child. 'I turned the bell for the babe, and for Mary eight days later,' he'd once told her, like a line from an old, sad story.

She'd always liked the sad ones best. 'Tell me about the town that drowned,' she would demand, and he'd stroke the hair from her forehead with the ball of his scratchy farmer's thumb and relate the tale of Dunwich that was swallowed by the sea, with its eight submerged churches, and the ghostly bells that rang out still on foggy nights to warn away sailors, keeping them off the treacherous ruins that would have ripped a hull.

Tonight, after tea and before bell practice, she'd gone to visit him. All her life he'd lived next door, helping out when he was needed and later being helped out in his turn; until last winter, that is, when he left Mum's neighbourly care and became instead her professional charge as deputy manager of the Lilacs Residential Nursing Home. Illness had reduced him, working loose the flesh from his bones beneath skin that took on the greyish sheen of greasy chip paper. Jack couldn't look at the pale, stretched triangle at his throat or the pucker of his forearm where the tube went in, but focused instead, when they were open, on the rheumy eyes which had kept their spark, or on his hands, still warm and capable and unmistakably old Jack's.

The little room this evening felt overfull of heated, antiseptic air. For a while now he'd been sleeping more and more in the daytime. She used to hope he'd be awake when she came to see him, but recently the space between the two states was becoming blurred, along with his perception. Still, she could sit by his bedside and talk him into sleep, as once he'd sat by hers and done the same.

'It's ringing night tonight,' she told him, uncertain if he knew it was a Thursday. 'Danny's done his wrist in. It's only a sprain, but it's quite puffed up.' Danny kept goal for the village football team. 'It's in a sling, so it seems he won't be ringing for a while. He said he'd come and watch, though, anyway. For moral support.' She grinned to herself. 'Or something.' Danny and Liam liked to hit the bar at the Ship after bellringing, especially on these warm summer nights, and sometimes Walter did too.

Old Jack swallowed, his throat working, and the closed lids flickered.

'We'll just ring the back five, I expect,' said Jack. That way, the fourth became the third. She leant to press his hand, where it lay square and heavy on the turned-down sheet. 'I like it when I'm in the middle – the third of five, you know. It feels more... symmetrical, somehow.'

Mothers talked to infants in their buggies, didn't they? She'd seen them in the aisles at the Co-op in Wickham Market, regaling their babies with the price of frozen peas. One end of life and the other. Was this the same, or was it different? If old Jack could hear her, at least he understood.

One more set of changes, and they'd call it a night, said Willie. 'I'll just hunt the treble down to the bottom and back again. Watch your striking spaces, everyone, and let's make those changes nice and clean. Straight past me on the next handstroke when I give you the word.'

It went like clockwork. Liam didn't ring fleet at all for once, and the team seemed to move in perfect partnership, as well-oiled as the wheels and bearings up aloft. Danny sat on the ladder and beat time in the air with his uninjured hand while the captain brought the second from its place at treble past each other bell in turn, and back up to the top to resume rounds. Walter sent the tenor swinging deep, so deep that the lighter bells were almost at the balance, and they rang like that for maybe a minute more, in stately, even rounds, handstroke and backstroke, their sallies chasing one another round the circle in metronomic order.

'That's all,' said Willie, with a frown of quiet satisfaction. 'And stand.'

Second and third came up to the balance, and gently over on to their stays. Jack applied the slightest of extra pressure to her rope: the smallest tweak was all it needed, and she'd follow them up to set. Olive and Walter behind her were already readying to finish. Suddenly something wasn't right. The fourth, though normally the most well-mannered of bells, seemed to give a jerk, the rope to twist between her fingers. As she gave the extra tug to bring her to the set, Jack's bell didn't stop but continued to swing, sixteen hundredweight of metal borne on by its own momentum. Up above her in the bell frame, stay hit slider with a buck and a leap, the ripping of bolts and the splintering of timber, and all at once the sally was wrenched from her grasp, sending the bellrope rearing and careering, lassoing out wildly amid the circle of ringers.

Hands raised to cover her face, Jack stepped backwards,

the instinct saving her from the lethal whip of the rope. The other ringers, having set their own bells, had already stepped away, summoned from stupefaction by Willie Woolnough shouting, 'Get back – back, all of you,' as he made a grab for the rope's lashing tail.

Jack felt sick, with a tightening of fear that was more than the delayed awareness of danger averted. Sweat sprang between her breasts and in the creases of her elbows, and tears rose from nowhere, making her blind. Her heart flailed wild and loose inside her chest. With a lurch she fled for the stairs, stumbling and tumbling down the narrow spiral, taking the worn stone steps two, three at a time, hardly knowing how she didn't fall, only that she had to escape from the savage clang of the bell above her in the loft. Then she was down in the church, feet grateful for the flat stone flags of the nave, and making for the south porch door, turning the great iron ring with a shaking hand, and letting the heavy felted oak swing closed with a clatter behind her. And out – out into the churchyard and the still hot night, and she was running now, running for home.

Up ahead, through the wash of tears, she saw her mother's torch come swaying towards her over Bellpit Field, while behind her in the tower the fourth bell, old Jack's bell, brought back to control now by the tower captain's expert hand, fell into a steady rhythm – the slow, implacable rhythm of the funeral knell.

THE WATCHER OF SOULS

The third cup of tea at breakfast was the mistake. The daily walk was a promise that Rebecca had made herself, along with more fresh fruit and learning to text the grandchildren, following the latest all-clear. Straight after breakfast was a perfect time for walking – unless you'd sat a little longer over the *Telegraph* crossword and squeezed a third cup out of the teapot.

It was bad enough having to spend a penny in the open, but surely nobody could manage it if they were being watched. Rebecca certainly couldn't, in any case. She was a good way from the road – ten minutes or so into the woods – and she'd found a quiet spot that was screened from the footpath by a belt of elder and hawthorn. It was too warm for tights, and her old cotton twill skirt was certainly easier than trousers. But she just couldn't rid herself of the sense of an onlooker. The feeling that someone was watching.

Someone – or, as it turned out, some*thing*. She wasn't sure how she became aware of it because she was certain it hadn't moved, and in spite of its paleness it blended well enough into the background hatching of twigs and leaves and sunlight. Maybe the same way she knew it was there watching her in the first place: there was something about its stillness that drew the eye, once you were still yourself.

It was a barn owl. Rebecca was no great ornithologist, but everybody could recognise a barn owl. It was so distinctive, with the flat, white plane of its heart-shaped face above shoulders speckled grey and fawn, and those wide, unblinking black eyes. Glistening, mineral eyes, as round and glassy wet as the pebbles they used to find on the beach at Aldeburgh that Janet always hoped were real jet. But if the eyes were hard, the hooked beak nestled protectively inwards among the pillowing down and the bird bore an overall countenance of calm – an air if not of benevolence, precisely, then at least of quiet, unthreatening vigilance. What nonsense, though, Rebecca chided herself, to be attributing to the creature these human feelings, these human characteristics. It was only a bird, after all.

But she still couldn't spend a penny with it watching.

After that, Rebecca found her feet often tending to that particular path on her daily constitutional. Pretty soon she admitted to herself it was a deliberate choice, in the hope of seeing the owl. On one or two mornings when she got herself up and out early for her walk, while the sun was still struggling to break above the under-canopy of brush and bracken and send its rays to slant in stripes between the trees, she was halted in her tracks by the sight of the owl at its hunt. Its chosen killing ground was a little distance from the tree where they'd had their first encounter, clear of the band of trees in an open area of scrubby gorse bushes interspersed with heather. At this in-between time of year, as March slid towards April, the new green growth fought for light and space in a landscape still dominated by last year's contours of woody black and brown. It was hard to believe that in three short months this would all be a carpet of brilliant purple, the hard-packed soil of the pathways crumbling back to a scuff of sand. For now, whatever small scamperers and scurriers were the focus of the owl's attention from its vantage point on a branch of gorse sought out for their protection the resinous clumps of overwintered heather, springing tough and resilient above the slowly warming earth.

The barn owl hunched motionless: watching, watching. Then it threw out both its wings and flung forwards, not in the smooth dive of the hawk but a clumsy flurry of feather and claw – yet almost eerily noiseless in the still of the morning. And down, its bleached belly a gleam of white against the dark vegetation, its wings two intersecting arcs of gold. It must have struck its target, because it did not rise again but disappeared from sight beneath the mounded heather. Rebecca turned away and hurried on, finding she had no stomach to confront even in imagination the transaction's natural end.

On days when she rose late and lingered over breakfast, she'd find the owl already roosting, always on the same tree as before, on a stubby oak branch some eight or ten feet above the ground. It jutted horizontally from the tree – the lone oak among a group of rowan, ash and hazel – before ending abruptly in a splintered wound, broken off, presumably, in some long-past storm. The trunk of the tree was fractured too, riven with a deep, angry V-shaped gash, perhaps another ravage of the same storm, though to Rebecca's mind it looked to have caught a glancing blow from the axe of some woodland giant, splitting kindling. Was the bird's nest in there, she wondered, inside the hollow? You thought of barn owls as nesting in... well, barns: in roof spaces, and empty farm buildings. She must look it up.

Rebecca had always been a library person, but the nearest one was Leiston, and you could hardly expect the mobile library van that stopped in the village once a week to have a reference book on owls. However, Janet had recently persuaded her mother online. She'd set her up with a computer – it was just an old one she'd finished with but it was a decent size, with a proper screen and keyboard, not like those fiddly things Josh and Ellie had that they called their 'notebooks', was it? – and showed her how to look things up. Silver surfing was the current phrase for it, apparently. 'Sounds a bit energetic for me, Jan,' she'd told her, 'and I'm more of a mousy grey.' But once you got started it was rather addictive – a terrible swallower of time. People thought you had a lot of time when you were older but in fact it was quite the opposite, Rebecca found. It raced away from her in a way she found ever harder to keep pace with, even without the lurking stopwatch of cancer. But if it devoured the hours at a disorientating rate, the web was a goldmine of information. There were pages and pages about the barn owl.

Tyto alba was its Latin name – the white owl, confusingly, in spite of its largely golden-brown plumage, and in spite of the existence, too, of the snowy owl, or *Bubo scandiacus*. In flight at dawn or dusk, though, she supposed her owl was so pallid as almost to appear white. 'Ethereal' was the word that came to Rebecca's mind. In some Inuit dialects, she discovered, the word for barn owl was the same as the word for ghost.

The hollow oak could certainly be its nesting place. They seemed to adopt not only man-made sites but holes and crevices in rocks and trees – anywhere with a flattish

45

ledge, concealed from view, on which to raise their young. But wasn't the websites outlining the habitat and breeding patterns of the owl which drew Rebecca to read on, but those which told of its mythology. The Lenape peoples of the Delaware and Hudson rivers believed that if they dreamed of a barn owl it would become their guardian and protector of their soul, while to the south-western Pima tribe the pale bird in flight at dusk was the newly released spirit of the departed. Death was known as 'crossing the owl river'; the feather of a barn owl would help the soul of the dying to pass across. Its crepuscular hunting habits and reputedly keen night vision imbued the owl for many with the power of intuition, the power of inner sight. It became the totem of prophets and clairvoyants, a messenger between the hidden world of death and shadow and the world of light. The one who hears what is not spoken and sees what is unseen. The keeper of secrets, the watcher of souls.

Rebecca stared into the owl's unreadable black eyes and the owl stared back. Softly, she moved closer, keeping hold of the bird's gaze, careful not to put it to fright but at the same time visited by a strange sense of seeking permission. Another step and she was near enough to look into the hollow bolus of the tree, and there it was, the nest site: a protruding ledge above the level of her eyeline, its rim encrusted with droppings and snowflaked with down. Lower down, in the base of the V where it narrowed to a point some two or three feet above the forest floor, she was surprised to see that grass and ground elder had taken root and were growing there in the partial sunlight, taking their sustenance from the accumulation of debris, of dead leaves and earth and every state between. And no doubt, too, from the fabric of the oak itself, as it rotted from within, the outside returning to fresh spring leaf while the inside sickened and fell to dust. *Like cancer, like cancer, like cancer.* Except that it wasn't the same at all; the tree's putrefaction was fecund, a source of new life. A part of the natural cycle of things.

Still mindful of the silent watcher above, she edged closer once again, until she could stretch out her hands and feel the cool moisture of the vegetation in the base of the hollow. She ran her fingers in among it, parting the grass, disturbing more down and droppings as well as here and there a larger feather. Peering down between the separated stems, she felt a sudden chill as she caught a gleam of white more bleached than the feathers, and colder and sharper, too: the brittle white of tiny bones. They lay scattered in a deep layer among the roots of the grass, the remnants of a hundred owl suppers, picked clean or undigested – the mass grave of a hundred small animals and birds.

Rebecca shuddered but did not step back. Some macabre fascination made her want to sink her hands in the tumble of broken skeletons, as if to measure the tally of lost lives. And then her fingertips struck something smoother, flatter, larger: an unyielding something that was neither rock nor bone. Its glint, when she swept aside the bones and leaf mould, was unmistakably metallic.

Working with firmer purpose now – almost hurrying – she dug and scraped and brushed until a clear surface began to emerge. It was darkened by its years of entombment in the damp soil, but as she rubbed it took on colour, a geometric pattern of red and black with, in its centre, two intersecting limbs of rusty cream which formed the letter X. *X marks the spot*, she thought, with the childish thrill of unearthing buried treasure. On either side of the X were soon revealed two matching letter Os.

47

It was an Oxo tin. *Oxo cubes dissolve at once*, announced the legend below the name, and above it the instruction, so palpably unheeded: *Store in a cool dry place*.

Her mother had had one not unlike it only smaller, which she used to keep her buttons in. Mum's would have been from the 1930s but the design, she supposed, had remained the same for decades. How long had the tin lain here? Seventy, eighty, ninety years? Since before the war, she'd guess, at very least.

She cleared away the dirt from around the edges of the tin, exposing the catch on one side and the hinges at the other, all of them browned and scaled with rust. It would no doubt be easier to open if she lifted it free of its resting place, but she found she was loth to do so; she felt the unswerving scrutiny of the barn owl from above her and was deterred. Instead, with the box *in situ*, she leaned forward and felt for the catch, working her fingernails underneath, prising and tugging until with a snap the corroded metal released its grip. She lifted the lid.

Inside was a small, flat, oblong bundle some four inches by three, wrapped in a kind of thinnish, greying cotton cloth and tied crossways with string like a brown paper parcel. The knot was not tight but it was old, and took some time to loosen and undo, before she was able to pull back the folded material – which appeared to be an old-fashioned gentleman's handkerchief – and see, inside, a sheet of paper, closely folded. Buried treasure, indeed – she felt like Howard Carter. Or perhaps this was the treasure map. Take ten paces west and five paces north. Three hundred silver pieces; dead men tell no tales. But light as she might try to make of it, Rebecca found her hand was shaking as she reached for the folded paper.

It was a letter. There was no salutation, but a letter was clearly what it was, penned in fading blue-black

48

ink and the looped copperplate handwriting that the older mistresses still hoped to instil when Rebecca was at school, a rounded hand, too, painstaking and uneven, suggesting youth and hesitancy. A girl, she thought, or if a young woman then of only scant education. The paper was cheap and flimsy, worn tissue-thin along the folds so that she feared it might fall to pieces in her hands.

Oh, but Tuesday seems a thousand years away, the letter began, so that Rebecca half wondered if this was not the start, and there was a missing sheet. *A thousand years – how ever I shall I bear it? Of course you must go to Ipswich to see about the stock like you said, and tomorrow's being washday I'll be at the tubs, and Mrs Jillings chivvying from dawn till night, no chance to slip away. But two whole days and not to see your face – I swear I'll die! Yesterday in the woods was perfect heaven. There's some might think it wickedness to say so, but 'tis simple truth, and the Reverend says it be no sin if we speak the truth. For heaven it surely was, with your sweet kisses and the way you pulled my arm through yours as we walked along the path, and the posy you picked and set in my corsage so bright and brave, like as I were some fine young lady in her carriage. My love, I live for Tuesday when you'll come again – at the time that we said, and at our own special place, and I'll wear the blue ribbon again that you kissed when you pulled it from my hair, and you said was like to cornflowers in the barley. Golden brown as the ripe barley, that's what you said to me as you looped a lock about your finger, like in a poem – like words from a proper book of poetry. No one's ever likened my hair to anything before, saving for the belly of a weasel, which the butcher's boy used to say to bait me. But oh, two days, two whole days apart! I think of you all night and day. Your own loving Annie xxx*

Under the first letter was another folded sheet and beneath that another and another, a bundle of maybe ten or twelve in all. She could take them home and read them – could take the tin – but it felt wrong, somehow, like theft, or sacrilege. He had chosen to hide them here, the unnamed man or boy. Was this in fact their 'own special place'? And he'd put them here for another reason, an irrational conviction told her; he'd placed them under the patient surveillance of the owl.

Not this owl, her own owl, obviously, but a perhaps long-dead forebear. How long did barn owls live? An oak, of course, might live for a thousand years – but how long could it survive once split to the core? Life expectancies, however, as she well knew, were fragile and contingent things.

She laid the letter back with the others and refolded it in the handkerchief, closed the lid of the Oxo tin, then raked back the leaves and bones and soil. It could stay there for tomorrow, beneath the careful eye of the watcher of souls.

My love, began the second letter, *I was in heaven again today at seeing you, though it be for only one short hour. I took a scolding from Mrs Jillings for being so late returned with the duck eggs from Bradcock's, but I showed her the tear in the bicycle tyre just as you told me, and she said no more, only pressed her mouth together all tight and sour, and I dare say she'll have it from my eleven and six come Friday. Oh, but an hour was far too short, just sixty little minutes, so few you could near as count them going by! And then I had to go, and you as well, and we won't be together again till Tuesday, but I'll see the back of your head in church on Sunday, your dear head with your clean collar and your*

50

own soft, sweet hair that smells like a kitten's fur. I blush to write these words but I wish we could be together – be truly together, I mean to say, like a man is with his wife. Her ladyship has sixteen for dinner on Saturday and Mrs Jillings has had me polish the silver till my fingers ache and I've a blister on my thumb the size of a ha'penny. You'll think it foolishness I dare say, but it wasn't my own face that looked back at me from the spoons and candlesticks but yours, your sweet own face. I kiss all ten of your fingertips, my love, and wish the minutes gone till Tuesday comes. Your ever-loving girl, Annie xx

There was nobody at home in any case to show the tin to now even if she had a will to take it – not for five years, since Bob died. That was what she missed the most, still missed at times with an unexpected, almost visceral intensity which was just as sharp as the very first day: she missed having someone to tell the little things, to share the small excitements, the small frustrations. Yes, she could tell Janet about the letters, could even take one and read it to her when she rang on Sunday – she was a good girl and never missed – but it wasn't the same thing. Jan visited, too, whenever she could but London was a long way and she was very busy with her job, and Ellie and Josh had their friends and their exams. Besides, she shouldn't grumble because it wasn't just her and it wasn't just Janet. Everyone's families moved away. There wasn't a lot for them here in the village – and certainly nothing for a corporate credit analyst. Rebecca slid the second letter back in the pile and shut the tin. Then she stepped back and looked up to where the barn owl squatted, its round eyes fixed upon her, unmoving and unmoved.

In some cultures, Rebecca learned, the barn owl is an

ill-starred omen. Creature of the night, it is a malevolent force, a feared spectre, the harbinger of doom. For the superstitious minds of ancient Rome, to dream of an owl meant shipwreck; the cry of an owl foretold an imminent death. *Yesterday, the bird of night did sit even at noonday, upon the market place, hooting and shrieking.* Witches, it was said, could take the shape of an owl and suck the blood of the newborn. In Arabia, the stories told how owls were evil spirits and would carry off children during the night. To the Japanese, the barn owl is demonic, an unclean soul, believed to bring disease and pestilence, causing children to sicken and crops to fail, while in old Russian folklore the owl's twilight call speaks out the names of the soon-to-die.

Why did you not come today? I waited and waited in our special place, at eight just as you said, and watched and watched but you never came. I know it was eight – I'm sure I heard the church clock chime – or if it was after it was not long past, as fast as I could get away without Mrs Jillings thinking aught amiss. She's such a body for her snooping and prying, I swear she's like a prison turnkey, even in the evening when my time's my own, and I've cleared the grates in the morning room and back parlour and banked up her ladyship's bedroom fire, and she had no business to be minding where I went, the mean old shrew. And I ran all the way once I came to the woods and there was nobody to see, and I wouldn't for the world have kept you waiting, and when you weren't there I swear I felt quite cold all over, quite desolate like you said to me you feel when we're apart. But oh, my love, it was torture to wait and wait and you not come, and at last to have to go back home not seeing you. At first I thought of dreadful things, how you might have met some accident upon the road or on the farm, some bull run wild or the crush of a cart's wheels. But then I thought a thing more dreadful still, that you are turned cold and did not wish to come – that you love me no longer. And I could bear anything but that – could bear death or influenza or the scarlet fever, or fifty of Mrs Jillings' scoldings, or even to be apart from you, for ten or twelve or a hundred days, if only I can be sure that you still care for me. Your constant loving Annie xxx

'Mum?'

Rebecca thoughts were adrift as she picked up the phone, and it took her several seconds to register her daughter's voice.

'Mum. Are you OK?'

'Oh, hello, Janet.'

'Only you didn't answer when I called on Sunday. Where were you? Were you out? I was worried about you.'

'I was here. Maybe I didn't hear it ring.'

There was a pause on the line. The cottage was two-up, two-down; the telephone stood on the kitchen windowsill, two feet from the sitting room door.

'Are you sure you're OK?'

'I've just been busy. A bit distracted, that's all. Thinking, you know.'

Another pause. 'It's not... Mum, you haven't got symptoms back again? Have you been to the doctor? Had a check?'

'No, no – nothing like that. Honestly, Jan, don't worry. It's really nothing. I'm fine.'

You came! My love, you came, and I was so happy I could have danced, or laughed out loud or cried, or all

53

those things together. But the time for our meeting is always so short, so dreadfully short, that for all I try not to think of it, I am watching and fearing for its ending even as soon as it's begun. It was sweet heaven when you held me in your arms tonight, and pressed me against you, and under you, on the grass beneath the trees. If I close my eyes I can still feel the weight of your body and smell the smell of you and taste your skin, the warm salty taste of it like sweet gammon ham, and remember the touch of your lips at my throat. Does it shock you when I write these things, that I'd never be so bold to speak aloud? I swear I even shock myself, and tremble to think of the Reverend's Sunday sermons, though it felt no sin to be lying there with you, it felt only sweet and right and true. It is meant to be, my love, with all my heart I'm sure. And I can bear with comfort now the full five days and five long nights till we can be together again, though it draggle and straggle like half a lifetime – I can bear it with good cheer because I know you care for me. Your own, for always, Annie xxxx

Many legends portrayed the barn owl as entirely benign, in spite of its nocturnal aspect. Endowed in popular belief with the gifts of foresight and sagacity, the owl was the favourite and familiar of Athene, Greek goddess of wisdom. The bird's reputed magical inner light, which enabled it to hunt by night, gave it great vision and prescience, the power to ward off evil. The owl protector accompanied Greek armies to their wars; the sight of an owl on the eve of battle presaged victory. The Dakota Hidatsa people, too, saw the owl as a protective spirit for their warriors. For the Hopis tribe barn owls were the guardians of all hidden and underground things, the tenders of seed germination. More domestically and closer to home, in Yorkshire the barn owl is still a friend to shepherds and farmers, warning them of coming storms. Zuni women in New Mexico place an owl feather in their baby's cradle to help it sleep; the watcher in darkness will keep the infant safe while the mother takes her rest.

My sweet love... It was the last letter; when Rebecca lifted it out, there was the nothing beneath but the lower layer of cotton handkerchief. She was moved by a soft pang, like the sorrow of distant loss. The final page, where the book must close. The end of the story. ...*there was a light under Mrs Jillings' door tonight when I stole up the attic stair. I swear she must have heard me but, Devil take the old tattletale, in truth I no longer care. My only care is to be with you as we were together tonight in the wood, to feel your arms around me and press you to my heart. My only sadness is that we must part and kiss goodnight and not come home together, to one hearth and bed and be as man and wife.*

Ah, but now, my love, now I have such hope, such darling hope—

There the letter ended; or rather it was interrupted where the paper had been torn jaggedly across from side to side, so that a half-inch or so was missing from the end of the page. Frustrated, Rebecca turned it over, but the other side was blank.

Had Annie's darling hope been met, her dream of being with the unnamed lover at last fulfilled? Did that explain the end of the letters? She need no longer write to him if he was by her side. But Rebecca would never know.

Now the tale was done; it was time to tie the letters back inside their handkerchief, re-knot the string and consign them again to their resting place and the care of the watchful owl. But when she lifted out the bundle of letters and fabric she saw that there was one more paper underneath. It was of heavier weight and better quality than rest, and watermarked, a single sheet folded precisely into four. The writing was unfamiliar: a different hand, bigger and bolder, with a negligent forward slant. And the message was short, just a very few brief lines.

My dear Anna... A liquid chill began to percolate through Rebecca's stomach. 'My dear' was good – but 'Anna', not 'Annie'?

My dear Anna, I am returning herewith your letters. I think it best that you do not write to me again. I trust I may rely upon your discretion to make no trouble with my wife or daughters. If we meet henceforth, it must be in public and as befits a limited acquaintance; I think it unlikely that our paths should cross with any degree of frequency. I pray that God may save and keep you.

So cold, so imperiously cold – at least until that closing benediction. And still not even the avowal of a signature, a name. She'd had the wrong idea, too, all this time, she realised. It was not his tin, but Annie's: not he but Annie herself who had hidden the letters in the barn owl's tree.

Slowly, almost mechanically, she laid his letter back in the tin, and on top of it the cotton-shrouded archive of Annie's outpoured love. Sitting back on her heels she raised her chin, looking up through the branches to the broken bough where the owl kept guard. She wanted to stand, to jump and shout and flap her arms. Stupid, shiftless, impotent bird! What purpose was there in seeing more than men could see – or more, at any rate, than blind, deluded women – if it did not lead to action? What good was all the watching and waiting, after all – as Annie had watched and waited, and for nothing?

But she didn't stand up. Instead, she tipped forward into a squatting position, and laced her hands across her stomach. There was an ache there, a dull clutch in her lower abdomen. Not the returning pain of cancer – not that, thank God, at least – but something like remembered menstrual cramps. And yet it was different: a rhythmic clenching, like something else remembered, a pain experienced just once, over forty years ago.

Reaching once more into the hollow of the oak, Rebecca lifted out the box of letters and, as she did so, saw what lay there buried underneath. Clean, white and fragile, these were not the remains of some dead bird or mammal, an owl's discarded prey. These were no bones tossed down at random, but placed with reverence, laid down to sleep with a mother's loving care. And beside the tiny skull – so small, so very small – against its cheek, was the single feather of a barn owl.

MAD MAUDLIN

I'm looking at a piano. That is, I'm looking at the video image of a piano, because I'm in the half-light of a rented bedroom at the back of a pub after closing and it's just me and the laptop.

Some time between 1954 and 1979, I notice, a new piano has appeared. The one in the earlier documentary clip has scrolled shoulders and is flanked by a pair of hinged brass candlesticks; I can make out the discolouration of the keys, even in grainy black-and-white. No surprise either, since back then everyone in the bar seems to have a roll-up attached to their bottom lip, the singers included. By the late seventies they've installed the piano that's still there now, a functional modern upright in a satinwood case. The piano stool has survived the change. Its velvet seat and fanciful, fluted legs don't match the angular new instrument, but there's something admirable about their unconformity, like an old woman dressed defiantly in furs and silks to attend the Ritzy that's now a multiplex. Everything else has survived, too, even down to the straw pack donkey which stands centre stage on the piano top, presumably a memento of some former landlord's long-past holiday, its baskets the repositories of old ha'pennies, scoreboard chalk and a single featherless dart.

Pubs, I've always thought, can be divided into two camps according to the stability of their decor. There are those that undergo a complete refit once or twice a decade, reinventing themselves from Haywain kitsch through ebony veneer and mirrors and back again in accordance with the latest fashion (or in spite of it) like the shifting political colours over some volatile town hall. Then there are others, the ones you'll generally find me drinking in, where change is so incrementally slow as to be almost imperceptible, as gradual as the softening of the contours of a familiar face. To say that the Ship falls into the latter category is to sell it far short. It is, of all the pubs in my wide and motley acquaintance, in a class of its own.

Moving the cursor over the older of the two archived clips, I click to play it again. In the foreground a slight sparrow of a man, who might be anything from fifty to seventy-five, stands crookedly to play the violin, one thigh wedged against a table, apparently for support, while the other rises and falls in jerks with the tapping of his foot. It's an old Irish jig tune, and his fingers run like mice. But my focus is on the portion of the public bar that's visible behind the fiddler. So many things are recognisably the same in 1954 as in the 1979 footage. In fact, most of them were still there this afternoon when I was in the bar myself, capturing the floor session on my little pocket Sony.

Along the back wall behind the piano runs a wooden ledge and on it stands a row of old beer bottles, photographs and other memorabilia. There, just left of the piano, is the obligatory team photograph: five men down on one knee in the grass in front of six more, standing, all of them balloon-shorted and sporting shirts and moustaches of various shapes and sizes. One or two of the elder players could be grandfather to the youngest, a grinning lad of twelve or thirteen, as if every able-bodied male in the village had to turn out to make up the eleven – and perhaps it was the case, it occurs to me with a bit of a shiver as I spot the date inscribed below the picture: 1919. Next to the football team leans another framed photo of what looks a similar vintage: a man in a cornfield with a collie dog. He seems to be wearing too many clothes for what, by the height of the corn, is surely spring or early summer. His dark jacket strains out of shape at its single buttoned fastening. The man stares straight into the camera, his face impassive, but the dog clearly lacks its master's stoic patience: its head is a blur of motion.

The fiddle player has shifted tempo now and is playing 'Fathom the Bowl', the verses sung out by a florid man in a cloth cap seated at a side bench, then the chorus taken up around the bar to the accompaniment of stamping feet and the thump of beer mugs on tables. As the camera pans towards the singer it brings into view behind him the far end of the ledge and below it an empty, high-backed wooden corner seat. On the ledge, beside a Toby jug, stands a third photograph: no more than a snapshot, really, taken there in the pub. A regular, no doubt, in a full beard and collarless shirt, grasping the neck of what could be a shepherd's crook but is probably just a walking stick. A pint glass stands before him on the table – the same table, back to the left of the piano, where I sat this afternoon, because there in the photograph is the scrolled wooden sidepiece with one brass candlestick, and on the ledge behind him is the photograph of the football team, and the man in the cornfield with his fidgety dog.

But stout and strong cider are England's control
Give me the punch ladle, I'll fathom the bowl...

The singer is warming to his theme, his tankard now raised aloft and pitching hazardously, while his brow gleams beneath his cap. I shift the cursor to the time bar at the bottom of the screen and drag the little round dot to the right, stopping ten minutes or so further into the clip to let it resume playing. The soundtrack here is a muddle of scraping chairs and rumbling voices, loomingly loud and close at hand and then quiet again, before at length from out of shot another song begins. A solo voice, unaccompanied and uncertain at first as to key but swelling in confidence: male and, I'm guessing, elderly. I don't know the song, but its themes are familiar: love, betrayal, a girl with raven hair. The camera is on the move again, scanning the circle of faces, all angled towards the unseen crooner. A new section of the side wall appears and, hanging on it, one more photograph.

It is taken in the bar again but this time the subject is a woman. Her clothing is dark and nondescript, bleaching to white where the picture is over-exposed or perhaps has faded with the light from the nearby window, and her face, tilted away from the camera, is cast half into shadow. I feel the stir of recognition nonetheless. It's that deeply cleft, almost heart-shaped chin, unusual in a woman. I'm sure I've seen it, or an echo of it, very recently. Just this afternoon, in fact. That's it: a woman with the same chin sat in the corner seat – the one with the high wooden back which in this clip is empty behind the cloth-capped singer – and sang 'Tom o' Bedlam' in a soft but sure contralto. Looking more closely at the photo before the camera swings away again, I can see that the woman in it is seated at the same corner place that her counterpart occupied today. Family tradition, maybe? This afternoon's singer might be, what, daughter or granddaughter, great-granddaughter even, of the woman in the photo?

The film was made in 1954 but the photograph would be older, might date from almost any time in the century prior to that. It is difficult to place the age of either one of them. Both in their forties or fifties, at a guess, but that's all it is. For one thing, women's dress always distorts their ages in old photographs; I've seen pictures from the 1950s where two-piece suits identical to their mothers' make matrons out of girls of seventeen. Not that there's anything distinctively of their time about these women's clothes. In fact, now that I try to focus my mind back, I can remember almost nothing about what the singer wore today beyond an impression of something plain with long sleeves, and black or at any rate dark in colour. Her hair, too, as I recall it, gave little away, being that type of pale English dusty fawn from which the pigment seems to leach away gradually with the years, instead of any positive change to grey. The monochrome image in front of me on the laptop screen offers even fewer clues.

Abruptly, I click to freeze the film and select instead the clip from 1979. The bar of the Ship now springs to life in colour before me – or, rather, that peculiar version of colour which seems to be unique to video footage of the 1970s, strangely lacking in bold primaries and dominated by the in-between shades, as if the world back then was mainly orange, mauve and turquoise. Music flares, the soundtrack kicking in a fraction after the picture. An instrumental piece, a Morris tune I think I recognise, cranked out at a spirited lick by two melodeons in unison, with a third adding creaking harmonies.

On the ledge along the back wall the objects are much as before, although their order has switched here and there, and perhaps a few more bottles have accumulated.

62

The striped and moustachioed football team is still in its place to the left of the piano but the man with his collie in the cornfield has now shifted along, the space between taken up by an old Bell's whisky jeroboam half filled up with crown bottle caps. Around the room the cigarettes are now king size, filter-tipped, and the gathered locals also seem to be somehow larger, broader. Coastal Suffolk might not jump to every whim of fashion but the trouser legs, the skirts and sleeves and collars are all perceptibly wider, and in several cases floral. I even spot a cheesecloth blouse, draping a pleasingly ample female bosom.

The melodeon players reach their final chord more or less together and, after a splash of applause and some coughing, at length one voice emerges through the throb of conversation, low and singing unaccompanied. For a moment, my breathing stops.

For to see poor Tom o' Bedlam
ten thousand miles I'd travel;
Mad Maudlin goes on dirty toes
for to save her shoes from gravel...

The camera angle shifts and she comes into view, there in the high-backed corner seat. Same heart-shaped chin, same faded hair. The voice is the same as this afternoon, as well: the quiet, confident contralto. The tilt of the head, too, and the way she sings with her eyes half closed as if she's lost in the words of the song. How can it be the same woman, though, more than thirty-five years ago? The singer on the screen in her simple, long dark dress might not be old but is certainly not young. And then there's the other one, the woman of the photograph, already framed on the wall in 1954. Mother, daughter and granddaughter? If so, the family resemblance is quite uncanny.

Still I sing bonny boys, bonny mad boys,
Bedlam boys are bonny,
for they all go bare and they live by the air,
and they want no drink nor money.

Behind her, at the end of the ledge beside the Toby jug, stands the picture of the bearded man with his crook and pint, and on the ledge behind him no doubt, although too small to see, are the striped shirts of the football team. There rushes over me a sense of the sucking whirlpool of time, as each image folds in on the next, smaller and smaller, ever more distant, until I'm engulfed and anchorless, toppling towards the void. It's the same sensation, almost of nausea, I remember from when I was small, angling the three-panelled mirror on my grandmother's dressing table to see endless repetitions of myself, receding away to nothing. Too much beer tonight, before I turned in; that last pint was a mistake. I refocus my eyes away from the pale illumination of the screen and onto the solid wall of the pub's guest room, the squat jug kettle with its pair of upturned cups and, by the window, my coat on the back of the chair.

She has come to the end of her song now, and back on the laptop a stout man in corduroy trousers has taken possession of the fluted piano stool. He picks up a tune which is known to his audience and is soon joined with enthusiasm around the bar: *and the larks they sang melodious...* But at this point the picture freezes and the slowly rotating circle appears, buffering. When it resumes the film flickers and jumps, so I suppose it must have been damaged, and the soundtrack, too, because there's nothing but a fuzz of white noise. Then, suddenly bright and unblurred, the woman's voice breaks through again.

Still I sing bonny boys, bonny mad boys...

Has the tape been reconnected wrongly, or is she really

reprising the song? But the portly man still sits at the piano; his fingers still scamper over the keys. There seems no logic to it.

I sit back to uncrick my neck, and unfold from under me a leg that has gone to sleep. Which is what I should do, really, instead of befuddling my brain with these imprisoned versions of reality, these overlayered electronic pasts. But there's a strange magnetism about them that makes me want to keep on looking.

It's stupid to be perching on the bed like this, but there's no desk or table in the room. I think longingly of the bar, but it's late, and the landlord, Raymond, will have called time long ago and be cleaning out the pumps. A lugubrious type whose chief delight, from what I've seen, is in flooding, crop failure and the hope of bird flu, he's unlikely to be pleased to interrupt his bottling up to serve an after-hours drink, even to an overnight resident. Moving to the head of the bed, I raise the pillows to an upright position and settle myself against them with the laptop on my thighs.

I quit the Suffolk folk archive website which houses the two historic films and drag the cursor to the desktop file where I've uploaded my own video of today's floor session. It's funny, when I click to start it running, to see my own life of nine hours ago replayed on screen. There's an unsettling awareness of my divided self, of being both there in the video, the participant observer, and simultaneously here in the pub bedroom, watching from the outside. Timeframes, places, selves, with the walls between them dissolving... I shake myself. I'm not normally prone to these vertiginous fancies – it must be the effect of looking at the old film clips, and of course I'm tired, and there's the effect of the beer. I'd be better

65

under the duvet, and with the bedside light switched off. The screen's low gleam will be enough.

On the laptop screen, my afternoon starts to rerun itself, sharper than my memory of it, precise in every detail. There is Raymond, greeting new arrivals from behind the bar with a 'Town lost again on Sat'day, then,' before pulling their pints in gloomy satisfaction. There, side by side at the wooden settle beside the bar, are the two regulars, the ones I met later over a supper of Raymond's pie and chips, with Jim – or was it George? – telling some grumbling story punctuated by jabs of the forefinger at an imaginary antagonist while George – or was it Jim? – nursed his half of Guinness and shook his head sorrowfully. I must go back in a minute and see if I can spot them, youthful and floral-collared, in 1979. Then the music begins. Proceedings open with what must be a Ship standard, as from the velvet-seated stool a pianist, younger and slimmer than the 1979 model, leads the room in a hearty if somewhat ragged rendition of 'The larks they sang melodious'.

Behind the piano, the ledge and the photographs are all where they should be: the football team, the man and dog. The me behind the lens, like the other cameramen before me, pans right towards the end of the ledge, past the Toby jug, the man with the beard... and suddenly the me that's here in the room sits up straighter against the pillows. The corner seat is empty. She isn't there.

Perhaps she only arrived later. But even as I think it, I know it isn't true. Well then, she must just have slipped out to the ladies at this point and will be back in a minute or two. I pause the clip, slide the dot a centimetre to the right and release it to restart. But the focus here is on a younger woman at a table at the opposite side of the bar, near the window, singing 'Aweigh Santy Ano' and playing the melodeon. Impatient, I slide the dot further to the right, release it again. A white-haired man is on his feet and midway through lamenting his wand'rings in the woods so wild – and behind him, clearly visible, is the high-backed corner seat. Still empty.

When did she do her spot? 'Tom o' Bedlam' – when did she sing it? It was towards the end of the session, I'm pretty sure of that. I pull the dot a good way right this time, and yes, there are the three long-haired teenage girls with their unaccompanied harmonies. 'Tom o' Bedlam' came straight after them, I'm certain of it. I let the tape roll on. But as the teenagers linger on their final major chord, modulating to a plaintive minor, and applause stutters around the bar, the scraping chairs and rumbling voices are interrupted not by my woman with the cleft chin but by the piano again, and the final item of the afternoon, a rousing general chorus of 'New York Girls'. I must have missed it. Rewind, play. Twice more I watch back through the final section of the video, stopping and restarting, and still she isn't there. Did I stop filming for a while, and I've managed to forget it? But I have the clearest recollection of standing there hearing her sing with the Sony in my hand – of watching her through the viewfinder, checking her image on the little screen. A malfunction? But there's no jump in the action, no hiatus, no join.

Frustrated, I close the file. My fingers are clumsy on the trackpad: why are they trembling like that? I return to the Suffolk folk website and the archived film clips. 1979: I'll find her there – or her mother, rather. Searching through, I locate quite quickly the three melodeon players winding out their Morris tune. I let them play; she comes next.

Damn it. Just as the music dies away and the low between-songs hubbub starts up, the picture freezes.

Bloody buffering – though the pub's Wi-Fi connection isn't bad on the whole, and you can hardly expect superfast broadband out here in the sticks. I wait, watching the rotating circle, impatience mounting. Still buffering: it must be jammed. I exit then click back on, starting the video from a little way back, with the melodeonists still in full swing. They play their final bars, the last chord ebbs, conversation resumes— and the blasted screen freezes again.

Give up, I tell myself, aware that my left hand is tightly balled, the nails digging into my palm. It's just a glitch. Leave it alone, come back to it later. Closing the link, I go back instead to the earliest clip, back to 1954 and the smoky black-and-white. I start it at the beginning. At least this picture is moving, but for some reason now there's no sound, only mummers acting out silently the scene in the bar. The spry little fiddle player, fingers scampering, taps his foot to a noiseless jig. Then his bowing slows, and the man in the cloth cap opens his mouth and mimes the first verse of 'Fathom the Bowl'. The camera swings round, and my stomach lurches. The corner chair is no longer empty.

Her chin is the same, and the hair, and even the dress: dark, long-sleeved and austere. Her face is angled down, partly shadowed, but I can see her lips moving, and as I watch there's a pop and the soundtrack crackles to life.

So drink to Tom o' Bedlam,
he'll fill the seas in barrels.
I'll drink it all, all brewed with gall,
with Mad Maudlin I will travel.

To the left and forwards of her I can see the fiddler, still plainly fiddling, although no sound of a violin can be heard. It's all wrong, all nonsensical. She shouldn't be there, not in 1954; she should only be there as a photograph. She's like some sombre Russian doll: remove the layers one by one but her face still reappears. The shot moves back towards the left and there at the side bench is the cloth-capped singer, his lips still wordlessly moving, while instead of his song there is only the woman's soft, insistent voice.

Still I sing bonny boys, bonny mad boys...

Computers can play stupid tricks. The other video must have re-started, and that is the soundtrack I'm hearing. That'll be it. But when I quit full screen and check the other link, it's still locked, still buffering. Yet her voice twines on.

Spirits white as lightning
shall on my travels guide me...

I click on the double bar to halt the video and the violinist's arm is arrested in mid-motion, but not the woman's song.

The moon would quake and the stars would shake,
whenever they espied me...

With sudden urgency I click to close the whole page, leave the archive website, shut down the browser. I'm back to my familiar desktop wallpaper, but still the crooning voice won't stop. I go to the main menu, drag the cursor to 'shut down'. Yet something makes my hand hesitate, arrested above the keyboard. Perspiration slicks the creases of my palm, and my finger joints are stiff, incompliant. The sense floods back over me of the self that's inside the machine, the recorder recorded, contained within my own past. The notion is more powerful now, more urgent, almost engulfing. It's as though I'm trapped. I am the disappearing image, shuttled to infinity between two mirrors. I am the smallest Russian doll, enclosed inside my earlier self, and I can't break out. More than that, there's a tightening

69

conviction that if I shut down now I will somehow be extinguished, will somehow cease to be. If I shut down now... if I shut down...

No gypsy, slut or doxy
Shall take my mad Tom from me...

There's no choice, no other way out. I have to stop the voice. I steel myself, select 'Shut Down', and press.

Nothing happens. Again I press, twice, three times, jabbing savagely at the trackpad, until an error message appears. It's the browser that's failed to quit. *She won't go. Why won't she go?*

Wresting my eyes from the screen, I glance across to the far wall, where the Wi-Fi booster winks at me, two green lights and a red. Around it, after the brightness of the computer screen, the blackout is almost complete.

Almost, but not quite. From the shrouded oblong of the window comes a faint greyness, and as my eyes adjust I see it there, above my coat where it hangs on the back of the chair, the pool of deeper black, the shadow where no shadow should be. I mustn't look. Whatever I do, I mustn't look.

My hand shakes. Reopen or force quit?

I'll weep all night, with stars I'll fight...

The room pitches. Force quit. It's one of us or the other. The woman, or me. *Force quit.*

I close my eyes and press.

Still I sing bonny boys, bonny mad boys,
Bedlam boys are bonny,
For they all go bare and they live by the air...

NIGHTINGALE'S RETURN

Two hours sitting folded like a grasshopper on the aircraft and several more waiting at the terminal on those wretched moulded plastic seats, plus three trains and two taxis at either end of his day, had left a niggling soreness in Flavio's lumbar vertebrae. Or maybe it was the forty years before that with insufficient regular stretching, spent behind a desk at the *sede del Municipio*, because his knees were also stiffer than they had any right to be. Sixty-four was no age at all these days; the old cashier at the Banco Popolare who must be five years his senior had run the Ravenna marathon last year. But that man was short, with the compact springiness of a Piemontese while Flavio was tall, and height was nothing but a curse as you grew older. He could almost feel the protesting grind of cartilage discs unaccustomed to any greater exercise than the short walk to the office and back, with a regular detour on the way home to Maurizio's sports bar on the corner for a grappa and to catch the news headlines. Not that the news was ever anything but grim these days, but a man had a duty to keep on terms with the world he lived in. No – he'd been stuck in the same triangular groove for far too long, stretching to an elongated quadrilateral on a Saturday for his regular treats: a trip to the barber's for a proper wet shave or to the Trattoria dall'Oste for *braciole di maiale* and a carafe of house red. This trip to England was just the shake-up he needed.

Perhaps walking would dispel the stiffness. It was too late to change his mind now in any case, as the taxi driver he had paid off and sent ahead to the inn with his suitcase had already pulled away and disappeared from view between the convergent banks of cow parsley, which marked the curve of the lane ahead. He hoped he could trust the man, who had volunteered precious few words on the short ride from the station, offering in particular no account for why the little halt should call itself 'Wickham Market' when it was at a place called Campsea Ashe. Flavio's father, Salvatore, had always spoken warmly of the people of these parts, as being straightforward, honest folk. '*Veri contadini,*' he'd called them; guarded, it was true, but flintily fair-minded, even towards a man who was their enemy. But the world had changed in seventy years. Who was to say they might not take the opportunity now to rob an ageing foreigner with a bad back and halting, schoolroom English?

Nightingale Farm the place was called, and his father said they were really there, back in those days, the birds that gave the place its name. Flavio remembered hearing nightingales at his grandparents' house at San Cesario in the countryside of Emilia-Romagna – hearing them but never seeing one. They were anonymous little brown birds according to Papi, plain as Franciscan fustian, with a drabness quite at odds with the extravagance of their song, and they kept to the densest thickets, nesting deep in the heart of gorse or underscrub. There was, besides, some quality about their song which made its source and direction impossible to gauge. 'That's because it comes directly from the throats of angels,' his *nonna* told him, 'and not from the larynx of a bird.' Flavio himself had no religion, though he would soon be reaching a stage of life when he might start to wish for its solace. But it was true that the small bird's music expanded and swelled until it filled the air on every side, so that it seemed to rise with the dew at daybreak and descend from the stars at night.

Nightingale Farm. He'd written ahead of time to inquire about a visit. The name of the people was the same as when his father was sent there: Beck, one of those solid Anglo-Saxon names. He had no other address apart from the name of the farm and village but it had been enough for his letter to find its destination. Perhaps in England, too, they had no street addresses in these country places, and the postman knew the house and family just as everybody did, the same way it had been in San Cesario. It was a woman who wrote back to him, and he wondered what relation she would be. The couple his father spoke of back then had been the age of his own parents, Flavio's grandparents, so that might make his correspondent now a granddaughter, or a great-granddaughter? He'd arranged to call tomorrow afternoon – had received a gracious invitation to tea and no doubt some English cake – and was putting up tonight and for the few days following at the village inn. He would ask for directions from there. The Ship, it was called, which was also the same inn his father had mentioned – the 'pub' was the word that Salvatore used – where he'd drunk beer at sundown alongside the other village farmhands and learned to join in the choruses of their songs. Flavio recalled it for the curiosity of its name, which Salvatore said made no sense at all when the village was fully ten kilometres from the sea. It was probably some English joke that neither of them understood.

It was a beautiful evening for a walk; he could have no complaints on that score, at least. He'd packed his case with a thought to rain, which was what he was told you could expect in England in any month of the year, including high summer. The lush vegetation of the verges bore some testament to the truth of it as they were certainly far greener than you would see in Italy in June. But beneath them, tramlining the lane, lay a powder of fine, pale sand, and the air was warm and moved by a breeze as crisply dry as a glass of good *verdicchio*. His back seemed to loosen a little as he walked but his left knee joint kept locking unaccountably. The knees of an office clerk, he thought, of a *funzionario*. Once, he knew, he had enjoyed his job in the local business services department, had taken a quiet satisfaction in his own efficiency, but he knew it in a distant, abstract way. It was too long ago now to remember what the enjoyment felt like. He had never married. There had been girls when he was younger, and several of them would have made agreeable companions to warm his bed and share his table, but when it came to husbands they seemed to prefer men who were better dancers or had faster cars and livelier conversation. Girls, back then, and women, too, more recently – though none, admittedly, for quite some time. But as they all grew older, marriage (to him, or their own to other people) no longer seemed to suggest itself as a consideration. You could scarcely blame the women; he was no kind of catch.

Then Maria had died – his sister, Maria Chiara, aged only fifty-two, who'd had a lump in her breast for more than a year. They weren't the kind of family where such a thing was talked of between sister and brother, so he'd known she was sick but thought it some stubborn infection she would shake off when the spring weather came. Instead, the returning sunshine brought only jonquils and mimosa for her coffin. After that it fell to Flavio to move back in with Salvatore and their mother, Giuseppa, both of them now ailing and housebound. He'd pulled in his horns then, like the snails he used to hunt for in the damp orchard grass at Nonna and Papi's in San Cesario as a youngster, whose glistening antlers swayed in a slow dance like something under water but retracted with surprising speed the moment they were touched. Like them he had retreated into the calcified prison he had built for himself. But it was four years now since Giuseppa had died, and Salvatore had been gone a year, the house cleared out and painted and the top floor rented out so that he could afford at last to take his modest municipal pension and live quite comfortably according to his measured habits. Now it was time to crawl out from his shell and reconnect, to see a little of humanity and the world before he was old and bedridden as his parents had been in those last narrow months and years.

Pausing for a moment to straighten his spine and let his eye absorb the vista of well-tended fields and tidy hedges, it came to Flavio how little, at heart, this country was different from his own. Idly, he brushed one hand through the feathered tops of oat grass and meadow foxtail at the laneside, releasing a mist of weightless seed and lacing the air with honey. Then he slipped open the top two buttons of his shirt and, shaking free his locked knee, moved off again towards the village.

*   *   *

Planting potatoes was back-breaking work under any skies. All day long Salvatore had bent to his task, lifting from their pallets the chitted tubers, flaccid-skinned and small as a bantam egg, and burying them a hand's width

76

deep in the raised seams of earth, with their sprouting eyes towards the warmth. Now, as the low grey cloud, which had drooped overhead since morning, finally banked up and away to the east to let in slanting from the west the golden evening sunlight, he stacked up the empty pallets, straightened the kink from his lower spine and set off up the lane for Nightingale Farm.

Would they be singing tonight, the nightingales? It was almost the end of April and they had been back for a week or more: two cock birds, one who had staked his claim to a tangle of hawthorn and thick brambles between the lane and the corrugated pigsties, and one in the gorse bushes on the piece of sloping scrubland behind the farmhouse which led down to Stone Common. They sang in the morning when he set off for the fields and again at his return, and on into the dusk after supper, and if he stirred in his bed at night, the sound of their voices still drifted in beneath the open sash. You'd think they never stopped, but if these English birds were like the ones at home in San Cesario then they took a siesta in the heat of the noonday like good Italians. Could a nightingale have a nationality, though, the way a man had – be he soldier, sailor or farmer – when they split their lives between two countries, spending summer and winter three thousand kilometres apart? They arrived, and sang for six or eight short weeks, and found a mate and raised their young, and then they would be off again, to follow their ancestral airborne tracks to warmer climes. Perhaps these Blaxhall birds, though English born, had also the scarlet blood of Africa running hot in their veins. And who could say that they had not flown through Emilia-Romagna on their journey here, stopping off to rest their wings in the woods at San Cesario?

A life split between two countries. Was not Salvatore

himself now nationless, a migrant like the birds? His brief days as a combatant had begun and ended in 1942. On his eighteenth birthday, which fell in February on the feast of Saint Valentine, he'd signed up with the Regia Marina; after receiving his uniform and ten weeks' basic training at a naval base in Sicily, he boarded the destroyer *Espero,* a battle-scarred veteran of the first war, and was torpedoed off the Maltese coast on his very first voyage, bound for North Africa with a troopship convoy. For seventy minutes Salvatore fought his war in the churning, ink-black water, not for politics or the mother country but simply for his life. He and his fellow survivors were plucked from the foaming, oil-slicked flotsam by the British vessel which had sent them down, were issued with different, dry uniforms and escorted under guard to Gibraltar, and thence through Spain and France on a troop train with other prisoners of war to an internship camp in Portsmouth. By midsummer, just four short months after his enlistment, he found himself back out in the sunlight, riding cross-legged on the back of a carrier's cart towards the Suffolk farm where he was to be put to work.

From drilling in Emilia-Romagna in February he was haymaking in Suffolk in June. From seed time to harvest and with no blow struck in anger in between, his experience of the war seemed curiously like a dream, or something that had happened to another man entirely. This was his real life, this continuity of rising and washing, of working and sweating and tilling the soil, and laughing and talking and eating and drinking, and his face cool on the rough cotton bolster at the end of the day. The language was strange, and rose and fell in ways which jarred upon his ear at first, but he soon learned to follow and fit his tongue to its daily patterns. The soil was finer and sandier than back in San Cesario; the beer was russet brown with a thin, yeasty taste and there were potatoes every day and rarely macaroni; the soups and stews were under-seasoned but hearty, and Harry Beck was a hard worker and a temperate taskmaster. The rhythm of the farming day, the farming year, was much as it had been in Italy, his pleasure the same in simple tasks carefully accomplished. He would soon have been here one whole year round: when he arrived at midsummer the nightingales were still singing and now in April they sang again.

In the first days when, separated from his compatriots at the camp and unable to connect with his watchful hosts in anything but shrugs and smiling bafflement, he found himself missing home all at once with an intensity that was like a mallet blow beneath the ribs, it was to the stables that he had fled for consolation and companionship. The two farm horses accepted with patient equanimity his overtures of friendship, and with whiskery, velvet-muzzled pleasure the titbits of apple core or bread crust that he saved for them. These Suffolk punches had the same sweet-sour breath, the same stoutly muscled quarters and warm, dust-scented flanks as the working horses of Ferrara stock on the farm at home, though their coats were a ruddier chestnut and they were clean-heeled, not feathered at the fetlock like Perla and Pietro. Jack was the younger and taller, while the stockier of the pair was his mother, Jewel. A fanciful name, by English standards – though there were plenty of farmers round San Cesario who called their horses Pulcinella or Imperatore or even Greta Garbo. But the dogs at Nightingale Farm were Meg, Bess and Mick, and Jewel was Harry's one flight of sentiment. 'My precious ruby', he called her, in tones he rarely used with his wife or daughter, and 'my diamond girl'. One evening when Salvatore had been at the farm for less than a month, the two men coincided at Jewel's

79

stall. 'Just checking on the mare' was what Harry said, but his hand held fat sweet carrots, sliced with his pocket knife. He told the story of the night when Jack was foaled, presenting with feet forward and the cord around his neck, and how poor Jewel had sweated and strained for hours to no avail. 'I thought I'd lost her,' he said; and though Salvatore grasped no more of the story than one word in four, the sense of it was clear. We have our own jewel at home, our Perla, he wanted to say, but lacked the means. It didn't seem to matter – they understood each other just the same.

In the big brick barn beneath a tarpaulin stood a beautiful blue Standard Fordson tractor, relegated to a place beside the binder and the old steam thresher. Under its wraps, Salvatore could see that its paintwork had been kept polished to a shine that would have passed muster aboard the *Espero*. Once, before the war, it must have been the pride of the farm. But you couldn't get the diesel these days, so it was Jewel and Jack who were back in everyday service – and Harry, he guessed, none the sorrier for that. Salvatore had always had a knack with horses. They seemed to trust the unhurried sureness with which he adjusted straps and fastened girths; even these foreign animals pricked up their ears to his chirrup, or fell calm at his murmured Italian endearments. Right from a boy he'd had an eye for a straight furrow, as soon as he had strength to handle the plough. Slowly, through the damp misty months of the English autumn and winter, he had won the respect of the man who was his employer, host and gaoler, and with it that of the land workers round about – unexpressed, perhaps, but equally ungrudged. With so many of the young men gone, the burden of farm work had fallen on older shoulders or to women, and schoolchildren kept home from lessons to pick fruit or help bring home the hay. The war was just the war to these unexcitable country people, and once wariness subsided, Salvatore's broad back and deft hands counted for more with them than his southern skin and alien, black crow's-wing hair, for more than birth or military allegiance. Nations might rise and fall and treaties be forged or broken, but there still remained the soil to be tilled, the stock to be fed and the crops to be fetched in.

He was at the final corner now, at the top of the rise and within a pebble's throw of the pigsties and the bramble patch; there at the turn of the lane he stopped to rest his aching back and listen for a while. And there it was – starting with a characteristic low whistle and a series of repeated fluting peeps, it began its gentle woodwind warm-up, before the sudden, heart-stopping rush and rise as it launched its evening aria. *L'usignolo*; voice of heaven, angel bird. The nightingale.

As he stood he closed his eyes and let his mind trace out the melody as it rose and fell. He knew no other bird which could combine within a single phrase that round, full-throated tone like a thrush or blackbird before soaring up as impossibly high as the trilling of a skylark. But his favourite of all was a low, bubbling warble, a note so pure and liquid clear you felt refreshed to hear it, as if you had actually drunk the spring water the sound resembled, welling fresh from the rock. *Cool'd a long age in the deep-delvèd earth*. It was a line from an English poem he'd had recited to him that lodged in musical snatches in his mind. The poem was about a nightingale, he knew, and although he didn't completely understand the words or what they had to do with the little bird, their mysterious sound seemed somehow to match the

81

other-worldliness of its song. *Beaded bubbles winking at the brim...* With the late sun bathing his tilted face, Salvatore stood still and drank deep.

* * *

At the crest of a small rise where the lane swung left, Flavio stopped for a rest. He was more than a little breathless, though he hadn't walked far and the gradient had been slight. He sounded like an old man – and perhaps after all that is what he was, or shortly would be – an old man like his father. Not that Salvatore had lacked for breath, for his lungs had always been strong and it was his mother whose last months had been measured out in snatched and wheezing gasps. With Salvatore it was the liver and stomach that failed him at the end, so that he lay gaunt and sallow on the pillows and was constantly cold, clutching the quilt up high over jutting collarbones and ribs. There was a peculiar intimacy about the care of the old, bringing Flavio physically closer to his parents than he had been since a small child, or even a baby. Physically closer, but not, in the end, emotionally. Perhaps it was the preservation of self-respect which produced, as it seemed to him, with both mother and father in turn, a compensating withdrawal into self, into memory and an interior life beyond the immediate, mundane indignity of spooned soup, bedpans and the sponging of limbs. Maybe as eyesight faded there was a natural retreat into a past which stood preserved in fresher colours. Or perhaps it was simply an effect of the proximity of death. Whatever the reason, Flavio perceived the distancing and respected it, though it frequently left him feeling lonely even before he was finally alone.

It was almost evening now, and the twittering of

skylarks which had formed the background soundtrack since he alighted on the single platform at Campsea Ashe, seemed all at once to have ceased. They were like the cicadas in the countryside back home; you only noticed them when they stopped. The silence was suddenly palpable, so that the faint noise of one distant passing engine called attention to itself, like a cough at a funeral. Such a quiet spot. Could he live somewhere this quiet? His father had never mentioned the silence, but maybe the rest of the world back then had been less clamorous.

Then into the stillness came a sound he recognised at once in his stomach and diaphragm – although it took his mind a while to catch up, to register first that it was birdsong, and then that it could only be a nightingale. *Directly from the throats of angels*, he thought. It was his father, though, and not Nonna, who had told him about the nightingale's habit of returning to the same nest site. That was something Salvatore had found out here in England. All those thousands of kilometres of journeying, and they came back to the same small clump of bushes where they had reared their chicks the summer before, or where they had themselves been fledged. It was beyond the resource of science to understand, his father had said, how it should be so, what genetic patterning or undetected sense enabled these little birds, with their simple, elementary brains, to trace one-eighth of the globe's circumference and find their way back home. A miracle of nature.

Indeed, there was much, it appeared, that his father had learned in England on the subject of the nightingale. There was a poem – a poem in English, seemingly taught to him by the daughter of the house, the young Miss Beck, who had learned it by heart at school. *The self-same song that found a path*... Old Salvatore could recite phrases from its stanzas even as closer memory grew dim; Flavio's English was rudimentary and unadapted to the language of poetry but his father had repeated the words so many times that some at least had taken a flimsy hold. *The self-same song that found a path...* But it was no good – the rest of the line was lost.

Might he now in fact be close to the place where his father had stayed? Of course it was simplistic to assume that the presence of a nightingale must indicate the proximity of Nightingale Farm. Perhaps they were a common species in these parts, and they were singing all round the village at every lane corner. And yet something stirred inside him which was more than the growl of a stomach that had had nothing inside it but a plastic-wrapped airport sandwich since his morning espresso. Something told him he was near the spot, that this was the same nightingale, or rather, the great-great-great grandson of the one that Salvatore had heard. How long was one nightingale generation? A year, or two, or three? In seventy years, how many birds had hatched, and fledged, and flown?

The people of the farm, those earlier Becks, what had become of them? Of the older couple – the farmer, Harry, and Marjorie, his wife – and their two surviving children? Salvatore had spoken of one son killed outside Tobruk in '41, but another was away fighting in Singapore and Burma at the time of his billeting with the family and might have come through unscathed, and then there was the younger child, the girl – Eileen, was it, or Irene? – who was fifteen or sixteen and still at school. About her, Flavio's father had been almost entirely silent – except as the source of the nightingale poem. Their ages were not so very far apart. But a man of eighteen, nineteen, who had been to war – he doubtless regarded her as just a *bambina*.

After he left the farm, towards the end of '43 following the signing of the Sicily Armistice, Salvatore had lost touch with his English hosts. Flavio never understood quite why, whether there had been some breach or falling-out between them – though it was an irony if that were so now that they were no longer enemies but allies – or whether their connection was just another casualty of the upheavals of war. Flavio knew only that his father heard no more from the family in Suffolk and that it was a sadness to him.

* * *

Salvatore stirred himself from the reverie induced by the bird's song. It was growing late and he would be expected. There would be rabbit stew tonight to go with their potatoes; Harry had trapped a brace of them early this morning on the Five-acre, up near the edge of the little beech copse. He'd made a rueful joke of it at breakfast, self-mocking. Even a farmer can't be sure of pellets for his shotgun nowadays, he'd said, with everything commandeered for the Home Guard. Here am I, setting traps for my own rabbits like some skulking poacher, while we save our shot for Hitler. Marjorie had glanced up at that and sent her husband a warning look. We're past all that now, Salvatore had wanted to say. If I'm here then it's your side I'm on, if I'm on a side at all; when it comes to empty stomachs, war's the same for all of us. And maybe she'd caught the echo of his thoughts, because she laid a kindly hand on his shoulder and said, 'I hope your mum and dad have got a rabbit for the pot tonight as well.' Irene, at the end of the table, said nothing at all, but her smile was like a shaft of sunshine on a foggy day.

She'd be back in from feeding the chickens by now, would have her pinafore on over her school blouse and be helping her mother peel the potatoes for supper. 'Taters', the old couple called them; it seemed that half the time there were two words to learn in English for every one. They were proud of their lass in their gruff, unspeaking way – a scholarship pupil at sixteen when most girls her age were out in the fields or else in Ipswich, at Turner's on the munitions line – but she still had to pull her weight at home. Maybe, chores done, she'd be curled in the small armchair beside the kitchen range, with her algebra primer and that wrinkle of concentration between her eyebrows that made him want to smooth her forehead as if she were a cat – or perhaps with one of her books of poetry.

From behind him, as he turned into the sandy track which led down to the farmhouse, the nightingale's song still trailed on the breeze. *My heart aches...* Why should a sound so beautiful make you, hearing it, feel sad? But it did: the English poet knew it, and he was right. ...*where beauty cannot keep her lustrous eyes...* In his head the song of the bird merged and melded with Irene's voice, speaking the words of the poem: her soft voice, her soft blonde hair and softer eyelids, half lowered over eyes so liquid dark they made him think of *mirtilli.* ...*or new love pine at them beyond tomorrow...* He hardly knew what the lines might mean. He only knew that, like the birdsong, they filled him with a nameless longing – for peace, for family, for home in Italy, and for home at Nightingale Farm. Whatever the future might bring, he knew that when he reached the farmhouse door Irene would be there, and that she was beautiful, and he loved her.

* * *

There had been a picture on his father's bedroom wall, in the last months: a painting executed by his own hand. Its appearance had taken Flavio by surprise, since Salvatore had never picked up a brush in all the time he'd known him. It was pleasing enough in a broad-stroked, naive way, and Flavio wondered why it had not been out on view while his mother was alive. He'd asked his father as much, and received no more than a shrug in reply. Perhaps there had once been words between them. She had laughed at his artistic efforts, perhaps, and his pride had been wounded, and the painting stored away. Towards the end, when he was confined to the bed, Salvatore had gazed at it increasingly often. Flavio had caught him several times staring with tears in his eyes, and had wondered why – though old men could be sentimental and cry for no great reason. The subject matter, at any rate, was no secret: his father had told him it was Nightingale Farm.

Thus it was that now, as he stopped at the top of a sandy track and looked down the gentle incline, he recognised the house at once. There could be no mistaking it: the configuration of trees had shifted slightly, but the big oak was still there to the left of the gate, and the walls were painted the same warm shade of dusky pink. From the central brick chimney, in defiance of the season, there even spiralled a twist of smoke, exactly as in the painting. It was almost as if he knew the place himself; he could almost have been coming home.

His luggage would be at the inn by now; they would be looking out for his arrival. Mrs Beck or Miss Beck, whose letter was in his trouser pocket, was not expecting him before tomorrow. Surely it would be a gross intrusion to arrive unannounced a day early, and at this hour? The English, he had heard, were a conventional people, with particular ideas about good manners. But even as these logical, practical arguments rehearsed themselves inside his head, his feet were turning down the track towards the five-barred gate, familiar from his father's depiction, and approaching the farmhouse door.

The bell was an old brass one: a ship's bell, with a chain attached. He took hold of the metal ring and pulled, setting the bell swinging to emit a clear, resounding clang. A pause, then muffled footsteps; the door swung open and a woman stood before him on the step.

She was about his own age or perhaps a little older, with a wing of smooth hair that must once have been black. The berry eyes that lit on him held curiosity but no surprise.

'You've come,' she said.

The Level Crossing

One two, one two. It's not hard, it's not complicated. It's just a case of putting one foot in front of the other.

Starting out is always tough, though. There's the stiffness in my calves, and the way my feet feel heavy, flat-soled as if I'm wearing giant clown shoes: *slap slap, slap slap*. The movement isn't automatic yet, as running ought to be. It feels deliberate, the lifting and placing, having to think about each step.

I think of how it works with engines, how the oil needs to heat before it liquefies, before its levels rise sufficiently to wash over the moving parts. Until then it's metal on metal, grating and jarring, unlubricated. It was Matt who told me, while degreasing chain and sprockets on an old newspaper at the kitchen table.

I feel the unoiled grind inside me, ball in socket, bone on bone; I feel my tendons dry as an unrosined bow, more fit to snap than to give and stretch. But then it comes, the rising oil, the rising sap. I hit my stride. The beat establishes control, *one two, one two*, and it takes me over, drives me. My limbs are pure rhythm. My body working now on instinct, my mind is released for thought.

89

I've done some of my best thinking when I'm out on a run. It's why I've never been one for running with a radio or iPod – that, and the alien tempo of the music, always slightly out of step with my own measure, with the natural cadence of my stride. How often has running made the gearshift, bumped the circuit, freed the logjam: problems unknotted, conundrums solved? When I'm running I can hatch great plans, receive revelations, crack a mystery, write a poem. Or once I could, but recently... but now... Time to think is a knife that cuts two ways.

One two, one two. I focus instead on what I see: on the peace outside, instead of the tangle within. This road is beautiful in the early mornings, in any weather, any season. Today the tarmac under my feet has the silver-grey sheen left behind by an overnight frost, and the ice melt falls in heavy droplets from the hedges on either side of the lane, their patter accentuating the surrounding stillness. The air meets my trachea in round, wet mouthfuls, saturated with the flavours of autumn: leaf mould and mushrooms and the woodsmoke of early chimneys. Over the stubbled fields which slope away towards the river and the railway line, a low, damp mist is gathered, huddling in the dips and hollows like sluggish cattle, while, above, a watery sun gilds everything it touches in a chill lemon-white.

I am one with it all, one with the moist air, the dripping leaves, the palely gleaming morning. No thought – no space for thought. I am smoothly pumping legs. I am swinging arms and warm, resilient, spanking feet. *One two, one two.*

One two, one two. The frost was sharper last night, or maybe this morning I am earlier by a fraction or the sun more veiled, so that the thaw is less advanced

90

than yesterday. To the left of the band of tarmac, where sunlight falls, the strip of encroaching grey-brown sand is moist on top and yields where I tread, like putty; to the right, in the shadow of the hedge, it is crisply crusted and has no give at all.

One two three four... If I let myself count on, what number would I reach? It never differs, my running route. Through the cottage gate and up the track – close-packed and rutted now but kicking deep with sand in summer – then turn right and out along the lane; right and right again, past the village hall and down the hill; past the turning left to Stone Common and the church, and on towards the level crossing. That's where I turn, at the level crossing. It's where I've always turned.

It bounded my roamings, marked the confines of my girlhood cycle rides: the forbidden frontier. Forbidden, and thereby of course imbued with fascination. The hurtle of metal, its relentless, smooth-oiled piston power. It still draws my own mechanical strides, engine moving towards engine, each in its own tramlines.

There at the unmanned gates I reach out a hand to tag the gloss-white painted wood – slick to the touch this morning where ice has been – then swing on my heel and retrace my steps, heading for home. Thirty-eight minutes, more or less exactly, my pace unvarying: nineteen minutes there and nineteen minutes back. So, how many steps? If I take three strides a second that's a hundred and eighty per minute; for thirty-eight minutes, that makes six thousand and... six thousand and... *One two, one two.*

I always leave at the same time. My alarm, I should say, is set for the same time, always a quarter to seven. But then there are the little variations – the time it takes to down a glass of water; to pull on sweatshirt, leggings, trainers; to tie up laces. I know if I am late or early by the southbound train: the Lowestoft to Ipswich train, due at Wickham Market at 07:14. It passes through the level crossing at, what, 07:09, 07:10? If the signal on the bend is down, it's gone by already; if the signal's up, it's on its way.

Did she see it before it hit her, little Izzie? Great-aunt Izzie, my grandmother's sister – though there's something incongruous about the idea an eleven-year-old great-aunt. Was it the Ipswich or the Lowestoft train, I've wondered but have nobody to ask. Northbound or south? If northbound it would have been visible for longer, on the open stretch of track between the water meadows. She'd have seen it coming, surely, the child of eleven, on her way to Willett's Farm with the morning milk pail. Southbound, then – rounding the corner from the direction of Saxmundham, past Willett's barn and the clump of broad horse chestnuts. Great-aunt Izzie, whose name is my name. Isobel. It was Grannybel's name, too, but I never knew; in the family my grandmother was always Bel. I never even knew there was a sister at all, not until after Grannybel had died. Not back in the bike ride days – not even then, when Great-aunt Izzie could have been a bogle to scare the children, a cautionary tale, a graphic flesh-and-blood reason to *Keep Off the Level Crossing*. I only knew about Great-uncle Ted, who died when I was eight but whose whiskery kisses I remember at Christmases – and Grannybel, a decade younger than her brother Teddy and named for a big sister she never met, the pain of whose memory was such that Bel was never Izzie but always Bel.

'What was she like?' I asked Mum when I found out, when she was logging the family genealogy, half a dozen years ago. But she didn't know; she hadn't asked. 'They

92

never talked about it.' And now they're dead and it's too late.

The signal's down; the train has gone. I turn for home.

First one foot and then the other: *one two, one two*. This morning is wet, but I still go out. I always run, never miss. The rain slants down in oblique grey lines. Like stair rods, Grannybel used to say, but I think more of wires: the colour of zinc, it stings my skin and leaves a ferrous tang on my lips. The first part is the worst. Setting off in the rain in just a cotton sweatshirt feels all wrong; it makes me feel exposed. But once I'm wet, and warm, the two things cancel out and cease to matter. There's only the rhythm of my moving limbs, my pounding feet. *One two.*

Family secrets. *They never talked about it.* But then, nor do we, do we?

The surface of the lane is glazed underfoot where I skirt to avoid the puddles. The ball of one trainer slips away from me by a half-centimetre as the tread makes contact with the road, and I feel my weight pitch sideways for an instant before the forward momentum takes over and I regain equilibrium.

Careful. One two.

The risk of falling and the damage it could do, the catastrophic event it might precipitate. That's what the books all talk of now, the overbearing, complacent books. That, and the jolting and jarring, the diversion of blood flow from where it's needed. Before that – before the twelfth week – it was the threat of overheating, of all unlikely things: the raising of my core temperature at peril to formation of the major organs. The bun in the oven, overcooked. Such nonsense, though, it all was – such patronising nonsense. Paternalistic claptrap for pampered Western women, to be coddled and wrapped around in cotton wool with their feet up on a cushion, when throughout most of humanity and for most of history, women have toiled in the fields until the time of their confinement.

What could be more natural than running?

It hardly seems real, in any case – the small invader, the knot of cells, expanding and mutating in my uterus. Sixteen weeks and I'm barely showing, even to myself. If I stand front-on to the mirror and press my palms across my abdomen I can almost believe there's nothing there. The symptoms, imagined; the test results, a mistake, despite the grainy image from the scan. No one has noticed anything, not even Mum. The decaf, the fruit juice: she seems to think I'm just detoxing.

Maybe I'll tell her. Maybe today.

You'd think she'd see the signs, when she's been there twice herself. You'd think she'd recognise it in her own daughter.

If the train hasn't gone yet when I reach the level crossing, then I'll tell her. I'll ring as soon as I get home. Or perhaps I'll leave it an hour or so; Mum's never been an early riser.

It's November now. The lane here, where it runs down the hill towards the river and the railway line between overhanging willows, is thickly smeared with rotting leaves, like goose grease. Mid-November. That's four or five months to come of winter clothing: long cardigans and baggy jumpers. No one need know, not for a long time.

But I will ring Mum, I will. I can't do this alone. If the train hasn't gone when I get there, I'll ring.

My stride shortens as I start to slacken off, to pull up as I approach the crossing gates. My eyes drift right, towards the chestnut trees and the bend in the track.

It's down – the signal's down. I turn for home.

Today the lane is wrapped about by an enveloping mist. It is no longer confined to low-lying places but reaches everywhere, diffusing and refracting the spectral early light. The moisture-laden air distorts sound, appearing to trap and throw it back, causing my rhythmic breathing, my rhythmic footfalls, to echo within my skull. The whole world is muffled and remote. It is almost as if the whole thing – my running feet, the fog, the looming, half-occluded hedges, the clinging passenger in my belly – were all contained inside my head. If I closed my eyes, would I make it disappear?

One two, one two.

Was it foggy, I wonder, when Great-aunt Izzie died? Is that why she didn't see the train? The branch cut short on the family tree in Mum's album bore a date in June. But the railway track runs close to the river all the way along, and the valley of the Alde is prone to sudden mists at any time of year. Was there that morning, perhaps, some treacherous concurrence of humidity and temperature which spun to a plume of opaque white the evaporating morning dew? A trail, a wisp – enough to deceive the eye and mask for a fatal second or two the onrush of steam and steel? And at the final moment, did she see it come, did she hear the approaching thunder, the brakes' metallic squeal? Did she have time to feel it, the impossible mind-stopping breath-blocking weight of impact?

As I run down the hill from the village hall, the fog seems more impenetrable with every step. The turning to Stone Common is almost upon me before I see it, there on the left: the road that leads to Stone Common where the old house is, the house where Great-grandma and

Great-grandpa lived with Izzie and Ted, and later with Ted and little Bel. The house they brought her home to, broken, that morning – by cart, perhaps, or carried on a hurdle? And beyond Stone Common up the hill again to St Peter's church, where they bore her later, shoulder-high and no weight at all, eleven-year-old Izzie in her wooden box.

One two. I can't make out the crossing gates yet, though I know I must be close.

Matt won't be coming back. I saw his eyes, that night when I told him – the eyes of the quarry, the hounded fox, already seeing other walls, another bed. 'I need time,' he said as he climbed on his motorbike, but the weeks which have stretched to months have shown that it wasn't time he needed after all. I gave him time – or, rather, I gave him space, and he has clutched it between us like the buffering fog. I could have pleaded with him. I could have – should have? – said the words. *I can't do this alone.*

If the train has gone before I reach the level crossing, then he isn't coming back. I'm almost there. Denser white behind the white, a low rectangle forms itself across my path: the gates. Easing to a halt, I blink away the beads of sweat and fog and peer to my right towards the bend, straining to locate shape amid the indecipherable blank.

I see it. The signal's down – as if I needed it to tell me what I knew already, what I know. The train has passed. Matt's gone; he isn't coming back.

My legs feel leaden as I turn for home.

Frost again this morning: a hard, cold, iron frost. Tarmac is a forbearing surface but today it's concrete. Every foot I plant jolts up through bone and sinew, slamming joint pads, compressing cartilage, rattling teeth and jaw. I hold

96

myself together tighter against the impact, but it only makes things worse. Everything is taut, everything jars.

If I reach the level crossing before the train comes... But I can't tell Mum. If she hasn't noticed, it must be for a reason. She has her own life, her own problems. I'm not a child; I'm twenty-eight years old. I'm not a kid any more to run home for a plaster, for Mum to kiss it better, to make it go away. She has no sticking plaster for this, in any case – I'm on my own.

I can't do this alone.

If I reach the crossing before the train... Matt isn't coming back. His phone is always set to voicemail these days. I know he's screening, pressing the button that shuts me out. He won't be coming back.

But I can't, I can't do this alone.

If I reach the crossing before the train... What did she feel, my namesake, the child with the milk pail who was my great-aunt Izzie? Was there time for fear, for pain?

If I reach the crossing before the train. Nineteen minutes; two thousand seconds, give or take; six thousand paces. How many indrawn breaths, how many remaining exhalations? How many heartbeats left, my own and the smaller flickering pulse inside? Of nineteen minutes, maybe five to go now, or four, or three... If I get there before the train.

If I get there first, I'll wait for the train. I won't turn back, I'll wait by the rail. It would be so easy. So easy.

Down the hill now, beneath the willows: the gates are in sight. My stride is looser: long and loose and slow. I look right, towards the bend in the track.

It's up – the signal's up. I'm here first; the train is on its way.

The small pedestrian gate hangs to the left of the main barriers. I lift the wooden latch from its iron cradle, swing back the simple stanchioned bar on its sprung hinges and step through, letting it thud shut behind me. The single track slices the tarmac, twin blades of steel gleaming in the frosty air. So easy. I move forward to stand before the nearest rail. There's no making sense of it as I stare down: the cold, clean metal in its shallow groove, silver on grey, quite static, a mere geometric pattern of colour and lines. Is this it? Is this all there is? Behind me and to the side, from the corner of my eye I catch the warning red as the light begins to flash. *On off, on off.* I still stare down.

One step forward is all it will take. Just one.

The sound is dull when it comes, not nearly as loud as I'd imagined. Willett's barn and the horse chestnuts must mask and dampen it. But I feel the change of pressure, so that its approach is more of a surge of movement than of noise. The train seems to push before it a solid block of air, sucking out oxygen, sucking me forward, sucking me in. It squeezes my lungs, squeezes the air, squeezes time itself: my life and future lives, past lives, concertinaed into one.

One step.

The rail beckons. Breath compresses. Time teeters, I teeter. Just one step.

Then it happens. And when it does, it comes not as enfolding arms nor as a child's reaching hand – her grasping hand, the other Izzie – but as sudden opposite momentum: a backwards drag, a quiet, compelling force, pulling me back on my heels and away from the rail. I rock, and stagger back. The train roars up and by. Tears blind me.

Then it is gone; the train has gone. The shockwaves subside and the air is still again. Away to my right the signal falls. I am aware that I am cold.

I turn for the gate; I turn for home.

Halfway up the hill, in the shelter of the willow trees, I stop, transfixed. I feel it – I feel her, my daughter. Inside the circle of my womb, I feel her shift and turn. One kick.

No more running now. I lace my fingers close about my belly and inhale the sunlit, ice-edged morning air, my breathing deep and steady. I'll be all right; we'll be all right.

I walk towards home. It's very simple, really. It's just a case of putting one foot in front of the other.

One
two
three
four

ALL THE FLOWERS GONE

It was a perfect morning for cycling. The temperature must have fallen during a clear night and a dawn mist had formed over the fields. As Poppy bowled along Tunstall Lane it rose in layers, which seemed to lift and peel away without losing any of their density, and hung just clear of the barley so that sunlight filtered through underneath, tingeing them from below with watery gold. Once through Tunstall village and out on the road that stretched straight ahead into Rendlesham Forest, she rose on her pedals in her battered trainers, pushing down harder with each stroke, enjoying the stretch in her calves and the rush of cool air in her lungs, until the dark trees on either side were no more than a blur.

Perfect for plant-hunting, too, with dew still freshening the leaves, and the flower heads yet to fade and fall.

She locked up her bike by the main gate, still crowned with its scrolls of military barbed wire, and walked across the tarmac towards the cluster of mismatched, low-lying buildings, outlines only against the slant of morning sun. From amid the dazzle there emerged a figure which she had to squint to make out: clad in a blue serge flying jacket, he could have walked straight from any decade of the base's existence, from the forties to the nineties.

'Hi!' Poppy hailed him as he drew nearer. 'Which is it? Film extra, or ghost?'

The boy laughed – or if he was a man it was a boyish laugh. Then again, it could have been the uniform that marked him down as young. The pilots of Bomber Command, who flew from here and died in Germany and Holland or in the dark North Sea, had mostly just been boys. 'Neither, actually. I work at the Cold War Museum, over in the old command post. Just as a volunteer, you know, but we like to look the part.'

She'd bet they did. So no ghost, then, but only an aircraft enthusiast – a plane spotter with an upmarket anorak. Perhaps even a war enthusiast, she thought with a sinking heart – though she'd been picturing the wrong war.

'How about you?' He had stopped beside her and turned; the silhouette acquired colour and definition, and she took in sandy brows over flecked hazel eyes. 'Have you come to see the museum?'

It was her turn to laugh this time. 'No – not that. No, I've actually come to look for a flower.'

A war enthusiast, perhaps, but he did have nice eyes. Words came tripping back from a song her mum used to sing to her at bath time when she was a kid. *Gone for soldiers, every one.* And then, close at their heels, another line: *When will they ever learn?*

A member of the public had phoned it in. All too often, she'd been sent on a wild goose chase (though not as literally as in the case of her colleague, Andy the bird man) by an excited and well-meaning caller, but this time it had the ring of credibility about it. *Silene conica* – the sand catchfly or striped corn catchfly. To many people it

101

might be just another member of the campion family, an insignificant roadside weed, but for anyone who knew anything at all about native plants, or had opened a basic field guide, there was little chance of error. Those distinctive striated seed heads, fat and onion-domed, like extravagant turbans or the minarets of old Istanbul: there really could be no mistaking them.

The woman had sounded plausible – confident but not overbearing – and the habitat was right, too. Next to the old runway, she said, near where there'd been some recent digging. *Silene conica* favoured sandy soils in coastal regions: dunes and the landward margins of beaches, or the light, well-draining soil of the Suffolk sandlings. It grew most readily in bare or sparsely vegetated areas and had a particular liking for ground that had been disturbed by man. Like me, she thought, like my own name. The poppies of Flanders.

'A flower?' The sandy eyebrows lifted a quizzical half-centimetre.

'I'm a botanist,' she said, trying to block out the note of apology, or at least of self-consciousness. 'I work for the county Wildlife Trust.' As if by way of credentials, she unzipped her backpack to reveal the camera and the roll of plastic warning tape, fluorescent orange zigzagged with black.

'More like SOCO.'

'Sorry?'

The costume airman nodded at the contents of her pack. 'Like on the telly. A police officer, you know. Come to seal off the scene of the crime.'

'I hope not.' She was grinning, but it was no joke, really, the damage people did, deciding to pick wild flowers. 'Quite the reverse. I want to protect it, if it's what we

102

think it is. Look—' He seemed a willing sort, and his job was helping visitors, wasn't it? 'I wonder if you might be able to point me in the right direction. Our informant said it's growing by the main runway. Maybe somewhere they've been doing some excavation?'

Turning to peer screw-eyed into the sun, back in the direction of the buildings, he gave a nod. 'For the remains of a Lanc.' At her hesitation, he looked back towards her. 'A Lancaster bomber. From a wartime crash.'

That would be it, she supposed. 'So, whereabouts...?'

He swung on the heels of his flying boots. 'I'll show you.'

It was *Silene conica*. Just a small, scattered colony, no more than a dozen flowering spikes, close to some mounds where the earth had evidently been turned over and then piled back.

'Oh, wow!' Poppy yelped with delight. 'It's actually it. Sand catchfly is its name. This is the first time it's been spotted here on the base, though they've had some on the reserve at North Warren, and up at Minsmere, too, just a few specimens. It's pretty scarce – fewer than sixty sites recorded nationwide last year...'

He wasn't really listening. His eyes had strayed towards the perimeter fence, the wire mesh and concrete pillars, tilted outwards at the top to support three parallel strands of razor wire.

'I came here when I was a baby,' she said, caught off balance herself by the sudden change of tack. 'In a papoose, and then in a buggy, later on. My mother was a peacenik, back in the eighties. CND and all that.'

Ban the bomb. Mum's placard was self-consciously retro, even then, among the others with their *No nukes!* and *Send Maggie on a cruise.* Funny to think the familiar photos in the album back at home were taken somewhere

103

out along that fence, just outside the wire. To think of what was happening inside the wire then, too – so secret, so deadly – and now she could walk in the front gate and stroll about photographing flowers.

There was one particular snap she'd always loved: it showed her mother gazing dreamily half away from the camera, hair loose about her shoulders and topped with a daisy chain, the perfect hippy chick, like something out of Woodstock in 1969. And she was in the picture, too, baby Poppy at a few months old, although you couldn't see her face, which was hooded by the shawl which bound her, squaw-style, to her mother's body. Except it wasn't a shawl, exactly, but one of those Middle Eastern scarves, a *keffiyeh* – worn, no doubt, in solidarity with Palestinian resistance, but strangely at odds with the floral skirt and Indian cheesecloth blouse, the strings of wooden beads and threaded seashells. Behind Mum's head, in and out of the mesh of the fence, were woven posies of flowers – cranesbill and scabious and meadow clary and more she couldn't identify from the fuzzy photograph – like people leave at the roadside, on a fence or lamp post, at a place where a child has been knocked down and killed.

'Well, they've all gone now.'

She blinked at the young volunteer and slowly nodded her head, uncertain quite what she was agreeing had gone: the American bombers, the peace protestors or the flowers.

* * *

It was a perfect morning for cycling. Overhead the larks were already peppering the sky with their barrage of twittering as Lilian bowled along the Tunstall Lane. The temperature must have fallen during a clear night and a dawn mist lingered over the fields. The pilots in last night's raids would

104

have had a good sight of their targets, but been sitting ducks for the enemy ack ack; she hoped that any stragglers had managed to land before the mist had formed. When she reached the road that stretched straight ahead into the cool darkness of Rendlesham Forest, Lilian rose on her pedals in her old lace-up brogues, which she'd had since school and weren't fit to be seen but were the only thing she owned you could possibly ride a bike in. She'd always raced when she got to the woods, right from being small, fleeing from storybook bogeymen even before there were Nazi spies and paratroopers to haunt the edges of the imagination.

She propped up her bike by the main gate and walked past the barrier, keeping her eyes down as the corporal on guard duty glanced up from his *Picture Post* to give the compulsory wolf whistle. At least there would be no whistling in the mess – the commissioned officers were too well-bred for that, even now that the cumulating losses meant they were recruiting pilots from all sorts of walks of life. She'd shared a smoke with one last week who'd been a brewer's drayman back in civvy street. 'I've swapped four hooves for four props,' he'd said, as he leaned in to light her cigarette. 'But I know which I'd rather be relying on, if it comes to limping home on three.'

It wasn't to say they didn't look, though – men are men, her mum always told her, and even officers have eyes. Some of them liked to rib her, too, and try to make her blush; Lilian hated how easily she blushed. She wasn't a child, after all, she was seventeen. Boys she'd been at school with were out in Italy and North Africa now, driving tanks, or down in submarines and goodness knows what else, and she was doing her bit, as far as you could, stuck out here in Suffolk, helping on the farm now that Arthur and Geoff were gone, and cleaning the mess hut and cookhouse at the base. Seventeen – but she knew she must look younger in her well-worn cotton print dress, let out on the bust and hips and down at the hem until there were no seams left to turn. On mornings like this, after a raid, the pilots rose late and would still be lingering over a second mug of tea while she got going with her bucket and mop; she tucked in her tummy and pushed out her breasts in the new brassiere she'd had from Auntie Vi in London, a proper bullet bra that made her feel like Veronica Lake, until she had to put on her old dress and cardigan, and her flat school brogues.

There was one particular one: the others called him Charlie, which baffled her at first, but it turned out his plane was C for Charlie and his real name was Joe. He had blond hair that flopped down over his forehead however much he tried to slick it back, and greyish, greenish eyes. Nice eyes. Joseph Woodhall was his full name – she loved how it sounded – and he came from a place called Market Drayton in Shropshire. It was so near to Wales, he said, that on a quiet Sunday you could hear the singing. Joe was always saying things like that, funny things, so she never quite knew if he was joking or not. He reckoned it was 192 miles by road from Market Drayton to Bentwaters, or 170 as the Lancaster flies, which meant they could get there in forty-five minutes at normal cruising speed, have a pot of coffee and a chocolate Kunzle cake in the Red Lion Hotel, and be back in time for lunch.

'Go on with you,' she said.

'Don't fancy it? Ah well, you may be wise. They're mainly beetroot and gravy browning, anyway.'

'Mainly...?' Confused, she was probably beetroot herself.

'The Kunzle cakes.'

It wouldn't do to look round for him – wouldn't do to be looking round at the officers at all, bold as brass the way some girls would. That's not how Lilian had been brought up. But she could sneak a quick glance about while she fetched her bits and pieces from the closet, and there he was, playing cards with T for Tommy.

When she went round the back to empty her bucket at the outside drain the way Sergeant Bulmer liked her to do, Joe was suddenly there behind her, up so close she could smell the rolling tobacco, and something harsher, like carbolic. And somehow he'd got hold of flowers – a great overflowing bunch of them like a proper bouquet from the florist, as if she'd know what to do with flowers when she was meant to be cleaning. Except they weren't real flowers, of course, not the hothouse kind or even from someone's garden, they were just wild flowers he must have gone out and picked earlier. Weeds, really, her mum would say. But they were all colours, bright as you like. The blue ones she knew were cornflowers, but she didn't know the other sorts.

'Call yourself a country girl?' he teased her. He seemed to know them all, and the names as he reeled them off to her were so beautiful it was just as if he was reading her poetry: knotted cranesbill and corn chamomile, arrowgrass and fragrant agrimony, musk mallow, ragged robin, wild marjoram and mignonette.

* * *

It was a perfect morning for cycling. Rosa loved those days in early summer when a clear night left a trail of dawn mist to be burned off by the brand new sun. The sort of days, she thought as she bowled along the Tunstall lane, when you almost couldn't believe how fragile all this was, this beautiful, precarious balance of gases and liquids, or water and air, of soil and plants and animals which sustained the life of this planet of ours.

It was hard to remember that the sun might one day, perhaps one day soon, be blotted out by a lethal poison cloud unleashed by the gigajoules of explosive power, the limitless megatons of chemical death, stockpiled on either side of the Berlin Wall – including at Greenham Common and RAF Molesworth, even if not yet here at Bentwaters.

She could still not quite accustom herself to riding a bike with two. Poppy was too small as yet for the baby seat which Rosa had fitted during a burst of energy in the early weeks of her pregnancy, so she rode with her strapped against her breast, the scarf wound tightly around them both. Bound there, Poppy almost seemed to become a part of her again, less the small independent person she was slowly and perplexingly coming to know and more the extra weight she had been for the long months in the womb, tipping her forwards disproportionately over the handlebars. Heat, too – she was aware of her as heat, that busy, concentrated infant heat, warmer than her own blood – and a heartbeat, merging with her own. This was for her, the protest, the campaigning: keeping the sun undarkened, keeping the earth alive for Poppy. As she reached the leafy fringes of Rendlesham Forest, she rose on her pedals in her buffalo sandals, pushing down harder with each stroke until her anklets jangled.

She dragged her bicycle behind some trees and leant it up with a tangle of others, then stood straight for a moment to ease the crick from her spine and adjust her weight to the vertical. The scarf shaded Poppy's closed eyes and puckered, slightly open mouth as she slept on, re-dreaming the lulling motion of her ride. Lightly, Rosa touched one finger to the downy head, as close as she ever came to prayer.

By the wire, there was quite a crowd already: Kate and Anne-Marie and Linda and most of the Aldeburgh group, some teenagers she didn't recognise, and a couple of carloads from Christian CND in Woodbridge, complete with doved and rainbowed banner. Older, most of these, and standing slightly apart, looking awkward – but Christians could always be relied upon for singing, once everything got going.

'Where Have All the Flowers Gone?' That was Rosa's favourite; it had so much more to say with its gentle, haunting lyrics than the angry chanting that Linda always liked to start. They were all going to link hands, they'd decided, around the perimeter fence, like they'd done at Greenham last year when she didn't yet know she was carrying Poppy, and thirty thousand women gathered to 'embrace the base' – even if here, today, they were closer to thirty than thirty thousand, forming no complete, unbroken circle but only a brief and flimsy chain. They sat cross-legged on the strip of gravel beneath the wire, its stones already half reclaimed by grass and wild flowers, like the graveyards in the song. One of the teenagers had picked some and threaded them through the fence, and then they all had done the same, so that the mesh was wreathed and garlanded in green. Rosa had taken daisies and slit the juicy stalks with her fingernails, pushing in the severed ends and sliding them through to the hilt of the flower heads, stringing them together like the hand-linked chain of protestors, and had laid it around her head.

'Uh-oh. Look out, here comes trouble.' Linda's voice held a note that was more of excited glee than warning; she was always spoiling for a fight, was Linda.

The company loosed hands and turned, some of them standing up and brushing themselves down, as the young serviceman approached. He was SP, by his uniform and beret flash – security police rather than an airman. They were always the ones sent out to deal with demonstrations.

'Hello there, you guys' was his opening – carefully casual, unconfrontational. 'Lovely day for it.'

Like nightclub doormen, they were always taught to keep things light. This one, though, seemed almost to mean it. He hardly looked older than nineteen or twenty, with Huck Finn freckles and a flop of dark hair in front, even though he was shaved to regulation rawness at the back. And his eyes held a genuinely friendly light. Nice eyes, thought Rosa.

'Not thinking of making any trouble, I hope?'

'We've every right to be here,' said Linda, although he'd given no indication that he thought otherwise. 'A right of peaceful protest. You can't make us leave.'

'No indeed, ma'am.' He played it deadpan, but Rosa had an inkling he might be laughing at her friend. 'As long as you don't start making free with the wire cutters.'

Linda harrumphed, trying to look as if she just might do that. One of the Aldeburgh contingent, a man called Terry, began to make a speech, all the familiar arguments about escalation and proliferation, the risk of accidents, and destruction of the planet. Some people thought you had to try and convert them, even the military: sow seeds of change from within. But this was hardly the way; the SP's eyes had lost their warm and open look, grown guarded. It was in the hope of bringing back the gleam that Rosa unwound the chain of daisies from her hair, and held it out to him, fingers reaching out to touch his through the wire.

'What d'you do that for?' Linda demanded, later. They had moved to a quiet spot in the shelter of the trees so that Rosa could feed Poppy. Linda was eating her sandwiches. 'I mean – a daisy chain,' she said, through a mouthful of humous and alfalfa. 'Like some dorky kid at primary school. 'Bloody 'ell, Rosa' – they'll think we're all feeble-minded.'

'Because he was cute.' Not the whole truth, perhaps, but a partial version of it that Linda might understand. *Peace offering* would have sounded trite, or even like derision, in the circumstances.

Another harrumph – a speciality of Linda's. 'Cute or not – he's on the other side. He's what we're fighting against, for God's sake. The enemy.'

Rosa watched in entrancement the slow, methodical working of her daughter's mouth at her nipple, felt reverberate through her body the sweet, deep, primal tug, as old as the tides. Wasn't that the point, she thought – not having sides? Not having enemies?

Obliquely, she found herself saying, 'My mother dated an airman. A British airman, that is, back in the war when Bomber Command were here. At least, I think she did.'

Linda put down her sandwich. 'Lilian? In the war? Was she old enough?'

'She'd have been seventeen.' Just a child.

'But why only "think"?'

'Oh, I don't know... She never talked about it, you see, not until after the first stroke, and by then she was confused.' The impaired blood flow had dragged her mother back in time, back to when she was young and living at home, as a child. She talked about the pigs, though the farm was broken up and sold in 1947. 'She didn't know where she was or who she was, who any of us were. She kept calling my dad by other names, you know, towards the end. Joe, she kept saying, and even, once, Charlie. His name was Fred. Imagine that – thirty years married, and your wife doesn't know your name.'

Poor Dad. Poor all of them. Mum was still young, not yet sixty, when she died last year – too young to

111

be felled by emphysema, and then the double strike of cerebral thrombosis. It was a close-run thing, but in the end she couldn't quite hang on long enough to see her granddaughter born.

'But you think it was true? You think she really had this boyfriend in the RAF?'

'Maybe. But she'd never mentioned it before, not to Dad, not to anyone. She never even told us she'd worked at the base, let alone met anyone there. And as you say, she was really just a kid.'

Just seventeen – a whole ten years before she met Dad. It was all such a very long time ago, and maybe the truth of it didn't matter, not now that Mum was gone. *Gone to graveyards, every one.* Rosa gave an involuntary shudder, so that Poppy's pale blue eyes flung wide in consternation. *Long time passing.* Bending over her child, she was caught quite unawares by the springing dew of tears.

* * *

The boy from the museum lingered to watch as Poppy took her photographs of *Silene conica* and unrolled the fluorescent tape to cordon off the site.

'Is that it, then?' he said as she stood back, returning her camera to the rucksack.

'Pretty much. I'll need to log it, of course. For local and national records.'

He nodded, the tawny eyebrows gathered in a slight frown, as if he was trying to think of something suitable to say. And then he apparently abandoned the attempt. 'So, d'you want to come and see the Cold War Museum?'

It seemed a reasonable exchange.

What detained her, however, was not the battle cabin with its airlock and decontamination shower, nor the signboards chronicling the history of the 81st Tactical Fighter Wing, but something almost incidental, a relic of an older war. A small wall cabinet in the entrance way displayed a black-and-white photograph and beneath it a card of explanatory text. It was actually the background of the photograph, blurred a little by the enlargement, which caught her attention first: something about the configuration of grass and tarmac, of Nissen huts and perimeter wire. It was surely taken where she had been just now, out there beside the runway. In the foreground were a series of disjointed, jagged shapes, which she took to be the lumped and broken pieces of an aeroplane; scored across the width of the photograph was a great dark furrow, gouged through the soft sand by the blade of a wing, like a grotesque parody of the plough. *Swords into ploughshares*, she thought.

Moving closer, she read the short, close-typed notice. An Avro Lancaster bomber of No. 64 Squadron, returning from the Ruhr, had attempted a landing in heavy fog on just two of her four engines, and crashed beside the main runway on 19th December 1944, killing her captain, Pilot Officer Joseph Woodhall, and all six crew.

It must have been the crash site they'd been excavating, in the place where the sand catchfly had appeared: the plane whose debris they were digging for.

Seven young men, and all of them somebody's loved one. Seven young men and an early grave.

* * *

A year on, and the war was over. Those who were coming home were back now, or would very soon be on their way. Lilian took one flower stalk from the handful she had gathered and threaded it carefully through the

113

mesh of the wire; then she did the same with another, and another. She had found them growing back there, there where it had happened, six months ago today. It wasn't a flower she remembered ever noticing before, not one of the ones that Joe had picked for her, his cranesbills and his chamomiles, and the others whose names were fading already from her memory. She was attracted by its starry pink flowers, and the funny striped seedpods like the domes of a sultan's palace.

Those who were coming home were back, but Joe's body had been laid to rest in the cemetery at Market Drayton by a family she'd never meet, while C for Charlie was buried where it fell, in the sand beside the runway.

Lilian turned away. As she walked back to the gate where her bike was propped, a slight breeze rose, thrumming the wires of the perimeter fence and vibrating the seed heads of the sand catchfly, splitting open one fat, ripe pod and sending puffs of gossamer seeds to trace their dance steps on the sunlit air.

WHISPERS

Dr Theodore Whybrow stepped out through the college gate, tightened his scarf, set his sights on the tower of the University Library and contemplated his failings.

Cathedral of the fens. It was various East Anglian parish churches which usually laid claim to this contested title: the church of Walpole St Peter in Norfolk; St Mary Magdalene church at Gedney, Lincs; not to mention the 'cathedral of the marshes' at Blythburgh in his own native Suffolk. Yet somehow the phrase always connected itself in Dr Whybrow's mind with the imperious outline of the University Library. Awareness of the true, prosaic purpose of that tower – for it was in reality no more than a vast bookstack, a repository of copyrighted materials of infrequent interest, encased in a column of brick – did nothing to lessen its power to cow. Perhaps, indeed, the thought of all that weight of learning was part of its oppressive moral authority. 'Who are you, little man?' it seemed to be saying to him. *Little* man: as insignificant beside those great scholars whose works were housed about its feet as any medieval worshipper before the company of saints and angels. What were the spires and pinnacles of churches and cathedrals, after all? Symbols of the hand of man, reaching towards the heavens for grace? Or, in reality, watchtowers, set over a weak and wayward population – visible reminders of their frailties to the frail.

Twenty-two years ago, fresh from a brilliant PhD, he had been the outstanding young academic in his particular field of literary biography, the emergent expert on his man: William Colstone, the Regency soldier-poet, essayist and dreamer. From his doctoral thesis had sprung a flurry of articles, published in the leading periodicals to universal acclaim, winning him his Fellowship, a university teaching post and national recognition. The next step, naturally, had to be the book. The Whybrow biography was to break the mould, to reset the ground rules for Colstone scholarship; for him personally, it was to be the magnum opus, the masterwork to secure his Chair and a permanent place in the canon.

That was then. Now, he carefully fixed his eyes and mind upon the immediate foreground. The library tower reared up above the line of trees which divided Queens' Road from the green of the Backs. It split opinion, that tower. Whybrow himself, however, had a sneaking admiration for the style he thought of as 'monumental fascist' when encountered in Milan, and as 'red-brick God' at Guildford. There was a sense of something cleansing about a spot of unabashed modernism, especially in this city so absorbed by its own past, a place so smugly not red-brick. But the sense was, he feared, illusory. The University Library could intimidate its congregation as effectively as far more ancient hallowed halls. It was a pure conceit, of course, to imbue a building with the animus of its past users, but one with a persistent hold on the popular imagination and to which Whybrow was not immune. And if the vaulted spaces of a church could murmur with the prayerfulness of generations – or their disapproving judgment – then why not also a library?

The short walk from his college rooms to Gilbert Scott's controversial edifice was the one he had undertaken every weekday morning at 8.45 am throughout the Long Vacation, this summer as for the twenty-one preceding summers: every working day in fact, since the last examination script had been marked, moderated and put to bed in June. Nor, this year, had his routine been interrupted by the onset of Michaelmas term, because Dr Whybrow was on sabbatical leave.

'Enjoy your freedom.' That was the greeting tossed his way by the head porter, Ernie, this and every morning since term began, after he'd picked up the mail from his pigeonhole. But it certainly didn't feel much like freedom. He had lingered as long over Weetabix and the *Today* programme as he could allow himself on a working day without the creepings of guilt. His email, disappointingly light in anything requiring a response, he had dealt with before leaving his rooms, carefully avoiding the recriminating gaze of the icon that crouched in the corner of the computer screen as soon as he booted up. The Book. It must be three weeks since he had even opened the file, though he was intent upon not counting. Much easier to shut down the computer, arm himself with old-fashioned paper and pen, lock up his rooms with the wretched thing inside and head for relative safety beneath the library tower. There, at least, lay the promise of surrounding calm – even if not inner tranquillity.

It was an irony not lost on Dr Whybrow that his personal bolthole – in that deplorable contemporary phrase, his 'happy place' – should, like the University Library, also be a tower, and also built of brick. The land certificate recorded him as registered proprietor since only the end of May, but it was many years since he had first become accustomed to think of it as 'his' tower. Since early one morning of the Easter holidays in fact, when he was eleven or twelve, back home in Suffolk from the purgatory of boarding school and reclaiming the pleasures of solitude and unmarked hours. Home on leave, was how he came to think of it: each school term a fresh tour of duty, a posting into hostile terrain, and each homecoming shot through with relief at having survived.

It must have been Easter because it was too mild for Christmas and too damp for July or August. The mist as he recalled it was no light summer sea fret but a tenacious spring fog, lying low over cold earth saturated from the night's rain. It was early, too: the sun, just visible through the veiling cloud, was low and bloated, bleeding a mauvy-pink. He wouldn't have been up and out at an hour to watch the sun rise if it had been the summer holidays. He was on his bike, he remembered – or rather, he had his bike with him, because out there across the muddy fields and the wetlands which lay beyond there were few places where tyres would not be soon bogged down. There were stiles to be hoisted over, too, and through the salt marshes the wooden duckboards were frequently so narrow that to wheel a pedal cycle became a precarious operation, promising at any moment a skinned ankle or a foot submerged sock-deep in foetid black silt. But it had been a present, that bike, a reward from his father for passing the school entrance exam, and he was too young, or too stubborn, for the double edge of this to dent his pride in the machine.

He was going fishing, an activity he understood for other boys was a means to congregate but which Whybrow did to be on his own. None of them caught anything, either way. They had no rods or tackle apart from a stick or a garden cane, perhaps some bait wheedled from an older brother and such pieces of line as could be found snagged in brambles or bulrushes along the path. Today he had not even that. The dewed strands festooning the reeded banks had all been cobwebs, not knotted nylon. He had stripped himself a likely willow switch some way back along the river but abandoned it again while tugging and hauling his bicycle through a place where vegetation had invaded the footpath from both sides so as to make it almost impassable. He had been heading for the curve of the estuary, where the ebbing tide left spits and banks of gravel which were almost like a proper beach, and where the pretence of fishing could be dropped in favour of skimming stones across the water. But the mist and the fight with the brambles must have disorientated him. He had missed his way and come too far right, but instead of turning back had trudged doggedly on while the path bent round to the south and east, towards the marram dunes and the sea.

That's when he had first seen it: his tower. Not loomingly tall, at least until you came close, but solid, squat and low, it resolved itself from out of the backlit brume and stood sombre against the skyline. At more or less the same time he became aware of the sound of the sea effervescing on the shingle. His tread quickened as he walked towards the apparition. Perspective clarified and he could see that it was a round fort, flat-topped and unbattlemented, emerging from below the embanked pathway on the beachward side and reaching above it by some twenty or thirty feet. Its brick walls, the colour of damp sand and slick with moisture, were unrelieved by any doors or windows visible from this aspect. It was the

Dark Fortress; it was Minas Morgul; it was Cair Paravel. It was his and his alone.

In the farthest corner of the University Library Reading Room sat Dr Whybrow, at the stretch of table that was his habitual hiding place.

The library had a quality like no other place, a paradoxical power to make the reader feel himself subsumed into the greater body of collective intellectual endeavour and at the same time secluded, walled off from the world. Once, not so very long ago, he'd been able to bury himself in its studious embrace and focus only upon the quiet hours between himself and the time of its closure. The thing about scholarship – in his youth a frustration and then, for many years, a comfort – was that there was always more to be read. Reading became its own end: a self-justifying virtue. Here in the sheltering silence there was no need to think of the days, the weeks and months going by, nor to measure any larger progress – or the absence of it. No need to acknowledge that his reading had become an alibi, a substitute for writing: the work of others a defence against his own. But in this last year even reading had lost its power to quell the demons which whispered against him. The stone clerestory and panelled oak ceiling of the Reading Room, even the long rows of desks, were a-hum with their denunciation; censure purred through the central heating, and every soft step on the deadening blue carpet was a new indictment: of his shortcomings as a scholar and the deficiency of his output.

He pulled the journal he was reading closer towards him, running a finger along the fold to press it flat. More than once he had found that his eyes had run over a paragraph without anything registering upon his mind at all. It was as if some functional connection had worked loose in his brain, so that the words upon the page no longer linked to their corresponding mental images. Reading was what he did; it was his life. For a moment he entertained a fantasy that the relevant synapse might break apart completely and print become mere patterns of ink, no longer decipherable into ideas. He would be left adrift: his pathway to this world, his only world, irreparably severed. Dad, after all, had been little older than Whybrow himself was now when his neurons had first begun to misfire, taking him away from his son. Out of reach, the way William Colstone seemed beyond his reach these days, too. There, but not there.

If it happened to me... He would have to retire, and go and live in his tower by the sea.

It was nonsense, of course; his faculties were perfectly sound. He glanced down at the pad of A4 narrow feint at his right hand. Apart from a heading, carefully inscribed with a wiggly underlining at 9.05 am, the page was a blank. Dragging his eyes back to the text, he tried to force his mind to follow, but its meaning slipped and slithered past the edges of his consciousness.

Perversely, when interruption came it was still unwelcome.

'Dr Whybrow.'

Above almost all else, he abominated the library whisper. Quieter than its stage cousin, it nevertheless shared with it an irritating overstated quality – as well as containing a sibilance that made him want to swat at the whisperer like a buzzing fly. The culprit in this case was someone who should have known better. Someone in fact whom, in the usual run of things, Whybrow was inclined to view with favour, and even a modicum of personal affection: his former doctoral student and now a Research Fellow of his college, Dr Jenny Lassiter.

He raised his head at her salutation and offered a suppressed smile which he hoped conveyed the discouragement of further conversation.

Evidently not. 'How's it going?' hissed Jenny.

He rearranged the smile into a frown. Disapproval did not prevent him, however, from sliding a guilty sleeve across his empty page of notes.

With a waggle of her own notepad, she turned to continue her progress towards the inquiry desk. But not before jangling his nerve-ends with a parting whisper.

'Enjoy your freedom.'

It had felt like fate when it came on the market. Not that Whybrow had any truck with such a superstitious concept, but even hard science could allow for patterns, for balances and synergies, for things falling into place. He saw the photograph in the estate agent's window in Saxmundham and recognised it instantly, although the angle – from the seaward side – was unfamiliar. *Opportunity to own a piece of history*. And that felt strange, as well: as if a person might own a slice of the sea or the sky.

The price was not prohibitive. Two decades of living rent-free or almost so in college rooms had facilitated the accumulation of a sizeable nest egg, even after allowing until recently for care home costs, and even on his modest academic stipend – not a *professorial* stipend either, as he required no reminding. And it was after all just a derelict shell, for all its historical interest, and lacked vehicular access into the bargain. Even the agent had not had the gall to describe it as 'ripe for development'. It was itself, and unapologetically so: his tower.

122

The printed details relayed facts and figures which the academic in him filed away for reference but which seemed remote from the living image he carried in his mind. *The most northerly of twenty-nine Martello towers erected along the east coast by the Board of Ordnance between 1808 and 1812 to defend England from the threat of invasion by the forces of Napoleon. The towers' design was inspired by the round fortress at Mortella Point in Corsica, unsuccessfully bombarded by British warships in 1794.* Most, like his own tower, were cylindrical in shape, the flat roof concealing a single interior dome – in contrast with the grander specimen at nearby Aldeburgh, which formed a distinctive quatrefoil, its four great towers now tastefully partitioned and rented out to holidaymakers. The Martellos were built to withstand cannon fire; a million bricks, it was said, went into the construction of each.

It was his period, he told himself, rationalising a decision he knew was already made. William Colstone's period. And his man, like Whybrow himself, was from that part of Suffolk: Colstone was born in Wickham Market where his father, Frederick, had the living. William held a commission with the regulars, the East Suffolk regiment. He'd served in India and the Dutch East Indies and at the capture of Mauritius, but was garrisoned in England for a time after 1810, lending backbone to the local militia. His letters, and an essay of 1811, were regarded as prime sources on the invasion panic which gripped the nation at that time. Posted back home to defend our shores from Boney – why not, indeed, in Whybrow's very tower? It was a tangible connection, as solid as anything to be found in books.

To arrange the viewing had been a guilty thrill, but it was also unreal, incongruous, to be noting an appointment

123

time and who would meet him with the key, as if he were looking round a three-bedroomed semi. *A million bricks.* Only on the drive over did excitement make way for the lurching fear of disappointment.

He need not have worried. As soon as the heavy oak door swung open he felt it, that almost electrical charge which tingled the nerves in his scalp and set all his senses to hyper vigilance. It was a hard thing to describe exactly. A special quality of silence, certainly, the kind you encounter sometimes in an empty church or an underground cavern; the kind to make you understand properly that overused phrase 'you could hear a pin drop'. It froze you to stillness; it set your ears on edge to listen for the pin. But it was more than that. Much later, he found the analogy which conjured it best: it was like being inside a giant bell. The high vault of the brick dome created a resonance which served to amplify the slightest sound and send it circling around and around. The least movement of air was translated to vibration, a thrum which reverberated almost below the frequencies of audibility. Even when nothing stirred, the air within the belly of the tower seemed to arc and crackle with life, as if detecting the presence of a listener. It was a place made for secrets.

'Wait for the best bit, though.' It was the girl from the estate agent – the young woman, as he knew he was supposed to say – who had demonstrated the tower's special magic. 'Stand over there. Put your head near the wall.'

She chose the spot directly opposite him across the line of diameter and leaned her face close to the bricks. He watched her lips move and for a fraction of a second heard nothing – and then the whisper came and it was if she were right beside him with her mouth to his ear, but in the same moment the single word rebounded about his head as if reflected from countless invisible surfaces, multilayered, at once both as loud as timpani and quiet as a sigh.

'*Echo...*'

To look it up was a professional reflex for Whybrow. He had personally witnessed the same effect in the Whispering Gallery of St Paul's cathedral, but now he found mention of other examples: the Church of the Holy Sepulchre; Santa Maria del Fiore in Florence; the Gol Gumbaz mausoleum in Bijapur. Even, apparently, a gallery outside an oyster bar in New York's Grand Central Station. As so often, theories competed to explain the phenomenon, with argument going back to the nineteenth century. The Cambridge physicist Lord Rayleigh – a Trinity man – claimed that sound travelled round the surface fabric of the dome along its inner perimeter; the Astronomer Royal, the appropriately named Airy, contended that the waves bounced across the space inside the dome, moving through the air. Neither theory had been proved conclusively to be correct. Whybrow read of the recreation of strange acoustic effects in artificial whispering chambers, both circular and ellipsoid; he read of hot spots of acoustic symmetry and points of focus, and the observation of bizarre reversal events, where sound flipped round and seemed to be coming from the opposite direction.

While all this knowledge might bring logic to the tower's properties it did nothing, he found, to reduce its powerful hold on his imagination. More and more, as he camped out on the dusty boarded floor that summer and into autumn, he found himself preoccupied by the notion of echoes, of ancient confidences which arced through brick or spun through space, of communication leaping through earth and air and time.

It never occurred to him to reflect on the most wasteful

aspect of the acquisition of his gallery of whispers: the pity that he should always be there by himself.

'I'm worried about Dr Whybrow.'

Jenny Lassiter was settled comfortably before the coal-effect electric fire in the back parlour of her college porter's lodge, resuscitating toes which had suffered the double assault of a cold bike ride from the Faculty of English and unsuitably frivolous footwear. Shoes, as Jenny enjoyed confessing to people, were her Achilles heel. From her cycling helmet downwards she was prepared to adopt a style of dress appropriate to the filthy Cambridge climate and the expectations of colleagues and students, but her feet she regarded as her own to torture as she chose. The pair she had just eased off was a recent acquisition: peep-toed wedges in soft Italian leather of a delectable shade of cranberry. As feeling returned to her liberated toes, so Jenny, with a pleasurable sigh, reverted to her theme.

'He's never here.'

Ernie, the head porter, took a carton of milk from the mini fridge and gave it the obligatory sniff. 'Well, he is on leave. Professor Elwood ran a lecture course at Princeton when he was on leave last term.'

'That's different.' Jenny raised her left foot towards the fire and performed slow circles from the ankle. 'Dr Whybrow hasn't gone away. He just isn't here.'

Ernie dunked teabags and pondered this distinction before handing her a mug with a considered, 'Ah.'

The back parlour of the lodge was the inner sanctum. Designed to serve as rest room for the porters on duty, especially at night, it provided a place of occasional resort for staff and students alike: part sanctuary and part confessional. Ernie's substantial shoulder had been cried on by homesick first years and by Nobel laureates, and his pronouncements had an oracular quality about them which meant there were very few troubles within the college which weren't eventually brought before him.

'I mean, he was always here. Always has been, ever since I've been at the college. A permanent fixture – like the portraits of all those old giffers in hall. Earthquakes might come and mountains crumble to the sea but you could always rely on Dr Whybrow being in his rooms of an evening if you needed a bracing chat and a shot of nasty sherry.'

'But now he's not.'

'Right. First it was only weekends – and fair enough, everyone's entitled to a weekend away – although I'd never known him go off anywhere before. But I thought, well, maybe he's acquired a lady friend or more likely an old mum with a dodgy hip or Alzheimer's or something that he has to go and visit.' She cast an appraising glance at Ernie over the rim of her mug, and a tiny flicker in the jaw made her think she'd stabbed close to the truth. But he only said, 'A father. He died last year.'

'Anyway, recently it's not just the weekends. I dropped round three times after dinner last week and knocked and knocked. Nothing – and no lights on either. And it was the same the week before.'

Her eyes strayed to the open door of the pigeonhole room. Ernie caught the movement and answered her question before she'd asked it. 'Hasn't cleared his mail since last Tuesday.'

Out there in the real world it was milk bottles left out on the doorstep, wasn't it? If anyone actually still had their milk delivered. But in college there were cleaners who went in daily, at least to empty bins and tidy round. He could hardly be lying undiscovered in a pool of blood. Nevertheless...

'Thing is, he's one of those old-style academic workaholics. Never takes a holiday. Lives for his work.' You could set your watch by him, normally, coming and going from the library. 'It's just so out of character.'

The head porter was volunteering no opinions. 'Jaffa cake?'

'Thanks.' Jenny nibbled frowningly at one chocolaty edge. 'Also—' She didn't want to be disloyal, but the pause spread out until it was impossible not to fill it. And her concern, after all, was genuine. 'Also, to be perfectly frank, I don't think his work has been going too well.'

There – it was said. Ernie's face remained impressively neutral, so she pressed on. 'He hasn't published anything in years. I mean, *years*. And I know it's because he's working on his monograph, this definitive biography of his, but...' It all created its own pressure, didn't it? The work that was to be a lifetime's achievement, the crowning glory of a career – and meanwhile the lack of those smaller, regular outputs which maintained scholarly momentum, which kept your head in the game and your name in the public eye, and ticked boxes for research assessment purposes. The more time passed the better the book had to be. By now, this one had to be pretty much perfect.

'I don't think he's been making much progress lately. There was a half-day Regency Literature conference in the faculty at the start of term, slap bang in his field, and he didn't offer a paper, though you'd think he'd have had a draft chapter or something he wanted feedback on, at least. In fact, he only showed his face for the first session and then disappeared before the Q&A. It was one of our own research students, and she was really disappointed.' No wonder – his early departure had bordered on bad manners. And Dr Whybrow's comments were enormously respected. For Jenny, her supervisor's gently insightful criticism had been the making of her doctorate.

'And lately, if I ask him how it's going, even in the most general sort of way, he goes all weird on me. Defensive, you know. Clams up, changes the subject. I think he might... well, I think he might be...'

'Blocked.' It sounded dreadfully final, the way Ernie said it.

'I suppose so, yes. And what with that, and then not being here, it makes me anxious about him.' She prodded one cranberry sandal with her toe and stared at the glowing plastic coals. 'I'm afraid he might be running away.'

The fire into which Dr Whybrow gazed threw out a much more hesitant glow, and from time to time he stretched forwards from his squatting position to insert another twist of dried marram grass at the seat of the flame. The driftwood bonfires of his boyhood had lit easily and burned with a brisk intensity – but those memories were of breezeless summer afternoons, a far cry from the damp of a late October evening on an exposed rooftop.

A wooden ladder afforded access, via a vertiginous climb from the main chamber of the Martello tower and thence through a heavy trapdoor, to a roof terrace which must once have served both as lookout and gun emplacement. Four square stone platforms commanded the view to north, south, east and west, each presumably once surmounted by heavy cannon: 24-pounders, according to his reading, at least if his tower was similarly equipped to the one at Aldeburgh. Of the timber gun carriages there remained no sign, but embedded iron rings still marked where they were shackled against recoil. Between the stone blocks were four rectangular recesses in the brickwork of the parapet, vented behind and above, which he took to have housed braziers. It was in one of these openings, on an improvised scrap of corrugated tin, that he was coaxing his fire to life.

A light drizzle began to fall, and he moved in closer in an attempt to shield the half-hearted blaze. Even on a clear night, and stoked by more accustomed hands, this hearth can surely have supplied precious little warmth to the soldiers sent up here to keep watch. A lonely, fearful watch by Colstone's account: his essay spoke of a 'dread presentiment' which 'ran like flame before the wind' to seize the populace, and to which even battle-hardened regulars were not insusceptible. With the *grande armée* massed at Boulogne one hundred thousand strong and the Frenchman bragging he would plant his imperial eagle on the Tower of London, along the English coast all eyes were trained upon the horizon for signs of the invasionary fleet, a new armada to eclipse the historic might of Philip's Spain a dozenfold, a hundredfold. The fleet that would never come.

From past the parapet, below the tower, came the soft slap and hissing withdrawal of breakers on the shingle. A fragment of Colstone's verse slid into Whybrow's mind: '... while old man Strand / suck'd brine through rattling teeth...'

He was here. The conviction was as unalterable as it was unexpected: the sudden, hurtling, headlong certainty that he was here, that William Colstone had stood here on this roof, chafing frozen fingers at this fire, his gaze fixed out beyond this rampart on the same black, empty, breathing mass of sea.

Back in the inner sanctum again two weeks later, Jenny was taking the weight off a pair of eau de Nil vintage kitten heels.

'I know where it is he goes now, anyway.'

The head porter was sorting keys on a panel of hooks on the wall. The college was endowed with excessive numbers of keys, none of them seemingly ever in the right place, and Ernie was engaged in a one-man game of perpendicular Chinese chequers. Without turning, he gave a short nod. 'Oh, yes?'

'Yes. He's bought himself a castle.'

The shuttling hands paused, though he still didn't turn. 'A castle?'

'Well, all right, not a castle exactly. More of a fort. A Martello tower, to be precise.'

'Ah.' Impossible to tell, with Ernie, what his familiarity might be with the military architecture of the Napoleonic Wars.

'Out on the coast in Suffolk, near where he's from, I gather. Where his family was from, I mean. And he's been staying in it – though goodness knows how. It sounds a complete wreck from what I can make out, been empty for years. In fact, I'm not sure it's ever been lived in at all – not properly, not by a family or anything, not since it had the army in it, back in the day.'

Ernie, having achieved some arcane symmetry in the disposition of the keys, joined her beside the fire. 'Is there electricity?' Trust him, with the obvious practical question that it hadn't occurred to her to ask.

'I think so. I'm not sure. He mentioned something about the place having been used by the Home Guard for exercises during the war, and also for animals at some point – cows, I think it was. He said that's why there's water there: the farmer had a tap put in. Perhaps he put in electricity as well.' She traced a hazy arc with one hand. 'A generator or something.'

'Red diesel.'

Jenny blinked. 'Sorry?'

'Red diesel would be the thing. Farmers get it cheap, for registered agricultural use. And you can run a generator on it.'

'Right. Um, he didn't say.' Dr Whybrow hadn't said much, really, in the way of functional detail. Nothing about how you reached the place, which was right on the beach: quite literally down on the shingle, so it seemed. Nor about furniture – if you could even have got it there – or whether the roof leaked, or what he was doing for heat. There wouldn't be a cleaner and three hot meals a day provided like he was used to in college. But if he'd been sketchy on the practicalities there was nothing unforthcoming about the way he described the tower, and especially its early history. How hammocks were slung from hooks set in the walls of the main barrack room, and tarpaulin sheets to partition off the officers' sleeping quarters from those of the men. Even the smell of the place, salty with seawater and dried sweat and fish hung smoking above the fires to supplement their rations – though quite how he knew all this was another matter. In fact, it was odd, when you came to think about it, the contrast in him from the polite evasiveness with which he'd fended off her attempts at gentle probing earlier in the term and this newfound loquacity. There was an undercurrent to his voice she'd never encountered in him before: an edge of excitement, almost of zeal.

'Colstone served there, he reckons. You know, William Colstone, the poet he's working on. The one who's the subject of his book. It seems he was actually billeted in this Martello tower.'

'Ah. He knows that, does he?'

'Yes. I suppose so. I guess he must have found a mention

of it in the literature. Or maybe – I don't know, maybe he's come across some evidence there in the tower.'

Ernie's eyebrows lifted a notch. 'Evidence?'

'Oh, you know.' She giggled. 'I don't mean he's found the bloke's initials carved into the doorframe or something. Fingerprints, or traces of his DNA. I meant evidence in the historian's sense, not the TV detective drama sense. Papers – a letter, receipts, some old army paperwork. In fact—'

It was a word he'd used about himself, unremarked at the time but which afterwards had stuck in her mind. The word he'd used was 'witness'.

'In fact, I wonder if he might have found some writing of his own. Of Colstone's own, I mean.' A diary, even? A diary would be gold dust, the biographer's Holy Grail. Why not? Such shafts of unexpected light did strike occasionally, in research. The extraordinary, serendipitous find.

But in a disused cowshed?

Apparently satisfied, Ernie leaned back in his chair. 'So that will be why he bought the place, then. Because of its connection to this man.'

'Could be,' said Jenny. But she couldn't shake off the feeling that it was somehow, obscurely, the other way about.

In the cold belly of the tower, beneath the arching hemisphere of brick, Whybrow lay awake. The paraffin storm lamp, which served him for both light and heat, threw into uneven, ridged relief the inner surface of the dome which in daytime appeared only as a smooth curve. Strange, really, the way more detail and texture was visible by the dim glow from the paraffin wick than could be seen in the daylight. The slightest shift in his own position, even a turn of his head towards the lamp, and the movement, or his breath, would cause the flame to shiver in its glass chimney, sending shadows scattering over the bricks.

He could pick out the contours of the broad wooden door recessed in the wall to the inshore side; the only pool of black was the deeply embrasured window opposite, facing out to sea.

A pair of doubled blankets insulated him comfortably enough from the hard oak floorboards, and his folded coat made a serviceable pillow. It was only the cold which kept unconsciousness at bay. Not until the warmth from his hot-water bottle, filled from the camping kettle on his portable Calor stove, had permeated the wool of his hiking socks would his feet lose their chill and make sleep possible. Meanwhile he lay on his back and waited, counting bricks instead of sheep.

He remembered the care home, in his father's last days: the whispered words at the bedside that he knew Dad couldn't hear. He thought, too, of the University Library and all its store of cumulated knowledge – but distantly, as if from another time, another life. How human voices were captured there, frozen, mothballed in ink and paper. And here? How many words, how many memories, could be held in a million bricks?

It had been a calm night outside, overcast and starless, the sea as close to a millpond as he had known it. But the tower was never silent. Even on the most breathlessly still of nights, there were whisperings in the bricks. He sometimes wondered if it was really the sea – some subterranean echo or vibration, rippling up through the walls from the shingle on which they stood. Or perhaps an illusion, a trick of the mind, like the echo of the waves heard in a seashell. Yet, for all that, there was a

134

paradoxical realness and solidity about the voices here, an immediacy – yes, that was the word for it: immediate, unmediated – which recalled with a sudden sharp pang the early days of his scholarship, that quickening of the blood he had thought to have lost. A connection thought severed, rejoined.

Slowly, the heat from his body crept out to fill the air pockets of his sleeping bag and, at last, he felt the first softenings of warmth in the stiff woollen fibres which encased his toes. He rolled on to his side and shut his eyes.

It might be cold here in the barrack room but it was never lonely. His brow, his nose and mouth lay close to the brickwork. Fleetingly, he thought he caught the scent of antiseptic, masking stale urine, but it danced away from him and instead he breathed in tar and damp canvas, woodsmoke, rum and spindrift. And the name that formed felt familiar on his lips.

'William?'

Into the stillness multiplied the murmuring reply.

It was Finlay, the young ginger-haired porter, who handed Jenny the lunchtime post from her pigeonhole the following Wednesday.

'Ernie not on duty today?'

'He's on nights this week. Be in later.' Finlay scratched a freckled nose. 'Anything I can help with?'

'Well... I suppose you might give him a message.'

What to say, though, that wouldn't be indiscreet? Finlay displayed a commendable Aberdonian caution in many things but he could be like a fishwife when it came to gossip.

Her source, at any rate, was beyond impeachment: the redoubtable Sue, whose duties included the cleaning of

135

both Dr Whybrow's rooms and Jenny's own study on the adjacent staircase, and who had switched off her hoover on the landing that morning to pass admiring comment on Jenny's lattice-laced black knee boots, before informing her mysteriously that he was 'back at it'. 'He' turned out to be Dr Whybrow, and the evidence that of his desk, on which, Sue explained, there lay beside the computer a stack of A4 printed sheets, topped with the felt pen injunction PLEASE DO NOT TOUCH. This, he had informed her warningly, was 'the book'.

'It hadn't shifted, not for ages. Of course he's been away a lot recently, but even before that, it hadn't been touched in months. Crying out for a duster over it. Anyway, evidently he'd been back on Monday – been through the room like a dervish, he had. And the pile was nearly twice as high. Lots of clean new papers, and not a speck of dust in sight.'

'Really? That's great. Thanks, Sue.'

It was proof. He was writing again; his mojo had been restored. Dr Whybrow was back on his book. And making great progress by the sound of it, too. Whatever he'd unearthed in that tower of his, it must be something big.

'Tell Ernie—' Jenny gazed thoughtfully at Finlay, then suddenly grinned. 'Just tell him Dr Whybrow is unblocked.'

* * *

A pale November sun rose from below the sea to speckle the beach with silver and send the elongated shadow of the Martello tower zigzagging away behind across the ridges and furrows of the dunes. It lent the tower's brickwork a milky glow, so that it almost appeared to be lit from within. The sea lay lulled, each soft breaker spreading and dying to silence before the next one rose.

Whybrow had wakened early, and sat, still in his sleeping bag and with his coat wrapped around his shoulders, leaning against the wall of the tower: on his lap, a pad of notepaper, his fountain pen on the blanket beside him. All around was emptiness and dust, which, although his gaze ranged over it, he did not see. The air was alive with listening.

He tipped his head back until it rested on the old, roughened surface; he closed his eyes and smiled. Then he picked up his pen.

A Curiosity of Warnings

Cycling in the countryside, along all those leafy Suffolk lanes had seemed a seductive idea when Bill was back in Finsbury Park with its one-way systems and potholes and tailbacks of the road-enraged.

The three-mile cycle ride from the little railway station was hardly an endurance trial but Bill hadn't been on a bike since he'd moved to London and it took a bit of getting used to again, whatever they said. As did rural navigation, not greatly assisted by signposts buried deep in summer hedgerows, nor by a station bearing the name of the small town of Wickham Market but situated in reality several miles from there at a village called Campsea Ashe. He wasn't convinced about the machine he'd been given either, by the rental firm. They'd brought it from Ipswich in a white van with a toothy, grinning cartoon bicycle on the side and the legend *Mister Bike – We Deliver*. It had far too many gears and made disconcerting grinding noises every time he tried to shift them, so he'd stuck doggedly to seventeenth for the last mile and a half.

A bike, however, had seemed appropriate to the purposes of Bill's trip. In fact, he felt self-consciously – almost ludicrously – like the protagonist of an M. R.

James ghost story. How else to arrive at the hostelry chosen for his short vacation, the avowed purpose of which was to visit the locations of 'A Warning to the Curious', than on a bicycle like young Paxton in the tale? The victims of James's hauntings seemed almost always to be academics like Bill himself, generally 'antiquarians' such as Paxton was described – which Bill supposed his own post as Lecturer in Early Modern History at King's College London might give him some claim to be. They pitched up in all innocence of dark events to come, with a backpack on their shoulders very much like the one that was threatening to unbalance him on corners now, except in stout canvas, no doubt, rather than grey-and-orange Gore-Tex. Dr Paxton in 'A Warning' had put up at the Bear in 'Seaburgh', which Bill took to be Aldeburgh, while he himself was booked in at a village pub some way inland. The Ship, it was called, though it must be six miles from the sea, and as he rested his calves to freewheel down a curved incline, there it was, swinging into view ahead on the right. The inn sign which hung from the gable end depicted the popular notion of a Viking longship, with its high prow and stern, striped sail and shields along the gunwales. In fact, he thought, as he slowed to peer up at the sign, the name was more likely to be a corruption of 'Sheep'. He'd have to look it up.

The motorbike came out of nowhere. Bill caught the blast of noise only as it screamed round the high-hedged bend behind him, and moments afterwards the powerful broadside cuff of wind as it sped narrowly past him at a giddying angle to the tarmac. Here in the dip of the road a dusting of sand lay loose across the surface and as he braked Bill felt its treacherous shift, just as he saw the motorbike's rear tyre slide sideways into the contours of a skid. For a breathless split second, time stood still as he waited for the inevitable tipping point: the wheels that spun in empty air as leather rasped over gravel, followed by the shock of impact, the sickening crunch of steel and fibreglass and bone. A split second only – and then the machine righted itself, before roaring away up the hill beyond the pub at full throttle. Bill wobbled to a ragged halt in the gutter, relieved to regain first his balance and then, by fluttering degrees, his normal pulse rate. Bloody desperado – a menace to sensible road users. And yet there was something approaching exhilaration in making it here in one piece, in defiance of protesting muscles and stuntmen on motorbikes.

He hauled the hired bicycle alongside a low wall at the front of the Ship and engaged in battle with the intransigent D lock supplied by Mister Bike.

The unaccustomed exertion of the ride had sharpened Bill's appetite for beer and pub grub and at soon after six he was first in the bar. Or almost the first: at the far end with her newspaper propped against the ice bucket and a half-empty pint glass in front of her leaned a young woman of twenty or so.

She glanced up at him, then pulled a face. 'Sorry about earlier.'

Bill stared.

'On the bike.' Her mouth corners plunged further: sad clown without the painted tears. 'I'm afraid I cut you up a bit.'

'Oh. Sorry. So that was...?'

He replayed the mental picture of the slight youth in motorbike leathers and black helmet, the mirrored visor, and tried to map it on to the ponytailed girl in front of him in summer dress and sandals, her face now resolving back to a smile.

'Me, yes.'

'Who nearly killed me?' Though actually, she was the one more likely to have died.

'Yeah, sorry about that. Buy you a drink? Oh, and the pie's bloody good, if you're eating. Raymond – the landlord here – is a miserable old sod, but his pie crust is poetry.'

So they shared a table and the last two portions of steak and kidney, brought over by an unsmiling Raymond, and she told him her name was Freya, and about the excavation she was working on, down at the churchyard.

'Seems to be the site of an earlier building. Saxon, maybe monastic.'

'So you're an archaeologist?'

'Well, sort of. Archaeology student. I'm just a grunt – gang labour, except there's only one of me. It's not even paid – but they put me up at the youth hostel and keep me in beer and steak pie.'

'Another antiquarian, in fact.'

'Sorry?'

Bill half smiled, shook his head. 'Nothing.'

Spearing a carrot with her fork, she flourished it at him. 'How about you? On holiday?'

'Well, I suppose you might call it a pilgrimage.' He hadn't supposed there'd be anyone he'd tell about it. It seemed rather eccentric, somehow, his literary jaunt – old-fashioned, even self-indulgent. But Freya listened without judging.

'So what did he do here, this Paxton bloke?'

'He found the missing Anglo-Saxon crown.'

'That was helpful of him. Who'd lost it?'

'Raedwald, King of the East Angles, so the story goes.'

She laid down her knife and took a swig of bitter. 'Isn't he the Sutton Hoo chap? The one in the burial ship?'

141

'It's a theory, I think, yes. Anyway, this silver crown of Paxton's was one of three that were said to be buried at intervals along the coast here to keep East Anglia safe from invasion. One had already been found and melted down, back in the seventeenth century, and another was supposed to have been swept away by the encroaching sea. But that left the third one, and Paxton fancied having it.'

'Careless of the fate of East Anglia?'

'Careless indeed. Anyway, he meets the rector at a church that James calls Froston – I think it's based on Friston, up the road there just past Snape. And this rector person tells him how there's a local family called the Agers, who were guardians of the third and final crown, sworn to protect it with their lives. There was an old father, William Ager, who died, and then his son, another William, who camped out at nights to watch over the crown and apparently caught his death that way, too, while still only in his twenties. He was the last of the line, the son, so of course his ghost takes over on guard duty.'

'Oh, dear – I think I can guess where this is going. Paxton tries to steal the crown and the ghost gets him?'

'Well, not straight away, oddly. He finds the burial place – a barrow or tumulus above the beach with a knot of fir trees on it – and he digs up the crown and takes it back to the inn where he's staying. But as soon as he touches it, he starts to see the ghost out of the corner of his eye – a man watching him, who disappears when he looks straight at him. Dark shadows lurking behind him, following him. You know the sort of thing. So he decides to put the crown back.'

'Quite right, too. Give the East Angles back their heritage. Like restoring the Elgin marbles.'

'Right. But then the ghost gets him anyway.'

142

'Bit harsh.' The sad clown face again. 'What's'it do to him? Scare him to death? Apoplexy of terror?'

'It chases him along the beach in the fog and he falls off an old pillbox and smashes his skull. A coastal battery, you know.'

Freya had finished her pie and was sitting back in her chair, retying her ponytail and looking thoughtful.

'When was this story written, then? I was imagining Edwardian gothic.'

'1925 – or that's when it was published, anyway.'

'And they had pillboxes here in the First World War? I think of them as being built to keep out Hitler.'

'Some, evidently. I suppose they thought the Germans were coming in 1914 as much as in 1940.'

'And 614 – or whenever it was Raedwald was knocking about. Except that would be my lot, not the Germans.'

Momentarily puzzled, Bill frowned at her.

'Vikings – Norsemen. Freya's a Norse name.'

'And you're from Denmark? Or your family are?'

She grinned and shook her head. 'Basildon. Another pint?'

It was perfect weather for the cycle ride to Friston the following afternoon, and Bill was getting the hang of the bike; he was using a range of gears from fourteenth to eighteenth. But the church, when he arrived, was disappointing: pretty enough, but heavily restored in the nineteenth century. The porch was plain and bare, with none of the 'niches and shields' that James described – and certainly no sign of the coat of arms with the three Anglo-Saxon crowns. In the graveyard, wading knee-deep through yellowing grass and meadowsweet and overblown, head-heavy poppies, he found no Ager tombstones. It should be no surprise – fiction was fiction,

143

after all – but he felt a sense of deflation nonetheless, and on the way back the hills seemed all to be against him and the sun was oppressive on his back. His collar chafed and he was sure his neck was burning.

After a shower he found himself hoping that Freya would be in the pub again, to commiserate on his failed mission. She was.

'There's more pie,' she informed him by way of greeting. 'Turkey and ham.' But through a mouthful of béchamel and shortcrust pastry she tendered little sympathy. 'So Froston isn't Friston. It's somewhere else – or he just made it up.'

For some reason her robust dismissiveness rather cheered him up. 'What about you, then? Did you despoil any historic treasures today? Rob any good graves?'

'We don't do that any more.' For once, she really seemed in earnest. 'Archaeologists – we're not like the gold-digger in your story. Those days of pot-hunting are long past – plundering the pyramids, stripping bare the sacred sites of other civilisations to sell the loot or cart things off and put them on display. Self-enrichment, self-aggrandisement.'

'Cultural imperialism? But it's Suffolk you're digging up, not Byzantium or Asia Minor.'

She nodded, her brows drawn to a small crease. 'But it's just another sort of imperialism, isn't it? The know-it-all present lording it over the past. The Victorians were terrible for it – and right through to the twenties and thirties, too.'

'So what are you doing now, if you're not trying to know everything?'

At that, the crease smoothed away and she smiled at him. 'Oh, don't worry, we're still appalling know-it-alls. We dig things up, but then we photograph and catalogue, record and document, and as often as not we put things back. It's not the finds so much as the findings. Not the objects but the stories they tell.'

'So – you're no longer looking for the Holy Grail?'

The smile widened. 'Nor the Arc of the Covenant, either. That Indiana Jones has a lot to answer for.'

Now it was Bill's turn to be sober. 'I'm not sure the ghost of William Ager would make the distinction. I suspect for him it's disturbing things in the first place that's the sacrilege. The past just needs leaving well alone.'

For a while they attended to their pie in silence. Bill thought of fields where the soil had yielded its ancient possessions not to the archaeologist's trowel but to the tractor, working them up to the surface to be broken and scattered beneath the blade of the plough. He thought of artefacts lost to the wind and rain and sea: to coastal erosion, as at Dunwich, which he had visited as a boy with his grandmother, and seen broken headstones and human bones, shockingly naked and white, sticking through the sandy cliff at grotesque angles like trauma-shattered limbs, so that he'd thought it must be a battlefield until Gran told him it was just an old cemetery, going over the edge.

Recalling him from his meanderings, Freya said, 'There are still holy grails, it's just that they're not things any more.'

'So they're... what?'

She shrugged her shoulders. 'Explanations? Connections?' She must have been working in a vest; there was a line of fragile white at each side in the golden brown, further out along her collarbone than the straps of her dress. His own neck prickled.

'Like us, then – like historians. Except my delving is all above ground. In county record offices, not tumuli. I do the Civil War. It's all old documents – letters, court rolls.'

'Less muddy, at least.'

'Just a bit of dust and mildew, sometimes.'

'No risk of sunburn.'

His gaze loitered on the bronzed shoulders. 'No. No sunburn.'

'And you dig up secrets, not Anglo-Saxon crowns.'

He nodded, sitting back in his chair and sipping his beer. It was true: betrayals and chicaneries, dark deeds dragged out and exposed to daylight, these were his stock-in-trade.

Freya leaned intently forward. 'The thing about secrets is, they're not like a silver crown. Once you've unearthed them, they cannot be put back.' She sought his eye and he saw that she was only half laughing. 'So you see, it's you the vengeful ghosts of the past should be pursuing, not me.'

'I read your story.' Tonight's pie was chicken and leek, and they had carried it outside on to the terrace, leaving the bar to a leather-hatted melodeon player singing a song about a foggy night at sea. Freya was attacking her plate with vigour. 'Online, yesterday evening. I read "A Warning to the Curious".'

'And? What did you think?' He found he really wanted to know.

'Well, I ended up going to sleep with the light on, if that makes you happy.'

He grinned. 'Sorry about that.'

'*And since that day*,' announced the melodeonist through the open bar door, '*we'll roam the bay, until we find the Navy Island gold.*'

Freya waved her beer glass. 'I was thinking, though. He was spookily prophetic, wasn't he, your M. R. James? The barrow on the hill, overlooking the water where the enemy ships might come. The buried Anglo-Saxon treasure. Even the possible Raedwald connection. It's all exactly like Sutton Hoo, isn't it? But you say he wrote the story in 1925. That's more than a decade before they started to dig at the Hoo.'

'Yes... But I suppose they knew there could be something there. I mean, the mounds were pretty obvious, sitting there for all to see. And there'd been looting in the past, things already found. Coins and so on.'

'*...a man names Bones took a chest ashore...*'

Freya impaled a potato and nodded eagerly. 'Right. And did you know they'd found that ship at Snape as well?'

'At Snape?'

'I looked it all up last night. Don't you love the Internet? They found an Anglo-Saxon burial ship on Snape Common – it was excavated back in the 1860s. Not as big as the one at Sutton, and the grave goods were missing – probably been raided by earlier looters. But I wondered if maybe James knew about it.'

'*...he killed his men, and cursed their souls; to roam as ghosts, and protect the gold...*'

'Maybe he had even visited the site there, at Snape,' Freya persisted.

'An archaeology fan?'

'Well, why not? He was a medieval scholar, wasn't he?'

One evening on Wiki and she seemed to know more about it all than he did. 'It's true that's very nearby,' he said. 'To the places in the story, I mean. Snape Common practically backs on to Friston.'

'There you are, then.' Her eyes gleamed triumphantly. They were, he noticed, a sun-dappled hazel green.

Inside the bar now an elderly woman was singing, strongly but tunelessly, about a lover gone to sea to face the foe amid the blund'ring cannons' roar. There was history, he thought, that wasn't buried in the earth or hidden in old papers. He would have made some observation of the kind to Freya but, before he could frame the thought, she said, 'Speaking of archaeology fans, you should come and visit my dig some time. It's only me and the prof – not even her, some days – and I'm sure she won't mind. Come along and I'll give you the tour. If you're interested in a hole in the ground three metres square and a bit of old wall.'

'Since you sell it so well, how can I resist? Thank you. And actually, I've been meaning to get down to the church. It's the other reason I came – apart from M. R. James, and a holiday, of course.'

'Oh?'

'My family came from here, you see – my grandmother's family. I used to come and stay when I was a kid. She lived in Southwold then, but she was born here in the village. I thought I might take a poke round the gravestones, maybe look at the parish register, and see what I can find.'

'The old family tree thing?'

'Not quite that.' He had an historian's disdain for fashionable genealogy, with its obsessive box-ticking. Pure snobbery, no doubt. 'But family history, anyway.'

'Parish records...' Freya's mouth, above the rim of her pint, was flirting with a smile. 'Do I scent dust and mildew? A busman's holiday as well as a pilgrimage?'

By the weekend, even Freya had had her fill of pub pie. 'D'you fancy a barbecue? A proper beach barbecue, I mean?'

They bought the fish from one of the fishermen's sheds on the beach at Aldeburgh: little flat dabs, locally caught, six of them for a fiver.

'*Six?*'

Freya wafted a breezy hand. 'Oh, we'll need three each, there's nothing on them.'

'What are dabs, anyway?' He'd never seen them in Sainsbury's.

'No idea. But you'll see – they taste like the North Sea. 'Cept without the sewage, obviously.'

She was right. The driftwood they gathered had been salted and seasoned by the sea until it was light as balsa; once they'd persuaded a match to light and not blow out, it caught like straw, and the shingle drew in air to whip the flames. Freya had brought kitchen foil, a lemon and a penknife; she gutted the fish with a nonchalance that was almost alarming. They were cooked in minutes and, eating scaldingly with his fingers and through mouthfuls of small bones, Bill had never tasted anything more delicious.

If the fire had lit readily and burned quickly it nevertheless died slowly, leaving them to lie back on their elbows and stare into the winking embers, or watch for the occasional flurry of rising sparks. It was strange, he thought, how the assortment of broken planks and branches kept their shape: empty, glowing crimson hulls, hollowed inside to little but hot air, first by the seawater and then by the fire. One touch and they would no doubt fall to ash.

Dust to dust. Like the timber ribs of the exhumed burial ship at Sutton Hoo, which turned to powder as soon as exposed to air.

'Is that the Martello tower? The one in the story?' Freya's words seemed to come to him from another time and place rather than from just across the fire. He blinked at her through the trickle of smoke.

'I think so, yes.'

It lay along the beach, beyond them to the south, a massive squat cylinder of sombre grey brick – or in fact more a quatrefoil than a cylinder, with its four great clustered towers.

'No wonder they were worried about invasion, those Ager blokes. The ones who were guarding Raedwald's crown. I mean, it's everywhere, isn't it? The physical threat of it. Those concrete pillboxes in all the fields on the way down here, waiting to defend the coast from two lots of Germans who never came. And then that bloody big thing, too. Whole garrisons of soldiers, watching for the French who never came either.'

Before that the Spanish, who'd sailed straight past, already defeated and in tatters. 'Luckily for us,' he said.

'Right.' Through the darkness and the shimmer of rising heat he could make out the light in her hazel eyes. 'Or maybe not lucky. Maybe there really is some powerful protective magic at work along this coast.'

'What about your lot, though?' He offered a smile, hoping to see her return it, but her expression remained distant, dreamy. 'The Danes – the Vikings. They came, all right.'

Came and saw and conquered; or rather, they came and raided and went away – or came and married and settled. But it was tempting to believe in Freya's talismanic sorcery, even so. Lying here in the glimmer of the dying firelight, hearing the slop and suck of breaking waves at the waterline, there was a powerful sense of the collapsing telescope of time. He felt he knew what they must have felt, those long-dead ancestors, as they listened for the lap of the feared Norsemen's oars, or watched for lights where no lights should be, out in the shifting mass of indigo and grey that stretched from beach to horizon. Did the cries of gulls and terns transform into the far-off calls of warrior sailors, hastily hushed, as they hauled up the sail to drift in stealth towards the shore? But there was no seaborne invader now to threaten these shores. It was a long time since Bill's parents had lived with the threat of the Soviet tanks rolling westwards towards them across Germany and Holland. These days the spectre was just a lone stranger with a rucksack – or even a neighbour, student, colleague – though surely not here on the Suffolk coast.

There was still some warmth coming from the burnt-out husks of firewood as well as from the seared pebbles surrounding and beneath. But August was more than half over and the sun was gone already, and with it much of the day's heat. It felt suddenly like summer's end. Maybe the sea cooled slower than the air – or faster (Bill was no physicist) – or perhaps it was the sudden drop in temperature, but whatever the reason, a sea mist had formed above the breakers. At first there were only wisps of haze, like steam over a heated outdoor pool, but gradually they merged and increased in density, before starting to rise and roll up the banked shingle of the beach. The Martello tower was already shrouded in white to halfway up its walls. Then towards them, as Bill watched, there stretched a slow, unfurling, vaporous finger.

Freya was staring in the same direction. Her bare shoulders hunched in a shudder.

'You're cold. Here – take my sweater.'

Instead she sat up, brushing sand and pebbles from her jeans and vest. 'Thanks, but this shingle is bloody uncomfortable, anyway. I think I might head back.'

There were no evening buses to or from the village, and Bill had balked at the idea of riding pillion behind Freya on the motorbike; besides, she had no spare helmet. So he'd met her here with the hired pushbike, and now faced a lonely eight-mile cycle home. He kicked shingle over the remnants of the fire – a good Boy Scout – and walked with her back to where they'd left the bikes, behind the sea wall. The path along the top of the wall was deserted, so he might have kissed her then, as he'd have liked to have done, but as she bent to free the disc lock of her motorbike she shivered again, as if a shadow had crossed her grave, and Bill was filled with the unformed, haunting sense of its being too late.

The sea fret hugged the shoreline, so that as he rose on his pedals to mount the hill out of the town it fell away behind him and he was out into pale, clear moonlight. But, glancing back as he paused at the summit to catch his breath, he saw that the mist had shifted and risen, too, so as to create the sensation that it was following him. The road wound between tall hedges and the moon cast shifting, fractured shadows across his way. There was no sound but the creaking of the bike's saddle springs and the whir of its wheels, so that when a pheasant, startled from sleep, rose beating from the hedge he was as shaken as the bird, and his heart hammered hard in his chest. The bicycle's front light gave out a watery beam, lighting a small patch of tarmac which served only to throw everything around it into deeper darkness. The pattern of the filament resembled a skull as it ran and jumped along in front of him; he found himself trying not to look directly at it.

From his right loomed suddenly the huge, dark outline of a pylon, and behind it a phalanx of others, marching in from the sea at Sizewell armed with countless gigawatts of atomic power, crackling and buzzing, seeking the shortest route to earth.

All he could think of, all the long way home with the mist at his tail and the leaping shadows tormenting him, was the story, the 'Warning to the Curious'. How the narrator, walking close between hedges, would sooner have been in the open, where he could see if anyone was visible behind him. And young Paxton muttering over and over, 'I don't know how to put it back.' Then, finally, Freya's voice. *You* dig *up secrets, not Anglo-Saxon crowns.* And, *Once you've unearthed them, they cannot be put back.*

The final week in August – the last week, too, of Bill's holiday – built to a fever of oppressive heat. The fields around the village lay dusty and inert beneath a haze of heavy air; even the stateliest trees appeared to droop and wilt. It was far too hot for long cycle rides. His room was airless – too airless even for reading in comfort – and in the bar of the Ship the only company was Raymond, the publican, growing gloomier the more the thermometer rose, and two indistinguishable regulars, George and Jim, who were scarcely more cheerful and sat playing endless games of cribbage. He saw almost nothing of Freya, who took to downing a quick pint after work and disappearing to the youth hostel to sit in the cool and write up her notes from the excavation. That, too, was coming to an end.

'We're clearing out early. I uncovered a layer of ash. If we haven't found much, that's maybe why – it might have been sacked by the Danes.'

'By your lot.'

'Yeah – by my lot.'

The Friday was the hottest day so far, a treacly, damp, impenetrable heat which felt too thick for breathing. With his return to London looming, Bill remembered that he hadn't yet been to the church, either to visit the archaeological dig or to research his grandmother's family. A knock at the rectory door had furnished him with the key to the vestry in which the parish registers were kept; the pretty and heavily pregnant young woman whom he took at first to be the rector's wife but further conversation revealed in fact to be the rector assured him

153

that they dated back to the eighteenth century. Dragging the bicycle out of the side shed where Raymond had grudgingly let him store it, he set off towards the church. It was almost five, but he had put off his expedition until he hoped the swelter might be starting to subside, and to an hour which Freya had mentioned as being more conducive to digging in a heatwave. In fact, if anything, both heat and humidity were worse than before, but cloud was massing from the west and the sky had taken on an angry, greyish-purple hue which surely meant the weather was soon to break.

As he locked up his bike by the church gate he could almost smell the approaching rain. The breeze had stilled, leaving the air dull and leaden. Even the birds had quietened. There was no activity at what he took to be the excavation site; the square trench near the tower was covered over with tarpaulins. They must not have been working this afternoon at all, or else were starting very late or had knocked off early to avoid the storm.

Inside the church it was cooler, which was some relief, but the air tasted stale and held no stir of movement. The vestry door was to the left of the chancel arch, just as the rector had described to him: a heavy oak door below a simple gothic arch, the old wood much patched and repaired. Beside it, in the final bay of the nave, was a stained-glass window – early Victorian, by the colouring and manner, with its elongated figures and elaborate folds of drapery. It depicted Mary in the centre panel, holding the Christ child as if he were made of Dresden china – which, indeed, he did somewhat resemble. On either side stood unknown saints with extravagantly curling beards; one held an open book and one a giant golden key. But what caught Bill's attention was something above and behind the three principals, where stylised leaves and lilies wreathed the upper portions of the lights and among them a banner unfurled, its ends elegantly scrolled. The field was a brilliant blue and on it a simple blazon: three repeated images in silver-white argent, each with three distinctive trefoil tines, familiar in heraldic design. There was no mistaking them – the three Anglo-Saxon crowns.

Bill saw that his hand was trembling as he slotted the vestry key into the lock, and resolved to pull himself together. It must be the hot weather: too much sun, addling his mind and making him a prey to foolish notions. He'd find Gran in the parish registers, make his notes, then return to the pub and take a long cool bath. If he hurried, he might even make it back before the storm broke.

It was in the third book of the marriage register that he found the entry. Manning, his mother's maiden name. Edith Ann Manning – that was his grandmother. He read the lines twice, three times, but the information refused to be grasped; it dodged and danced and taunted him, defying comprehension.

15th June 1938

Charles Edward Manning
bachelor of the parish of Little Glemham
son of Thomas and Jane Manning

to

Edith Ann Ager
spinster of this parish
daughter of William and Elizabeth Ager

Bill closed the register with a snap that sounded abnormally loud in the stifling air. Consumed by an urgency for which he couldn't fully account, he pushed it back between the other volumes on the shelf, then blundered from the vestry, fumbling in his impatience to lock the door, and on out into the churchyard, Freya and the dig forgotten, almost running now to where he'd left his bike. Already the first few bloated drops of rain were beginning to fall, wetting the path in haphazard splashes and saturating the unnaturally early dusk with moisture. It was suddenly cold.

His fingers shook so that he struggled with the bicycle lock, and by the time he was mounted and pushing off along the lane the rain was coming down in earnest: a fierce, unrelenting downpour. It was rain so dense that it almost had solid shape, like vertical columns of water. The surface of the road fizzed and steamed beneath his tyres where cold liquid met heated tarmac, while overhead the power lines sputtered and hissed in warning. Bill's hair and face were soon drenched, water cascading down his brow and temples and into his eyes. It tasted metallic on his lips; it ran from his chin in rivulets.

The secrets of the past, he thought. Family secrets. *You dig up secrets and they cannot be put back*. He was an Ager. No Paxton, but an Ager; the watcher, not the watched. Why was he impelled to flee? If there was a ghost at his heels, it could only be his own.

For a moment the slate of the sky was lit to an eerie yellow. Then came a rumble that could be the first roll and judder of thunder, or the growl of an approaching engine, blurred by the drum of rain. Blindly, with head down and eyes screwed tight against the stinging torrent, Bill pedalled into the storm.

THE INTERREGNUM

Parochial Church Council of St Peter's, Blaxhall
Minutes of a meeting held in the village hall on Tuesday 24th November 2015 at 7.30 p.m
Present: Sheila Mott (vice-chairperson and church-warden), Dorothy Brundish (secretary)...

Dorothy had served as secretary of the PCC for more than forty years. During that time she had graduated from her old Smith-Corona portable typewriter through, successively, an Amstrad and a Macintosh desktop the size of a Ford Fiesta to the current MacBook Pro, slim and silver, provided by the deanery. Over the same period she had moved through several pairs of spectacles, each with progressively fatter lenses. The MacBook allowed you to enlarge the font and twiddle around with differently coloured backgrounds but, even so, typing these days was rather a strain. A pity that deanery resources didn't run to the supply of new eyes.

Item 1: Arrangements for the interregnum
Miss Ivy Paskall has been appointed on a temporary basis to provide cover during the absence of the rector...

Although, strictly speaking, it wasn't actually an interregnum. That would have been a commonplace enough phenomenon, of which there had been three during Dorothy's tenure as secretary – following, respectively, the retirements of Harry Camplin and Bartholemew Leach and the untimely death from pancreatic cancer of poor David Tuttle at the age of only sixty-two – and procedures for covering services in such circumstances were well established. But six months of maternity leave, necessitated by the pregnancy of the Revd. Kimberley Jackaman, who'd not been married a year – this was an eventuality unanticipated by diocesan synods of the past.

Dorothy moved her mouse back over the text on the screen before her, selected 'arrangements for the interregnum' and pressed 'delete', before substituting 'arrangements for maternity cover'.

The congregation would all rally round, of course, to support the churchwardens, and old Harry Camplin still lived in the village and had volunteered his best offices, but at eighty-seven and with his prostate issues there were limits to what they could expect, even now with the new plumbing in the choir vestry. It was the Rural Dean who had suggested Ivy's name; he had met her at a dinner at his old college over in Cambridge. She came with impeccable credentials: sensible and fifty, with a career in teaching behind her, followed by a double first in Philosophy and Theology, she was completing a doctorate on the early Christian church in East Anglia before training for the ministry. It meant she was only a licensed lay reader where they might have hoped for a deacon or even a retired priest, but what she lacked in terms of investiture she more than made up for with the forthright energy and old-fashioned common sense that had struck them all so forcibly at the informal interview held around Kimberley's kitchen table at the rectory. Even Air Vice-Marshal Fitzpatrick had been impressed. And while a lay reader wasn't authorised to celebrate weddings or baptisms or administer the sacraments, she could at least conduct a funeral – that being, it often seemed, the rite most in demand at St Peter's. The most immediate thing, too, was that Ivy would be here for the busy Christmas period, and it didn't take an ordinand to rally tots in dressing gowns and tea towels or lead the carols round the crib.

She obviously couldn't move into the rectory, as old Canon Whiterod had done during the last interregnum. Kimberley and her husband were very much in possession, and busy pasting Peppa Pig wallpaper in the first floor box room. But the Air Vice-Marshal had offered the use of Church Cottage at a preferential rent, and Mrs Suggett said she could easily manage to do for Ivy in the way of cleaning as well as for the Reverend. Not of course, as Dorothy reminded herself, that it was an interregnum this time.

* * *

Village die-hards might not like it, but Dorothy thought the Epiphany Burning was rather fun. The kiddies always loved a bonfire, after all, and they could all do with something bright and cheerful to think about, with the Christmas merriments done and packed away for the year and the brunt of the winter weather no doubt still to be faced.

The idea had been Ivy's, but Sheila Mott had jumped on board with enthusiasm, organising the jacket potatoes and the hot fruit punch – non-alcoholic, so no objection could be raised on that score. The appearance of the Rural Dean to apply the taper and bless the flames had added the incontrovertible seal of approval.

159

The practice was a long-established one, according to Ivy, in the European protestant tradition. The taking down of Christmas trees and other evergreens which had been brought indoors to celebrate the season were taken out and burned. The cleansing fire represented purification, the sacred funeral pyre from which rebirth would come: for the ancients, the cycle of death and regeneration in nature; for Christians, sin, absolution and amendment of life.

'The ancients?' Dorothy had queried, gently uncertain, through the candy-twist steam which rose from her punch.

Ivy had flourished an expansive arm, scattering buttery raindrops from her foil-wrapped potato. 'Oh, yes. Epiphany is like all the Christian festivals – steeped in the lore of earlier faiths. Look at the Christmas tree itself, if it comes to that. Bringing evergreens indoors at the winter solstice and decorating them was very much a pagan custom. It was condemned in fact, by the Prophet Jeremiah. *Thus saith the Lord: learn not the way of the heathen, for the customs of the people are vain; for one cutteth a tree out of the forest with the axe. They deck it with silver and with gold.* But you have one here in the church porch every year. The tinsel is in a box in the vestry, underneath the offertory plates.'

She'd talked about forest fires, too, and how they were a natural and necessary part of the woodland ecosystem, removing dead materials, releasing nutrients back into the soil that have been locked up in mature plants and creating space for new growth. 'You must surely have witnessed it on the common here,' she said.

Happily, however, the Epiphany Burning had not taken place on the common – which must be a tinderbox, even in January – but on the hill behind the churchyard.

160

Willie Woolnough and the other bell-ringers set them on their way with a short set of changes ('The ringing of bells,' said Ivy, 'was known to the pre-Christians for the driving out of demons'), and the church porch spruce, denuded of its gaudy, idolatrous trappings, was borne in processional from the churchyard along the Holy-gate Path which led up Silly Hill.

Ivy had a theory about this, as well. 'Its derivation is probably the same as that of "Silly Suffolk" – a corruption of the Old English "*selig*", meaning holy or blessed. So Silly Hill is really Holy Hill. What better place for a religious celebration?'

Looking round at the faces of the Sunday school children, toasted in the fire's glow, Dorothy had no heart but to concur. Besides which, the bonfire performed a useful social function. Everyone in the village had a dead conifer to dispose of, and this had to be better than all that shredding, or a hundred trips to the tip.

* * *

Parochial Church Council of St Peter's, Blaxhall
  Minutes of a meeting held in the village hall on Tuesday 26th January 2016 at 7.30 pm

  Item 1: Candlemas celebrations
  A budget was approved for the Candlemas celebrations to be held on Sunday 7th February, including £150 for candles and a £100 subsidy towards the cost of the Wives' Feast. Those attending will also be asked to bring either a sweet or a savoury dish, and drinks as appropriate.

Dorothy removed her spectacles and gently pressed both eyelids with bunched fingertips, then waited for the

161

sparkling to subside. Curious, she thought, how it was the Wives' Feast that had most keenly divided the meeting.

The Harvest Supper was always subsidised, as Sheila Mott had pointed out, and the annual Sunday school picnic.

'But those events are open to all,' objected Martin Cowling, the church treasurer, 'and not just one section of the congregation,' while Dorothy, seated beside Air Vice-Marshal Fitzpatrick, had distinctly heard him mutter the word 'feminist' – though it wasn't something she'd ever heard him say about the Mothers' Union, whose speakers' expenses were regularly met and who had recently persuaded Martin to a new slide projector from eBay, when every other group in the parish just huddled round a laptop.

Dorothy's own doubts – not that they were exactly doubts; it was more just a faint, indistinct unease – were more what one might term doctrinal. Though you could hardly question Ivy's expertise on matters theological and historical. It was her specialist field, after all: the subject of her Cambridge PhD. They'd never marked Candlemas at St Peter's before to Dorothy's recollection, but it seemed irreproachably biblical when Ivy first explained it.

'The name comes from the Gospel of Luke, when Simeon and Anna met the infant Jesus in the temple at the time of his consecration. Simeon's prophecy declared Jesus to be the light of the world. That's why we light the candles. *A light for revelation to the Gentiles and for glory to your people Israel.*'

But surely the fact that it fell halfway between the Winter Solstice and the Spring Equinox was rather less pertinent to the Church of England? It was natural that Ivy should take an interest, but that interest seemed at times to shade less towards that of the academic and more towards that of what Dorothy could only call an enthusiast.

'Both the symbolism and the timing of Candlemas have continuities with an earlier pagan festival called Imbolc. It was one of the two great female fire festivals and sacred to Brigit, the maiden aspect of the triple goddess. The ancients told how Cailleach, who is the same goddess but in the form of an old crone, drank from the well of youth and was transformed into Brigit, her younger self.'

The rite of Imbolc, it seemed, was sacred to women and the power of the feminine principles of inspiration, illumination and prophecy – hence the candles. Hence, too, the modern Christian tradition of a feast for the women of the parish.

'It is a time of fresh beginnings,' said Ivy with shining eyes, 'and celebrates the renewal of the potency of the Earth Mother.'

It sounded to Dorothy dangerously like a fertility ritual – or a hen party. She caught a grunt from the Air Vice-Marshal, and some mumblings which sounded like 'claptrap' and 'women's lib'.

Replacing her spectacles, she refocused her eyes on the MacBook screen. Her bacon and mushroom quiche might do, perhaps – or maybe she'd take a three bean salad.

* * *

If it hadn't been Dorothy's week on the flower roster she wouldn't have been up at the church on a Wednesday morning, and if it hadn't been such a chilly morning she might never have paused to listen. She was on her way out to the compost heap with the dead crysanths and spent Oasis when she noticed the Sunday school

163

children sitting cross-legged with clipboards around Ivy Paskall at the west end door, and it did seem a terribly cold morning for some of the smaller ones to be outside sketching. It was half-term, though, and the mums, she supposed, would be grateful for anything which got them out of the house.

'The Green Man,' she heard Ivy telling her audience, 'is a very old legend. Far older than the Bible stories we tell you on Sundays. It goes right back to really ancient times.'

'Before Queen Victoria?' asked Alexander Marriott, whose parents sent him to the preparatory over at Brandeston.

'Before the Victorians, before the Tudors, even before the Romans – way back before Jesus was born.'

Little Millie Dodds, who was barely four and really shouldn't be sitting on that damp gravel in February, squinted up at Ivy. 'Before Christmas?'

Dorothy had never really noticed the Green Man before – if that's what the carving was supposed to be, that rather grotesque face emerging from stone foliage in the right-hand spandrel over the arch of the west door. And it did seem to her an odd choice of subject for the children's drawings, when there were plenty of nice saints inside the church where they would at least have kept their bottoms dry and their fingers a bit warmer. Dorothy herself had had a particular soft spot, as a little girl whose mind was prone to wander during sermons, for the somewhat bouffant Lamb of the World behind the altar in the tall east window. *Wool-gathering*, she thought, and permitted herself a moment's inner smile.

But Ivy, at least, was warming to her theme. 'Lots of churches have kept the iconography – that means the signs and symbols and images – of the old pagan religions, which the people around here had all believed in before the missionaries came who told them about Jesus and converted them into Christians. The Green Man is one of those pagan symbols. He was a god of plants and nature, representing the cycle of life. He was part of what we call a "pantheist" tradition – the belief that God is in everything, all around us, in the natural world...'

Well, in that case, I suppose we're all pantheists, Dorothy told herself as she let herself back into the church with her empty vases. Didn't the Bible teach the immanence of God? And the bishop's last newsletter had featured an article about Christian duty and respect for the environment.

When she re-emerged half an hour later, her fresh arrangements complete, Dorothy couldn't help glancing again towards the west door. Should the children, she wondered, really be whirling round and round like that, their arms outstretched and faces tipped towards the sky, cackling with wild laughter, while Ivy, standing in the middle of the gyrating circle, stood with hands spread wide and raised aloft, emitting an undulating, crooning hum?

At least, though, all that spinning about would get the little ones warmed up.

* * *

The talk in the village hall came at the suggestion of the Rural Dean. 'Such a waste to have Ivy here among us for this time and not share a little in her learning.'

Sheila had wondered about having her address a meeting of the Mothers' Union, since they were a couple of speakers short for their spring programme, but this time the gender equality lobby won the day – if it weren't too absurd to cast Martin Cowling and the Air Vice-Marshal

165

in that guise. An open meeting was decided upon, which the whole congregation, and indeed the whole parish, was welcome to attend.

The village hall, if not exactly packed, was certainly less sparsely populated than Dorothy had seen it in many a month, especially considering the frosty roads and the rival attraction of a midweek football international on the television. Mainly women, then, in the audience after all. And it was lovely to see the Revd. Kimberley making a rare public appearance, having, as she explained to Dorothy, left baby Jasper with her husband and a bottle of expressed milk.

'Pagan Suffolk and the Early Christians' was Ivy's title for the lecture, although she'd baulked at the use of that term when Sheila had suggested it for the posters.

'Oh, I do hope it won't be like a lecture,' she said brightly. 'I'm aiming for something much more open and participative. I hope there'll be plenty of questions and comments.'

Dorothy, who doubted how many questions the parishioners of St Peter's could muster on the subject of paganism – or that weren't the lurid sort about sheep's entrails and blood sacrifice – determined to do a little background reading herself beforehand, so that she at least would have something sensible to contribute. There were many present who were not attenders at church, and the pride of the PCC was at stake.

Ivy's opening text was therefore already familiar ground: the Christian conversion down in Kent of the seventh-century East Anglian king Raedwald. Diffidently, Dorothy put up her hand – 'Isn't he the one they found in the burial ship over at Sutton Hoo?' – and was rewarded with, 'So it's believed,' and an encouraging smile. She was perhaps a little more surprised to hear the speaker refer to 'the new cult' of Christianity.

'Raedwald and a portion of his followers certainly embraced the new faith,' Ivy informed them, 'but it was very far from being the wholesale and uniform conversion of the Anglo-Saxon population which popular history tends to imply. In fact, we now know that in reality the two mythologies – the new religion and the old – survived very much in tandem.'

Mythologies? Dorothy was on the point of raising her hand again, but Ivy by now was warming to her theme and the opportunity slid by.

'When St Felix built his Christian monastery on the spit in the river Alde at Iken, it was as much surrounded by hostile theological waters as it was by physical ones. Raedwald's own wife, for example, continued in the old faith. According to Bede, she remained a heathen throughout her life, and when Raedwald built a church just up the road from here at Rendlesham it was in fact a dual-purpose temple, containing two altars, one Christian and one pagan.'

A scatter of nervous laughter greeted this revelation, while a wag at the back – not a churchgoer – called out something about barbarian hordes over Woodbridge way.

Ivy, unlaughing, surveyed the assembly with serene assurance. 'Nor was it only Rendlesham,' she said. 'There were pagan altars, we now believe, in many churches throughout East Anglia in what we think of as the post-Christian middle ages. The Druid's Stone at Bungay is thought to have been one such.' They seemed to be circling perilously close to sheep's entrails. 'And what of our very own Blaxhall Stone? Its presence at Stone Farm has never been adequately explained. Such a large block of solid sandstone, in this area of light sandy soil with no indigenous rock. Could it also perhaps once have served as a pagan altar stone?'

'It grew'd here, didn't 'un?' The display of uneven teeth suggested that old Wilf Dodds – more regular in the bar of the Ship than at St Peter's – was enjoying his evening. His reference was to local legend, which had it that the stone, when unearthed by a long-past ploughman, was no bigger than the man's two fists but had grown where it lay ever since.

Sitting next to Wilf was another of the Ship's habitués, a man whom Dorothy had never seen without his misshapen corduroy cap. George something, was it, or Jim? 'Like one o' thun fairy toadstools.'

'Whether it grew' – Ivy bestowed an indulgent smile on the two satirists – 'or whether it was swept here by prehistoric glacial action, the theory of its ritual adoption and use seems equally tenable.'

Dorothy sought the eye of the Rural Dean, but found his gaze fixed determinedly on the far wall. The rector was simply looking shell-shocked, but you could hardly blame the poor girl, as she'd probably not had a proper night's sleep since November. Behind the trestle with the tea urn, Sheila Mott was shuffling the cups and saucers with an agitated air.

'Oh, yes, we can be sure that pagan observance in this part of the country continued to thrive for many years alongside Christianity. For many centuries, indeed. We need look no further than the Suffolk witch trials of the 1640s as a case in point.'

'But surely—' In her perturbation, Dorothy had omitted to raise her hand. She gave an apologetic cough. 'Um, excuse me, but I thought the witch hunts were just an excess of Puritan fervour? An excuse for people to denounce their neighbours.' Heresy as nothing more than intolerance and suspicion – or at very worst, the customs of Rome. Surely not actual idolatry? Here in the village?

'Who knows? It is very possible that what Matthew Hopkins and his co-inquisitors understood in Christian terms as communion with the devil may in reality have been worship of the pagan nature gods.'

'But—' This time Dorothy's objection faltered beneath the unswerving blaze of Ivy's regard.

'Of one thing we can be absolutely certain, which is that, in spite of Christian incursion, paganism in Suffolk survived – and still survives today. Its practice has never truly gone away.'

Into the pregnant silence which greeted this asseveration, from one side of the hall where a group of teenaged girls were gathered whom Dorothy didn't recognise, there fell like heavy stones three unmistakable words – 'Burn the witch!' – which triggered a ripple of gleeful mirth.

Dorothy had never been more relieved to hear the clunk of the tea urn switch, and Sheila Mott strode up on to the stage. 'Thank you so much, Miss Paskall,' she proclaimed above the hubbub, 'for your fascinating and most thought-provoking talk...'

* * *

Holy Week was always the high point of the church calendar at St Peter's, just as in every other parish church up and down the country. As usual, it began with the Palm Sunday procession which, in all previous years that Dorothy could recall, had involved the children marching up the aisle and back bearing small palm crosses (hand-made in Africa and sold in aid of development charities) and singing various modern

169

hymns of the type favoured by primary school teachers and featuring the word 'Hosanna'. On one occasion the event had been moved to the churchyard, due to the inclusion in a bid for biblical verisimilitude of Susie Wakeling's donkey. This year, however, Ivy had more ambitious plans.

'The donkey would be wonderful,' she told the PCC, 'if it's available again. But, with your approval, I'd like to take the procession out beyond our walls. I would like us to symbolise more graphically the entry into Jerusalem. The people brought branches, Matthew's gospel tells us, and accompanied our Lord towards the gates of the city. The procession should therefore take place outside the citadel, so to speak, and we should be walking up a hill. I had in mind to use Silly Hill.'

'Silly Hill?' the Air Vice-Marshal repeated, in tones rimed with scepticism. 'Like for that hoopla at Epiphany?'

'*There is a green hill...*' trilled Sheila rather ill-advisedly, ending in a splutter and adding, 'er, not too far away.'

Ivy threw her a smile of sympathy and gratitude. 'Why not? And I thought that this year we might save the money' – she turned her eyes on Martin Cowling – 'and use pussy willow instead of palms.'

'*Pussy...?*' The Air Vice-Marshal's voice now sounded strangely compressed; inside his button-down collar his neck bulged.

'Oh, yes. Matthew, you see, only specifies "branches", but not what kind; in some traditions, the people waved olive boughs. But neither palm nor olive trees were readily to hand in medieval northern Europe, so pussy willow was widely used. Palm Sunday was even known as Willow Sunday in parts of England.'

'Well, there's certainly plenty of it around the hedges at the moment,' said Sheila, settling the question. 'And the

170

kids will have great fun going out to look for it. The little ones can never resist those furry catkins.'

The Sunday morning was bathed in April sunshine, and you couldn't deny it was nice to be out of the pews and walking up the hill behind the chattering children with their willow boughs – even if the combination of warmth and gradient left Dorothy slightly puffed.

As she paused to catch her breath, Ivy moved up and stopped alongside her. 'Lovely view from here,' she said, with a sweep of her arm towards the church tower and the chequerboard of green stretching out beyond.

'Holy Hill,' said Dorothy, who was finding herself infected with the spirit of the occasion. 'Where better to begin our Holy Week?'

But Ivy, it appeared, now had a different hypothesis. 'On some old maps of the parish it is shown not as Silly Hill but Funny Hill.'

'Oh?'

'Yes. And I gather that "funny" might be a corruption of "cunning" – the "cunning folk", you know, were the pagan healers, practitioners of natural magic. So it may in fact be the cunning hill, a place of spiritual healing.' She drew in a lusty lungful of air. 'It certainly feels therapeutic on a day like this, don't you think?'

She had a further theory to impart, as well, about the willow branches. 'The willow was a tree that was sacred to the pagans. They knew it as the tree of water, tide and moon, of dreaming, of intuition and the current of deep emotions. Symbolically, it signifies the spring and the stirring of new life. Its Old English name, "*saille*" or "sally", you know, means a bursting out – a sallying forth.' And with that she sallied on up the path.

The fine weather held throughout the week but, even so, the exposed summit of the hill – be it Christian or

171

pagan, holy or healing – was a maverick choice of venue for the Maundy Thursday vigil. This was a practice which a few among the St Peter's congregation had observed in the past, but safely inside the church, in their own pews, and only until 10 or 11 pm before peeling off home for toast and cocoa. Ivy would have no truck with such half-hearted measures.

'*Stay here and keep watch with me!*' she cried. 'That is Jesus's invitation to us: to watch and pray, and meditate upon the events that await tomorrow, on Good Friday. The disciples slept – the spirit was willing but the flesh was weak. Let us not fail Him as they did. Let us stay awake, and not abandon or forsake him, even until cock crow.'

And Silly Hill, it seemed, was to be their Garden of Gethsemane. 'Won't it get very cold, after nightfall, up there on the hill?' Dorothy had put the question tentatively, thinking of her rheumatism. (And wasn't the garden at the foot of the Mount of Olives, rather than the top?)

'Don't you suppose the disciples were also cold?' was Ivy's counter to this. But Suffolk even in a clement April was scarcely Palestine.

In the end, there were only five of them: Ivy, Dorothy and Sheila, a sister of Sheila's who had come to stay for Easter and said she'd keep them company and the surprise last minute addition of Kimberley Jackaman, with baby Jasper strapped to her chest.

'I never get much sleep anyway, so I might as well be awake up here with all of you and get some good praying done, as at home in bed listening for his majesty's next scream.' Though in the event the baby was no trouble at all, and slumbered away peacefully in his cocooning blanket, lulled, perhaps, by the motion of being carried up the hill – unless, that is, he had frozen to death, poor mite.

It was Ivy's idea to hold hands where they sat in their little circle. Dorothy had brought the low three-legged stool she used in the garden at home when doing her edges – 'My days of sitting cross-legged on the ground are behind me, I'm afraid; I fear you'd never get me up again' – which made it slightly awkward to reach down and grasp Kimberley's hand to one side and Sheila's sister's to the other. But the contact felt companionable, and the warmth was certainly welcome.

'The early Christians often joined hands when they prayed together,' Ivy told them. 'It's a sign of inclusion, of fellowship – but the circle also has other meanings, both in Christian and pre-Christian syntactics. To pagans, the natural cycle of death and rebirth; for Christians, the circle of death and redemption from death, the crucifixion and the resurrection.'

Dorothy cast an enquiring look at Kimberley, but the rector said nothing, only nodded thoughtfully.

It was only at around two in the morning, after baby Jasper finally woke up and Kimberley decided to go back to the rectory and feed him in the warm, that Ivy suggested the humming. A gentle, low vibration of the abdominal muscles, she said; an earthy sound, of hidden caves, of buried tree roots channelling the sap of life, the resonance of the womb and the longing deep inside us for creation and renewal. Obediently, although feeling a little self-conscious, they hummed. *Ommmm.*

'Feel it!' Ivy urged them. 'Nurture the spark and feel the flame – feel the cleansing fire!'

Dorothy didn't know about rising sap or healing flames, but the humming certainly took her mind off the chilly numbness of her buttocks on the wooden stool.

Good Friday's services passed without incident, and the Saturday, of course, provided the usual hiatus in proceedings, a chance to regather one's forces for the joyful festivities of Easter Day. Kimberley had generously agreed to come along and celebrate the Holy Communion at eleven o'clock, which meant the cancellation of the usual Family Mattins at ten – so Dorothy, who was due to serve as sideswoman, was enjoying the rare indulgence of a Sunday lie-in. She had just been downstairs to make herself a cup of tea, had taken it back to bed and was sitting propped up on her pillows, watching dreamily where the sunlight patterned the bedroom wall through the lace of the net curtains, when the telephone rang. Sighing, she reached for her slippers again.

'Dorothy? I'm sorry to bother you so early in the morning.' The was something tight about Sheila's voice which halted Dorothy's protest that half past eight on a Sunday was certainly not early for her.

'Are you all right?' she found herself asking, instead. 'Is it your sister?' A stab in the dark. 'Is she unwell?'

'My sister? No, no.' Sheila sounded distracted, impatient. 'No, it's Ivy. I've had a call. We need to get down to Stone Farm.' There was no need, but she nevertheless added, 'Straight away.'

The Blaxhall Stone was located in the yard at Stone Farm, close to the perimeter wall, in which spot it had presumably lain, either growing or not growing, since it was cast down there by the ploughman of legend. Greyish, low-lying and flat-topped, it measured maybe eight or nine feet long by four feet wide and must have weighed at least a couple of tons. Its surface was lined and pockmarked by centuries of weathering, and dark moss clung in one or two of the deeper hollows, especially on the side most sheltered from the wind. Dorothy had come

174

to see it many times as a girl but she'd had no cause to do so recently, its novelty having faded with the years. For a moment she was recaptured by the astonishment of its sheer bulk, and of its incongruity in this place. No wonder it had spawned stories, or that the ancients thought it a marvel and invested it with mythic powers. But it was only for a moment. Because on top of the stone was something more marvellous still. The stiffly upright figure, with arms outstretched above her head, of Ivy Paskall.

Strangely, even then, it was her hair that Dorothy noticed first. Unfettered from its usual restraining pins, it fell long and loose about her shoulders, but with knots and tuffets here and there which stuck out at awkward angles, and matted, as though she had been running her fingers through it or had slept on it uncombed and wet. Intertwined with the strands of greying hair were the stems and leaves of various plants: Dorothy recognised cow parsley, vetch and columbine, and trailing strands of stinging nettle. It was the nettles in fact which finally drew her attention downwards, because she was thinking how they'd surely be bringing up welts on the naked skin of Ivy's back and arms. Naked – just like the rest of her. For Ivy was wearing not a stitch.

'Come, oh, great goddess Eostre,' came her chanted words, drifting across the raked gravel of the farmyard. 'Come, bright goddess of the radiant dawn, bringer of upsurgent light. Come, fill me with your tongues of fire, your sweet renewing fire. Come now and reveal yourself, oh, Eostre – come to your handmaiden on this, your glorious resurrection day.'

* * *

Parochial Church Council of St Peter's, Blaxhall
  Minutes of a meeting held in the village hall on Tuesday 12th April 2016 at 7.30 pm

Item 1: Approval of extraordinary expenditure
  The PCC unanimously approved payment of a non-recurrent fee of £50 to the diocesan officer for deliverance and exorcism, for services rendered.

Item 2: Revised arrangements for the remaining period of interregnum...

Except that strictly speaking, as Dorothy reminded herself again, it wasn't an interregnum; it was only maternity leave.

STONE THE CROWS

'Stone the crows,' my brother Johnnie used to say, although it was actually the last thing he would have done. Mother may have been half his size but she'd have tanned his hide. Rabbits, certainly, he brought home for the pot, bagged not with stones but lead shot from Father's old shotgun; pigeons, too, plucked, topped, tailed and gutted by the half dozen for a pie. But never crows.

It was from Sarah's boy Will, more than fifty years later, that I found out they were rooks, not crows. 'A rook by itself is a crow, Grandad,' he said, 'but a crow with other crows is a rook.' It's the way to tell them apart, apparently, though Mother never knew and we called them all crows, growing up. They roosted in the stand of horse chestnuts on the edge of Willett's farm, down near the level crossing. Still do. And Mother always reckoned that they brought good luck – or, if good luck was a stretch too far, that at least they warded off the bad. A sort of talisman, I suppose, like the ravens at the Tower of London, keeping England safe. I don't think we believed her, even back then. But that's why Johnnie was never to shoot them, even later when the war came and shop-bought food was short.

At the base we had plenty, mind you, even though it was grey and swimming in grease, so it could have been pork or beef or leg of ruddy Labrador. 'Snake and kidney', some wags used to call it, and chalk out the 'n' in 'mince'; real toads, they'd claim, in the toad-in-the-hole. Those boys in the mess tent couldn't cook. Most had been office clerks before the war, or schoolboys whose mothers packed their bread and dripping. Townies, a lot of them, who'd never seen a cow and wouldn't know her topside from her teats.

It was at the base that Johnnie picked up that crazy talk of his. Stone the crows, he'd say, and jumping Jehoshaphat, and everything'd be tickety-boo one week and whiz-bang-a-bang the next. Mother wouldn't have him using profanities, though, not in her hearing. There were boys down at Martlesham Heath from all over: Jocks and Irish lads and even Aussies, though no Yanks yet, of course – that was later. Slang was passed around like dirty pictures, and I think he picked it up at the movies as well. Johnnie loved the movies. They used to put them on in one of the hangars every Friday night, if we weren't scrambled. Errol Flynn was Johnnie's favourite, and he could do him to a tee. After a few beers he'd do Katharine Hepburn, too, and even Shirley Temple.

He started at the base before me, but only by a matter of months, although he was six years older. They soon needed every man they could get, and I was flying before I was nineteen. Boys of eighteen, nineteen, seemed older back then; we felt ourselves worldly-wise. A year was a ruddy long time in the war.

Pilot Officers John and Philip Root. I still have the photograph, taken by a ginger corporal called Tug who had a camera – a decent bloke even if he was a pen pusher, a desk wallah: in the chairborne division, as we used to say. The two of us are pictured squinting into the sun in front of Johnnie's Spit. We're standing by one blade of the prop and behind us is a section of the wing and the riveted underbelly of the fuselage. Johnnie's battle blues are all untucked, his cap tipped behind one ear at a rakish angle; the Wingco would have had his guts for garters. Someone, I can't remember who, has printed our names and ranks along the bottom in spidery white capitals. It was Mother who put the photo in its frame, black lacquer with the moulding picked out in faded gilt, and it stood in pride of place on top of Father's bureau, beside the kitchen range.

I used to listen to the crows – that is to say, the rooks – squabbling and shouting up above me when I went to look for conkers. You couldn't see the birds through the canopy, not at conker time when the leaves were still on the trees: edged with fiery yellow but not yet fallen. But you could hear them all right. Mostly it's a lot of quarrelsome *caa caa caa*, but they also make a shorter, harsher '*tshk*' sound, a bit like a creaking spring. They seemed an unlikely sort of good luck charm to me, with their noisy flopping and flapping in the branches. They're ungainly birds on the ground, too. I remember watching them with Will last week, feeding among the stubble on Willett's big wheat field. Such awkward-looking creatures they are, with their bald faces and outsized beaks, that splay-footed walk they have and often with their feathers all awry. And, underneath, those comical, baggy black pantaloons.

It's the droopy drawers, according to Will, that's another sure sign they're rooks. His own adage, that a crow with others must be a rook, is only a very rough guide, he says. Crows will flock together to feed, and in family groups in spring. But it's only the rooks that form

179

a proper colony like the one in Willett's horse chestnuts. In winter when the trees are bare, that's when you see them best, those great untidy thatches of sticks they build for nests, which look too big for the spindly upper branches that support them, and the birds gathered to roost, cut-out shapes against the sky. Still and silent in a December dusk, they do acquire some sort of dignity. Upright, hooded, they make me think then of brothers in some contemplative order, or watchmen standing guard. Or maybe of a crowd of mourners, hunched and frock-coated, gathered at a rainy graveside.

I knew I wanted to fly. I always knew, even before Johnnie joined up; even before that, when we were boys and it was me with the Biggles books and the picture of a Fairey Seafox on my bedroom wall out of *Practical Mechanics*. And when war looked likely, I knew it was a Spit or a Hurricane I wanted to fly, not a Wellington or a Lanc. There were bombing stations closer to home – over Rendlesham way at Bentwaters, and inland at Parham – but that was never for me.

You might put the choice down to simple cowardice, I suppose, although the boys who bought it in Fighter Command weren't noticeably fewer than among the bomber crews, especially in that late summer of 1940. If your number was up, it was up, whatever your mission and mob: that's how we all came to look at it. Death was no respecter of divisional demarcation, any more than of braid on a sleeve. But still... in a Spit you felt your life was just a little more in your own hands. With luck and a fair wind, you could dodge and dink and weave your way out of trouble nine times out of ten. And the tenth? Well, if I had to go west in a burning cockpit or a plummeting spiral of smoke, I'd sooner it was over friendly inshore

180

waters or a patchwork of English fields.

What do they see when they look down, the circling rooks? It's a different world, up there on the wing. Most of the time on an op you didn't look down at all, except to get a fix on your position, and to peer for the flickering goosenecks that marked the runway on your way back in. But sometimes, just once or twice that I recall, when the expected German fighters were late to the party or things went suddenly quiet, there was time to take stock of things beyond the task in hand. Beyond the immediate skies around you, your gun sights, and staying alive. Once, we were scrambled in the late afternoon. It must have been August or September and the sun was already low, turning heaven and earth the same soft, luminous gold. We'd flown north, hugging the shoreline, but travelled no great distance, and it seemed to have been a false alarm: for once, we had the skies to ourselves. I took a long, looping turn to the west ahead of the others, coasting at about ten thousand feet, and an unexpected sense of peace settled over me. The goggles, the hot rubber of the oxygen mask, usually so encumbering, were temporarily forgotten. Even the roar and judder of the engine seemed to fade to a distance. There was nothing but me and my kite and the empty air.

Beneath me were fields, some dark and mottled with stubble, others the yellowish green of late summer pasture, all criss-crossed by the darker lines of hedgerows and studded here and there with the neat circle of a tree, as if a child had drawn round a sixpence. There were few clouds, and those few were mere puffs, drifting high above my own altitude, so that as I banked and then straightened from my turn, shadows flickered briefly across the Perspex canopy of the Spit, and ran and jumped over the tapestry below.

181

That other world, the solid world of soil and wood and hearth and home, was like a shadow of itself, a projection on a screen. It could have been a thousand miles away, or a thousand years. Nothing in that evening landscape moved to give it life and substance – until suddenly, beyond my left wingtip, a miniature figure swung into view, straddling the midline of a field where it changed from the dull grey-brown of stubble to a deeper, richer russet, ridged in black. At first I had no sense that the figure was in motion, so slowly did it creep along the line of the last furrow, edging forward no faster than a sluggish beetle, dazed by the sun. I took another turn, dropping my height a little, to gaze down until I could make out the broad backs of a pair of chestnut horses, the glinting Y-shape of the plough and, behind it, just visible, the dot of a man's head. Somewhere in the plunging fathoms of space between me and the ploughman a flock of birds were drifting, no doubt scanning the freshly upturned earth, appearing from my elevation as no more than a pattern of moving speckles. Maybe it was the timelessness of the image – with diesel so scarce in those days, it was not unusual to see farmers resorting to the old ways of working – or the perfect stillness of the gilded evening, split only by the rush of my own machine, but that momentary scene seemed to me somehow to be eternal, to be out of the reach of war, safe from the horrors of dogfights and ack ack, of air raids and bomb blast, of gunfire and shrapnel and burning and death.

Only once have I ever seen one up close enough to touch – a rook, that is, or possibly a crow. I don't think even Will could have said for certain, not after it had tangled with Johnnie's port side cannon mounting, coming in to land from an early patrol. 'Lucky it didn't strike the prop,' I remember Johnnie saying, swinging the corpse by the legs like a chicken, and the Wingco whistled. 'Lucky for which one of you?' he said. Its wings dangled out and down at drunken angles but the feathers held their gloss, shining blue and purple as well as black.

This afternoon Will came over and took me for a drive in that little Vauxhall of his. I don't get out as much as all that, since I've been in the Lilacs, but Will's a good boy and comes when he can. He knows I like to drive round by the old house and sometimes, like today, we stop for a half-pint at the Ship.

It was well after four when we started back and they like you to be in by five for tea. Early hours, they keep. We went round by the level crossing and Willett's farm, through Stone Common and up towards the church, and there, over Silly Hill, the sky was full of birds. Will saw me looking, and he was looking too; he pulled over on to the verge and we sat for a while to watch. The hedge was low just there but you still couldn't see the field, not from sitting in the car, so there's no knowing what it was that drew them. It must have been something, though: there were dozens of them, circling round and round above the crest of the hill.

I thought at first that it was just the rooks, because the wheeling outlines showed up black against the pale sky; the whiter flashes I caught as they turned I put down to a trick of the light. It takes my eyes much longer than it once did to adjust for distance, and accommodate to darkness, or brightness out of doors. I was passed twenty/twenty by the eye doc when I signed up, but I'd be no darned use for night ops now. After a minute or two, though, I got my sights trained in on them, and I could see they weren't all the same. There were two different colours there, black birds and white. Dark and light: friend or foe, good luck or bad. And two different wing shapes, as well. The rooks' wings were broad and straight, splay-tipped, while the other birds, which were grey on top and white below, were longer and more tapered in the wing, with an angle back towards the tail.

'Black-headed gulls,' said Will.

On the walls of the Nissen hut, above our bunks, we had posters showing different fighter planes in silhouette. The Hawker Hurricane, the Spitfire. And the other lot, of course: the Heinkel He 112, the Focke-Wulf 190 and the Messerschmitt Bf 109. We had to be able to identify them in a fraction of a second, through cloud and haze, at dawn or dusk, or coming straight out of a blazing sun.

'...except their heads are only black in summer,' Will was saying. 'Or actually, even then, more like a very dark brown.'

The Heinkel's wings, according to the manuals, resembled those of an upside-down seagull – but in fact we rarely came across them. Once or twice, perhaps, in some early scraps, but after that it was always the Messerschmitts. They were nifty little craft, those 109s. They could dive away at the steepest angles and never seemed to stall – whereas with a Spit, if you pulled back too far the whole crate would start juddering or the engine cut out and you'd be forced to ease up. But our lot, both Hurricanes and Spits, were tighter in the circle. In a dogfight you could take a sharp turn to left or right and you'd soon shake the beggars off your tail.

The brow of Silly Hill was some way off from where Will had stopped the car, but when he wound the windows down we could hear the birds' cries carrying down on a gusty breeze: the low, rasping engine note of the rooks' *caa caa* and the higher pitched call of the gulls, which resembled no mechanical sound but had a piteous, almost human tone, like the distant voices of women and children, raised in inconsolable grief.

Was it a dogfight we were witnessing there over the hill? Were there battle patterns in the spiralling of the birds? You hear people talk about respect for the enemy, respect for our fellow flyers, but it wasn't like that. There was no time for respect, or hatred either. Your mind was a blank. Everything went into automatic. The control stick, the rudder pedals and the dials, the meshwork of tracer, the cross hairs of the sights and your thumb on the fire button. I hope Johnnie had no time to think.

It was early October, a Tuesday. A perfect English teatime, bright and breezy, much like today. We'd been sent to greet a formation of some twenty aircraft. Light bombers, mostly, with an escort of just half a dozen fighters, but those Dorniers were heavily armed and nearly as manoeuvrable as a 109. I'd been playing cat-and-mouse with one of the fighters; I'd got in a few short bursts but didn't think I'd hit him. Johnnie was somewhere off my starboard wing. The afternoon sky, in memory, was unbroken blue. There was no flame and no black smoke: just a pale plume, as innocent as vapour, trailing out behind, and the gleam of sunlight on my brother's plane as he fell like a stone.

SILVER-STUDDED BLUES

If you want to see silver-studded blues, you need to look for ants.

Symbiosis is what it's called. The caterpillar emits a sound that replicates the black ants' distress signal, prompting them to carry the caterpillar down into their nest, where they guard it and keep it safe from predators until it's ready to pupate. In return, the caterpillar secretes a syrupy substance on which the ants can feed. Mutual dependence and mutual advantage. It's win-win, as Dr Stebbings likes to say. He's full of these little phrases, the kind you get in 'motivational' books, and he's always cheerful and smiling, even when what he's saying seems nothing to smile about.

A lot of people, if you talk about symbiosis, either look at you blankly or else they think of wildlife programmes on the television: oxpecker birds that stand on the backs of rhinos on the African savannah and eat their ticks, or that David Attenborough film of the sea anemone and the hermit crab. I've noticed most people are only really interested in wildlife if they find it cute or funny, like the scuttling hermit crabs with their outsized sea anemone jockeys, waving their poisoned tentacles to

186

fend off octopuses. And everyone thinks of symbiosis as something in nature, something out there. They never just think about themselves. But we're all involved in symbiotic patterns all the time.

There are the obvious ones, like dogs. Joan and I feed Mungo and provide him with shelter from the cold and wet, and a cool kitchen floor where he can stretch out flat on his belly in hot weather. We twist out his ticks when he's been in the long grass at the bottom of my old garden next door. In return, he kills rats in the outhouse, and barks if anyone's coming up the path. Except Dr Stebbings, that is. When Mungo hears the doctor's car, he pricks his ears then lays his nose down on his paws, heaves his hairy ribs in a sigh and goes straight back to sleep.

Then there's the symbiosis that's invisible. Sometimes it's so small you'd need a microscope to see it, like the flora in our guts: a hundred trillion microorganisms, ten times more than the number of our own body's cells, digesting what we can't, releasing nutrients to feed both them and us. We couldn't live without them. Sometimes it's too big for us to bring in focus, like the delicate environmental balances we're busy fouling up. One butterfly flaps its wings in the forests of the Amazon and there are hurricanes we can't foresee. I talked to Joan about it, how they'd proved it all by mathematics, and she listened with a frown. 'What if it's here,' she asked, 'the butterfly? What if it's here on Blaxhall Common?' I told her I thought it must work here too. Maths is the same everywhere.

There are five hundred species of bacteria in the average human gut, but only nineteen butterflies of the family Lycaenidae occurring in the British Isles. Nine of those are blue. Once it would have been ten, before the

Mazarine blue died out. And nine could soon be down to seven, since both the long-tailed blue and short-tailed blue are now infrequent visitors.

The small blue is barely blue at all but more of a dusty brown with just the hint of bluish veins radiating out from its body. The chalkhill blue is a pale turquoise shade that is almost aquamarine and, as its name suggests, is found in chalky uplands and not on Suffolk's sandy soil. The remaining five varieties, though, are hard to tell apart. Small and inconspicuous compared with many native butterflies, with undersides of anonymous grey or brown, their habit of closing their wings when not in flight creates good camouflage. You'd mistake them for just another dead leaf – until they flicker open to reveal that splash of brilliant blue.

The butterflies at the museum make me sad. We don't have only native species here – the blues and whites and hairstreaks and fritillaries, the heaths and browns and tortoiseshells, the skippers and the swallowtail. Some of our specimens must actually once have flapped their wings in the Amazon – before being pinned to a card by Charles Randolph Badderley, English sportsman-naturalist (1847–1918). Their true colours are only to be guessed at, repainted in the mind's eye from gaudy online images. Even the familiar ones are faded shadows of their real-life counterparts. The peacock, eyes dulled, has lost its vibrant plumage; the admiral's red coat is rusty and threadbare; the purple emperor no longer boasts its deep Tyrian bloom. Sunlight and the years must have done their damage before the green felt flaps were added, too late, to the glass-topped wooden cabinets.

Charles Randolph also collected birds, both native and exotic. He bequeathed to the museum four volumes of painstaking notes, observing, identifying and cataloguing his specimens before he shot and stuffed and then imprisoned them, each in its cold crystal dome. I used to hurry through the bird room when Mum left me there on Saturdays while she went to do the shopping. (*Stay here and be a good boy.*) They were too still, and I was afraid to meet the accusation in their hard, glass eyes. The only ones I could bear to look at were the goldfinches. Charles Randolph, having killed a family of five, allowed them to be together in a large, rectangular case, furnished with a branch to perch on and carpeted with leaves. Two were placed so close to each other that they almost touched, while another was captured with its wings half unfolded, as if it were about to rise in flight.

Taking the job here made a lot of sense. I was familiar with the exhibits already. I could have recited the text on most of the caption cards by heart. I knew every photograph of old Saxmundham on the Green Room walls, from Edwardian sepia to fifties black-and-white. My favourite, from 1912, shows the colonnaded front of the museum itself, looking almost identical to its present self, while before it along the high street a herd of pigs pass by, driven, no doubt, by a farmer who is out of shot, but apparently strolling at their leisure. I could already have listed the Anglo-Saxon artefacts, rescued by archaeologists from the foundations of the new estate: the coins and clasp and rings, the bronze belt buckles, the spearhead and daggers which, according to the card, are 'suggestive of a warrior's grave'. My legs had stuck to the tip-up plastic seats in the small side room, on stuffy summer holiday afternoons, while I watched on an endless loop the flickery film of 'Saxmundham at War'. I'd loitered inside the replica railway ticket office in the foyer, exact in every 1940s detail, even down to the stationmaster's hat, the tape inside its rim worn oily smooth from many youthful foreheads. I must have tried it on a hundred times when I was small enough for it to slip and cover my eyes so that, in darkness, I could breathe the dusty smell of it, of soot and sweat and Brasso.

Besides, it's not far to Saxmundham on the bus. Before Joan retired we used to ride in together in the mornings, me to the museum and her to Knit Knacks. We used to get the back seat if we could manage it, to give her needle room. That's what she called it when I was a kid, if I leaned too close to her on the sofa: 'Sit up and let me have some needle room'. Back then she was always knitting something, even on the bus: wool was a vocation. At home we both have bedrooms full of vivid, multihued creations, hand-knitted before Joan's hands began to disregard the signals from her brain. Too numerous to wear, they remind me of Charles Randolph Badderley's victims: bright jays and hummingbirds and lorikeets, kingfishers and resplendent birds of paradise, piled high in cupboards and squashed into drawers.

Now, as often as not, I have the back seat to myself. Coming home I catch the 5.04, or the 5.44 if I'm picking up groceries from the list Joan gives me, for her to make our tea. She was a good cook as well as a knitter, was Joan. Her raised pork pie was famed at summer fetes and harvest teas. Lately, though, I do most of the work under her instruction. It's not so much the shaking – not since Dr Stebbings got her tablets right – as that her fingers lack the force. She hasn't the strength to grip, she says, whether it's knitting needles or the vegetable knife. So I peel and chop and grate and stir while she tells me what to do.

Sometimes even that is hard, these days. It was names that her brain began to scramble first, of people and of places, and then the ordinary names of things. 'Wash the trellis,' she'll say, when she means the lettuce, or, 'Shell the beef. The peef. The peas.'

Then the other important words began to slither from her grasp, the adjectives and verbs. 'Slice the tomatoes,' she'll tell me, 'and make them nice and skin. Nice and skid. Thid... Not thick – the other thing.'

'Thin,' I'll say, and she'll repeat the word as if committing it to memory. 'Thin. Slice them nice and thin.'

Still the in-between words seem to roll along all right, as if without attention on them they have to shift for themselves.

Seven thousand, eight hundred and sixty-seven days I lived next door, first with Mum and Dad and later just with Mum. I moved in with Auntie Joan after Mum went into hospital, and when she died it made sense to stay on. Since then it's been almost as long again: seven thousand, eight hundred and nineteen days. That's what counts – not Dr Stebbings with his 'not the next-of-kin'. I wish Joan had really been Mum's sister, all the same, and not just a neighbour. It would have made things easier.

'In seven more weeks I'll have lived here half my life,' I told Joan yesterday. She smiled and nodded. 'You're a good boy,' she said, but her eyes were glazed with tears.

With the help of a stick and my firm grasp under her other arm, Joan can still get out on the common for walks. Mungo trots ahead in his self-important doggy zigzags, throwing in the air for imaginary guns every bird in his vicinity. Butterflies, though, are off his radar just as he appears to be off theirs: they're mutually oblivious.

It's five years since we've seen the silver-studded blues, but we still go and look for them when the sun comes out, every July or August. There aren't many habitats left for them in Britain – only fifteen remaining places where they are known to breed. Lowland heath is what they like, with plenty of the heather on which they feed, and a sandy soil for the ants. The caterpillars need young heather, low-springing and tender, not the woody older growth. Many colonies, they say, were lost in the 1950s when myxomatosis came and swept through the population of grazing rabbits, which had kept the heather short for the butterflies. More symbiosis – with man, the scientist, wading in as usual to mess the whole thing up.

Blaxhall Common is ideal, and we always had a colony here. You had to know the place to look, between the sunken pathway and the pheasant covers, on a patch of open ground just past a cluster of silver birch. The adults don't fly far once they've emerged – no more than ten or twenty metres in any direction, according to the books – so we could always track them down. They're no size – nothing like the garden whites and tortoiseshells – and there were never major numbers of them. A small breeding colony, a few hundred adults at most. But on a blazing day, when the sun catches glints of blue as they bob and bounce above the heather like so many crazy ping-pong balls, they're an effervescence of joy. Every summer they have been there, beyond the silver birches, until these last five years.

Only the males in fact are blue. The females are a brownish-grey, on top the same as below, with little to make them stand out. All the blues are similar: the male bright blue above and drab below, the female just plain drab. There are variations in shade, but these are not to be relied upon, occurring within as well as between the species. The silver-studdeds down in Hampshire, for example, are a dull, matt mushroom colour underneath, while our Suffolk ones have a sheen of silvery grey. What distinguishes most clearly the different types of blue is the patterning that rims the wings. With silver-studded blues you have to wait until they close, and observe the underside. All the blues have a fringe of black-and-white dots but only those on the silver-studded contain at their centre the reflective, pale blue scales which catch the light like burnished metal – those telltale silver 'eyes' the books describe. When they settle for a moment on a tuft of heather and their wings flick and quiver, as fragile as an eyelash, they wink their silver at you as if in private confirmation. *Yes, you're right. It's me.*

We went last week to see if they were there. There had been a shower the night before, which had washed the heather free of summer dust, restoring its evergreen gloss and the sharpness of its violets and magentas. Do I mean magenta? Joan would once have named the colours with an expert's eye. The walls of Knit Knacks, lined from floor to ceiling with a honeycomb of small compartments crammed with wool, were better than a paint chart. The balls of yarns were ranged chromatically as well as by fibre, weight and ply, sweeping up through the rainbow and back down again, a visual glissando. A museum of colour. That's something else the disease is slowly stripping from her. Different shades have already started to merge and lose their clarity, she tells me, and Dr Stebbings warns that she may end up colour-blind. How will she spot butterflies when she can't tell blue from yellow?

Today there were common blues and brimstone yellows among the coppers, browns and tortoiseshells, but not the faintest whisper of a silver-studded blue.

I didn't study Latin or Greek at school but evidently Charles Randolph Badderley did. It's thanks to him, and the Internet, that I've picked up the odd few words. The family *Lycaenidae*, I've learned, means 'resembling gossamer' in Greek, and it's true their wings are as delicate as cobwebs. The sub-family Polyommatinae is Latin, referring to the many eyespots appearing around their wings, while *argus* – our silver-studded friend – is Greek again. It means, appropriately, 'shining', for their gleaming silver eyes. It's not my job, exactly, to know all that, but I like to have the facts behind the caption cards in case somebody asks. Not that the public do ask questions much, at least not about the exhibits; it's more often what time we close or where to find the toilets. But it means there's plenty of time to look things up.

Curare. That's another Latin word I've found, and it means to take care of or curate. Like my job, in fact: curator and caretaker, both. Every morning before we open I clean the toilets and refill the paper towel dispensers. Every evening after closing I sweep through all the floors with the big soft V-shaped brush, amassing in the foyer by the stationmaster's booth a tidy pile of dust and leaves, sweet wrappers and discarded ticket stubs. Once a year on 1st October I reignite the pilot light on the temperamental boiler in the basement, then work my way round eleven Victorian cast-iron radiators, releasing from the valve of each a scalding hiss of steam. And in between? In the hours between I am free to update the catalogue, or think, or look things up, or just to stand and dream.

Not only in Latin but in English too, 'care' has a slippery meaning. Yesterday afternoon after work, Dr Stebbings was closeted upstairs with Joan for longer than is usual. He came down without her, wearing that smile of his that doesn't mean he's happy. 'They'll take good care of her there,' he said. The Lilacs: a 'residential care home'. *Less of a worry for everyone. Much the best place.*

Not the next-of-kin.

The birds at the museum in their crystal cases don't alarm me now; I can look them in the eye. And although the faded butterflies are sad, they are so familiar that they feel like confidants. The butterfly room is on the top floor, beneath a high, arched ceiling crowned with an octagon of coloured glass. A card by the door tells people it was once an orangery. Sometimes after I've swept and locked up down below I climb back up the stairs, resisting the urge to tiptoe. I pull on my white museum curator's gloves and in the pregnant hush I run my hands over the cabinet tops, smoothing the green baize like a snooker referee. One time – just once – I folded back the cloth then raised the glass of every cabinet in the room. Closing my eyes, I took a step back and I'd swear I felt against my upturned face the stir of air from myriad tiny beating wings, and that had I dared to look there would have swirled above my head a living kaleidoscope, a fountain of scattering, flittering colour.

This morning we walked to the common again. The sky was overcast: not conducive weather for butterflies. Beyond the silver birch clump nothing stirred. The air above the heather hung silent and empty, and Joan's weight was heavy on my arm.

Mungo was a short way off on some quest of his own, sniffing at the roots of a patch of brambles, when suddenly with a scrabbling flurry a hen pheasant erupted, frantic, from the depths of the thicket and took off towards a distant band of trees, with Mungo close behind. Leaving Joan propped on her stick, I followed at a trot, afraid of losing sight of the dog. When in full chase he has a habit of overrunning himself and forgetting his way back. The course the bird had flown led us across uneven ground, tussocked with heather and studded with low gorse. It made for awkward going, which Mungo negotiated in a series of delirious leaps but which slowed me down considerably. My shins beneath my shorts were soon scratched raw. Above my left boot top the red wool sock – Joan's handiwork – snagged on a bramble and, as I tugged it free, began to unravel, a meander of unwinding scarlet.

When I reached the line of trees, Mungo was nowhere to be seen. I shouted his name and whistled, to no response. I plunged between the nearest trees and whistled and called some more, turning to skirt the edge of the wood first left, then right. There was no sign of the dog. After a while I stopped, took a final look round, then retraced my steps to the point where I'd entered the wood. To search for him further seemed a hopeless enterprise, so I thought it best to return to Joan. I'd been out of her sight for some minutes by now and she would be anxious on her own.

When I reached the group of birches I saw that Joan was turned with her back towards me and bending over something, which on drawing closer I discerned to be the errant Mungo. She was looking down at him, brows gathered in a frown.

'Monday,' she was saying to him. 'Bengo. Munkum. Munkum.'

The dog surveyed her steadily with liquid eyes, while his tail lashed slowly from side to side.

Then his gaze faltered and he lowered his head as he began to execute a strange manoeuvre, weaving and shifting his weight from paw to paw. Something on the ground was disquieting him, something in the sand between the knots of heather.

Ants. An army of black ants.

Then suddenly there they were, all around us as the sun broke free of cloud, rising from the heather like a flurry of blossom caught in a sudden updraught, while the light caught skittering patterns in their incandescent eyes. Our butterflies. The silver-studded blues.

THE WITCH BOTTLE

It began with the installation of a damp-proof course.

'These old houses,' said Nick, 'they didn't bother with anything like that. Just learned to live with it, I suppose.'

Nick was the builder she had found at Wickham Market through a recommendation from English Heritage. *Specialist in conservation work and period properties.*

The house had no foundations to speak of either – just the raft of its timber frame and a floor of trodden earth beneath the Victorian brick. If global warming hit and the sea level rose, Kathy imagined Parmenters breaking loose in one piece from its anchorage and sailing away to higher ground.

But building regulations were tighter now than in the 1500s, and Kathy less prepared than her Tudor antecedents to make mould and mildew her living companions. So Nick took up the bricks and the packed earth beneath and laid a bituminous felt membrane. And that was how, while digging up the inglenook, he came across the witch bottle.

'Hey, come and see what I've found.'

It was still half buried in the impacted clay, and her eyes adjusting from the dazzle of the computer screen in her brightly sunlit kitchen. Head bent close to his in the confinement of the dark fireplace, she was momentarily dizzy. His smell was hot brick and salt skin. Like the house, she was at risk of slipping the moorings she'd kept so closely bound since the shipwreck of her divorce, and floating adrift.

At the brush of his fingers, a curve of glass became visible, glinting darkly beneath its veneer of dust. He'd heard before, he told her, of bottles like this one, found buried under the hearths of medieval houses.

It was a talisman. 'It will keep you safe,' he said, but the air between them crackled with danger.

Later, exhumed and rubbed clean, it stood before them on the wooden picnic table in the shade of the apple tree, where Nick had been persuaded to join her for a cold beer before he went home. They both stared down at his find in curiosity: the translucent greenish flask, surprisingly undulled by age, with its contents of dark-coloured cloth, wound to a crumpled twist.

'Apparently they were pretty common round these parts in the seventeenth century.' Kathy had been on Google when she should have been chasing unpaid invoices. 'East Anglia in general, that is – but also just locally. There are stories about a witch trial here in Blaxhall.'

Nick picked up the bottle, held it to the light. 'And how did it work, exactly? You'd expect some eye of newt or toe of frog in there, not just a bit of old rag.'

Kathy surveyed him with interest. Damp-proofer and Shakespearean scholar: an intriguing concoction. But after all, why not? *Craftsman* was the word that came into her mind as she watched his long, square-tipped hands turn the bottle slowly round and round. Perhaps he caught some part of her thoughts, because he gurned menacingly. 'We did *Macbeth* at school. I made a pretty gruesome second witch.'

199

'Spine-tingling, I'll bet.' What the hell was she doing – flirting with her builder? Hoping the heat didn't show in her face, she rushed on at random. 'Wool of bat was the one that always puzzled me. You never think of bats as particularly woolly, do you?'

'Maybe you have to get up close. I expect they have secret downy places.' His voice held the pulse of amusement; he was laughing at her. And she deserved it: a man mentioned a bat's underparts and she found it stirring?

She pulled herself together. 'Well, anyway, a witch bottle didn't call for boiling and bubbling. It didn't hold some magical brew. The cloth would be a piece of the witch's clothing, I gather, if they could get hold of some. And they'd often put in some small sharp objects – thorns, or shards of glass, or needles.'

'Like pins in a voodoo doll?'

'I suppose so.' They both peered closely at the bottle, but there was nothing to be seen except the twine of fabric. 'And also, if they could manage to get anything actually from the witch herself, they'd put that in. A part of her, I mean.'

'Body parts?' He slurped his beer with salacious glee. 'As in, liver of blaspheming Jew?'

Grinning, she shook her head. 'As in toenails or a lock of hair, or...'

'Or?'

Or menstrual blood, but she wasn't about to say that. 'Or urine. That was the commonest thing, it seems. The cloth would be soaked in the witch's urine.'

'Oh, nice.' In pantomimed distaste he pushed his glass away. 'And how did they go about—? But perhaps we're better not to ask.'

Kathy was perilously close to giggling.

'So basically, you had a bottle of witch piss hidden under your fireplace.'

'First, catch your witch.' The giggles were tightening her chest, like hiccups. It was Nick's fault; he made her feel about sixteen. She swallowed, and took a hold on herself. 'But it's really not funny. There's no such thing as witches, never was.' And it wasn't, in truth, a thing to be laughed about. It was ignorant and cruel – or worse. 'She'd be just some poor woman that people didn't like the look of. An outsider, an outcast.'

'Perhaps she was promiscuous. I bet witches all shagged around like nobody's business.' His eyes glimmered like flame. 'Or maybe she was a lesbian?'

Ignoring this, she said, 'Probably had a disfigurement or something. Dragged her left foot or had a hare lip or a birthmark on her face and they decided it was Satan's brand.' Marked by the devil. She withdrew her fingers from the chill, beaded damp of her glass. The garden was suddenly cold.

Maybe Nick also felt it, since he was no longer laughing either. 'So why did they bury them, then, these witch bottles?'

'Oh, it was something about the fireplace, this website said. Being open to the outside air above. It meant the chimney was the way that evil spirits could get into your house. So if you buried the bottle under the hearth, it would ward the spirits off. Keep them out, I suppose, if the witch tried to invite them in.'

'Better give it back, then.'

She looked across at him, puzzled at the choice of phrase.

'You'd better put it back in the fireplace where it belongs, as soon as I'm done with the work. We don't want the demons to get you.'

Then the charm is firm and good... But on which side, exactly, lay the evil in this case – with the witch or her persecutors?

She was smiling again, but as she held his gaze her stomach turned a strange, slow dance. 'Let's hope so.'

I burn for him; my fever rises and I burn. And yet, for all, I know that it is mortal sin to think of him as I do. Has not the rector preached as much from St Peter's pulpit every Sunday? I know that this burning in my body is the burning of hellfire, the tongued flames which slicken my woman's parts are devil-sent, the lappings of Satan and his fiendish incubi. Oh, sweet baby Jesus in your innocence, and pure mother Mary preserve and save me, for I burn, I burn.

Kathy had fallen in love with Parmenters the first time she drove round the corner past the row of flint-faced cottages and saw it there at the bottom of the hill, lying low and pink and mellow between the pair of cedars, ankle-deep in the buttercups of its overspilling lawn. It was the colours which seduced her as much as anything: the warm terracotta of the pantiled roof and, most especially, the soft, earthy pink of the rendered walls between the struts of timber frame. It made her think of Italy, although they called it Suffolk pink.

'Pig's blood,' Nick informed her with unnecessary relish as he packed away his ladders. 'That's how they used to get the shade of pink: cut a pig's throat into the limewash. But don't worry – you can order it from Farrow and Ball these days, and I expect it's strictly kosher.'

It was a fortnight since the discovery under the hearth and he was working outside on the roof, repointing the chimney and renewing the lead flashings. 'You really ought to get a spark guard put on there, too, if you're planning on lighting fires this winter.'

The day had been dazingly hot. The heat, which in the early morning had shimmered with soft humidity, building slowly, layer by washed watercolour layer, by mid-afternoon was fat and thickly textured, laid on with a knife like oils. Even now, at past six o'clock, it still crouched heavy in the shade of the cedar trees and shimmered over the lawn. Nick's neck and forearms were sheened with sweat.

'Afraid I'm out of beer. But there's juice or Coke in the fridge, if you fancy it?'

'I'd rather have a proper drink. Raymond at the Ship makes Victor Meldrew look sunny, but he keeps a good ale.'

So they'd adjourned to the terrace in front of the pub, and he was on to his second pint while she tried to remember to take slow sips at her cold white wine. Inside the bar a man in a leather cap was playing the melodeon while an elderly woman, with greater confidence than musicality, sang a song about a wounded knight's quest.

'I've been reading up about the Suffolk witch trials,' Kathy found herself telling Nick. 'It was quite a bloodbath. Eighteen of them hanged in one day at Bury St Edmund's in the 1640s.'

The history class nerd. But Nick was a receptive audience and his blue-grey eyes didn't stray from her face. She took another gulp of wine, which was slightly tingly on her tongue and tasted of summer twilights.

'It was that man they called the Witchfinder General – Matthew Hopkins. He was based down south near the Essex border but his family had land at Framlingham, so this whole area was his stamping ground.' And stamping is what he did – along with burning and slashing and crushing beneath his heel. 'They came from all round here, his victims. Halesworth and Yoxford and Brandeston.'

'But not Blaxhall?'

'Not that day, at that particular trial. But another time, who knows? They claim this Hopkins was responsible for putting to death three hundred women.'

A low whistle. 'Bloody hell. Makes Jack the Ripper look a very dull boy.'

'And that was just him – just that one man. But there were others, lots of them, sniffing out imagined witchery at every parish pump.'

'*And clear was the paley moon,*' came words of the old woman's song through the open door from the bar, '*when the shadow passed him by...*'

'But what about the buried bottle?' Nick seemed really to want to know; at least, he was leaning forward across the table and his loosely laced fingers where they clasped the beer glass were almost touching her wrist. 'Doesn't it mean our witch can't have been burned or hanged or whatever they did to them? If there was a bottle, doesn't it mean she was still around to be her chucking about her spells and hexes?'

It seemed to matter to him, and, oddly, to her as well. *Our witch.*

'I honestly don't know. The book said they think the bottles were usually intended as a counter-charm against the black magic of a living witch. But maybe not always. Maybe... well, the thing is, once or twice a bottle has been found which appears to contain entrails.'

'Oh, God.' He looked genuinely aghast and a shudder ran between them like chilly electricity.

'I know – horrible.' Their witch, already dead; their bottle, a fetish to ward off sorcery from beyond the grave.

Another beer and another glass of wine, and Nick was

prepared to volunteer the information that he'd been doing some witchcraft research of his own. 'Just online, you know.'

'Oh, yes?'

'About how they spotted them, these women who were supposed to be witches. For a start, they all had their familiars. A familiar was the witch's evil spirit, which she sent out to do her wicked work for her, but they took the form of animals or birds. It could be almost anything – a fox, a jackdaw, a starling, a toad. If there was an owl nesting in your barn, say, then you were in big trouble.'

In big trouble... This glass seemed to be even tinglier than the last one; things were beginning to buzz and spin. The singer's toneless voice hung at the edges of perception: '...*below the hill were the brightest stars, when he heard the owlet cry...*' Kathy attempted to focus. 'Or if you were a bit too fond of your cat, perhaps?'

He grinned. 'Right. And then there was always supposed to be some kind of mark, somewhere on the witch's body. Beelzebub's sign and all that. It could be a birthmark, like you said before. But often it was just a wart, or even a mole. Just an ordinary discreet sort of mole, a cute sort of mole, the kind that anyone might have...' His eyes slipped down towards the open neck of her shirt, and the upper slope of her left breast.

Aware of the heat in her face, she clutched her wine glass tight against her chest. Her head felt unanchored, weightless.

'And then they'd claim it was a third nipple – Satan's nubbin, the devil's dug.' The blue-grey eyes were dark and dangerous. 'The place where the sorceress would suckle her familiar.'

'...*wherefore came you here? I seek the witch...*'

By an effort of will, Kathy forced herself to break

his gaze and lightness into her voice. 'So, what kind of websites were these that you've been looking at, exactly?'

At that he laughed and the spell, for the moment, was interrupted.

'Another glass of wine?'

I burn. At night it is that I burn the worst, lying alone in my maiden bed where I no longer know the peace of a maiden conscience. My linen constricts me, with its brazen coils which twist and cling close about my limbs. Each evening I slip out from its sleepless embrace and creep from the house while all are abed. As if by the tugging hands of demons am I drawn to the place, to Parmenters, to stand and gaze upon its walls. Its pink walls: such a pretty hue, but I did hear the maddened squeals of the pig when its throat was slit and bled into the limewash for the renderwork. I gaze upon the house wherein he lies, he for whom in sin I burn, and I picture him there. May God forgive me, I picture him lying naked there, there in the house whose very walls are soaked in blood and ruddied with the stain of death.

The name – Parmenters – was unusual, of course, but she had grown accustomed to it and ceased to give it thought. If she'd had any notion of the reason for it, it was of some kind of medieval craft, like pargeting or parquetry. Or she associated it with Parliament men, thinking perhaps this had been a Puritan house – which brought her back to zealotry, and witchfinding.

It was only when, after two months since her move here of telling herself she must, she finally took a visit to the church one Sunday that she realised how literal the name of her house must be. There were several stones of Parmenters – Victorian Emilys and Regency Janes – growing grey and gold with lichen among the drooping heads of cow parsley. And in the floor of the aisle, worn almost to smoothness by more than three centuries of devoted feet, was an older memorial, carved in pinkish sandstone. It was this one in particular which arrested her attention, because of its age and the woman's name – her own name.

Here lyes the Body of Daniell Parmenter, Dec'd 19th May 1656 aged 24 years. Also Katherine his wife, Dec'd 5th Octob'r 1685 aged 51 years.

Such a long widowhood, thought Kathy, to outlive her husband by almost thirty years.

'Don't you think it's sad?' she asked Nick in the half-lit heat of the pub bar. 'All those long, lonely days on her own in the house.'

'And lonely nights,' he said softly. 'Without a man to warm her bed.'

She sat up late that evening on the rug before the inglenook. September was only two weeks away but it was far too hot still even to contemplate laying a fire, so she found some church candles, fat and buttery white, and lit them around the grate. The Ship's Pinot Grigio still warmed her blood and cast a glow to merge with the candlelight, and she thought about chimney places and how they were the conduit of spirits. But the shadows that danced around the flickering light were friendly ghosts; dark demons seemed far away tonight from the encircling safety of hearth and home. She gazed into the candles' fire as people had gazed before her in this very spot for half a thousand years – her predecessors, the chatelaines of Parmenters. She thought of Katherine Parmenter and her thirty years in widow's weeds; she thought of all those who had sat where she now sat and conjured pictures in the flames, hugged close their memories or dreamed their future dreams. She thought of all who had lain where she now lay – had lain alone or lain with another. And, as sleep crept in to fade the light, she thought of Nick.

They say I am too base for him. They say that Spalls are low of birth, of simple Saxon stock – tillers of other men's soil, bondsmen and rentlings, quarter-day slaves – while Parmenters are fine and fancy folk, born of Norman seigneurs and overlords, that noble blood runs in their veins. But cannot a mouse raise its eyes from the ground and gaze upon a cat, a pauper look at a prince? I only look at him, at Daniell Parmenter in his house with walls of blood. I only look – and burn.

Another book arrived, an old one from the 1930s not currently in print, which she'd had on order from the library in Ipswich and picked up after work. From it she learned of the ingenuity of witches, of the monstrous range of mischiefs attributed to their hand. Stillbirths and miscarriages; childhood agues; droughts and floods and thunderstorms; fits in hogs, milk fever in cows; fruit that withered and crops that failed to thrive; drownings, poisonings, and even fires.

And that was when she found her: the witch in the bottle, her own Parmenters witch. *In the settlement of Blaxhall in Suffolk,* the author wrote, *another death by fire was laid at the door of a sorceress, a village girl of fifteen summers by the name of Patience Spall. The victim was Daniell Parmenter, a yeoman farmer. According to one local account, Daniell was awakened at night by the whinnying of his plough horse and went out to the barn to attend to the animal, thinking it perhaps to be sick of the colic from a surfeit of spring grass. When he did not return to bed, his wife looked out, saw the barn ablaze and raised the alarm. Too late: her husband's body was found next morning in the embers.*

'An arsonist?' Nick demanded. 'A pyromaniac? Our witch?'

'Well, all we know, I suppose, is that there was a fire and Daniell died.' If even that was certain, so long ago and on mere hearsay evidence.

'And she was the one who lit it? No doubt by sending out her familiar with a box of Swan Vestas. Of course she was – because she had a limp, or one shoulder higher than the other, or freckles in the shape of the devil's horns.' He sounded scandalised, but his voice was also strangely edged with glee. 'No question of his just going out there with a torch or a taper and putting it down for a minute to look at his horse, a bit too near some dry straw. Oh, no – it had to be black magic. It had to be our witch.'

But Kathy only frowned, and crossed her arms around her body to close out the chill that stippled her skin in spite of the breathless evening heat. *Slips of yew, sliver'd in the moon's eclipse... finger of birth-strangled babe, ditch-deliver'd by a drab.* And they had burned her here for her sorcery, right here in the village, above the church on Silly Hill – which the book explained meant holy hill, a name surely most inapt to this ungodly purpose.

'Her name was Patience,' was all she said, 'and she was just a child.'

I hate her, Kat Alward – Kat Parmenter that is to be. She it is, not I, who shall share his bed. 'Tis bitter bile to think of it, and yet, for shame, the devil does inflame and heat me with imagining of their wanton marriage bed. And Kat's flesh shall exult to his touch and she shall grow ripe of him, while I in my narrow bed shall shrivel and dry, an empty husk, untended and unfilled. And like the discarded chaff, the dry-parched straw, I am tinder to the spark and hungry for burning. And the flame that consumes me is the flame of hate for her: for she that shortly will become my Daniell's bride.

The sound that distracted Kathy from her book of witches came from inside the inglenook. A soft scuffling or scrabbling, its source appeared to be somewhere behind the shoulder of Tudor brick which angled back above the mantel. At her approach the sound ceased, and the air hung dense with silence for a full five, six, seven seconds, counted out methodically by the old brass clock which stood on the mantelshelf; then with a flurry it began again, the scratching and scraping, and now more insistent than before. Ducking beneath the lintel, Kathy found her vision doused by the darkness as effectively as by bucket of hot, black liquid. The heat and the smell of wood-ash choked her nostrils, along with something else, something more visceral, a tang more animal than mineral. She had only a moment in which to try to pinpoint it, to orientate herself and adjust her eyes, before the maelstrom was unleashed and the narrow space about her head was filled with the frantic whirling and beating of all hell's furies. Her hands sprang up to cover her face but her scream was silent; she dared not open her mouth for fear of letting in the demons. Against her hands and ears and neck and in her hair she felt the assault of a thousand tiny hands, a nameless, formless terror of fur or feather, of stabbing beak and clutching claw.

To burn in desire or to burn in hate – how lies it with us to tell between the two? A fire once well ablaze makes no nice distinctions – the flame devours all that come in its reach without regard for rich nor poor, for sin nor purity, good nor evil, the bride in Christ nor Satan's whore. In the heat of passion, hate is love and love flares high and is scorched to hate. I hate them both – Kat Alward and Daniell Parmenter, my beloved, both, in their bed of consuming lust.

On the Saturday of the August Bank Holiday weekend, Kathy invited Nick over for supper in her garden at Parmenters. His work on the house was complete, the floors and roof damp-proof and watertight, and the rendering renewed to a spanking fresh – and one hundred per cent vegetarian – Suffolk pink. The roses on the garden wall drenched the air in their sweet-shop perfume, as thick as Turkish delight, and the lawn hummed torpidly with insects and the musk of fallen fruit. Scalding late-summer sun looked set to hold for a few days yet, but storms were forecast for the following week. It might be the last chance for a proper outdoor summer feast, and she wanted to share it with Nick. Besides, she had another discovery to show him.

'It's indoors, in the inglenook.'

'Again? Not another genie in a bottle?'

'No.' No bottle this time – these were different ghosts.

'What were you doing in the fireplace, anyway? It's hardly the weather for laying fires.'

She pulled a face. 'Scraping up crap.' Her clawing hell-fiend had turned out to been nothing less ordinary than a starling that come down the chimney and been trapped. She had managed to drive it from the fireplace and out through the open French windows, but it had left behind a mess of droppings and snapped feathers.

'No wonder. Scared shitless I expect, poor thing.'

'It wasn't the only one. I felt like Tippi Hedren on set with Hitchcock.'

211

It was a joke now, but still brought a residual clench to her stomach: the confined space, the blind beating panic. *Lizard's leg and owlet's wing.*

'I really must fit you that spark guard,' said Nick.

'Anyway, come and see what I found when I was cleaning up. I want to show you.'

It was with some reluctance that they left the fragrant garden, but it was dark now and they had finished the Roquefort and the raspberries; they brought the remains of the Prosecco with them. Inside the house it felt sultry after the freshness of the outdoor night. They'd carried bottle and glasses through to the sitting room; Kathy drew deeply on hers and Nick refilled it.

'Here. Come and see.' She stepped inside the inglenook, lowering her head to duck under the mantelpiece. On the other side, there was height enough for them both to stand upright between the lintel and the smoke hood which hung behind. The space, as before – though mercifully empty now of birds – was dark as soot and heavy with the smell of woodsmoke. Kathy had a torch.

'There are two wooden beams, you see – two lintels. One behind the other.' She shone the beam as she spoke. 'It looks as if the back one is older.'

'Yes. I remember – I noticed when I was working on the floor. It looks as if they put the front one in later to strengthen the chimney breast. Nineteenth century, by the look of it.'

'Right. But look what I found on the old mantel beam. Here, in the gap.'

She pointed the torch into a cavity a few centimetres wide between the back of the Victorian lintel and the front of its Tudor predecessor, which would once have faced into the room above the fire. He had to lean his face very close to hers to see inside the narrow opening.

212

'It's a pair of carved initials, you see.' She moved her hand inside and outlined the ridged contours of the two swirling shapes. K and D.

'It's them, don't you think? It has to be them. Katherine and Daniell.'

He nodded, and above her torch beam, uplit, she watched his lower lip curve into a smile. 'It's them,' he agreed. 'And it's also us.'

'Us?'

'K is you. Katherine, Kathy. And D is me.'

'Nick? Aren't you Nicholas, then?'

A shake of the head. 'I'm Dominic.'

In the soft chiaroscuro of the inglenook, in the warm secret space between the two lintels, his hand joined hers in tracing the carved wooden lettering. 'It's the two of us,' he said, 'entwined.'

The final word hung between them, thick and smoky and charged. The heat and proximity were suddenly a heady potion; the torchlight trembled with her fingers. Her face was already tilting up to join him as his lips came down and found hers. The torch fell. They were in darkness, and there was only his mouth, still sharp with the fizz of raspberries, and the scent of his skin in her nostrils, hot and human and alive against the smothering staleness of old ashes.

The lovers spent the night on the old Persian rug in front of the fireplace. At some point, in between spells of touching and talking and laughing and loving, and another bottle of Prosecco, Kathy had fetched down the duvet from her bed upstairs; it was almost four before they finally fell asleep, half on and half under it, their spent limbs still slackly intertwined.

By six she was awake again, her body and mind far too

213

alive, too stimulated, for more than those short snatched hours of rest. Taking care not to wake the slumbering Nick, she extracted her lower body from the weight of his legs, her arm from under his head, and slipped out to the kitchen, where twice she filled a mug to the brim with cold water from the tap and drank it down. Already – or still – the breeze from the open kitchen window was shot through with heat. Picking up from the table her book on witchcraft, she walked out naked into the garden, and over to the bench beneath the apple tree. It was odd, she suddenly thought, how even thus alone she would normally have been too self-conscious for this display, yet this morning there was a simple, heedless pleasure in it; how strange, too, that she should feel completely at one with this body, for all the unfamiliarity of her stretched muscles, battered limbs and sensitised, tingling skin.

The editors of Kathy's book had not, in 1935, done much of a job on the indexing. There were entries for neither Blaxhall nor Parmenter, or else she would surely already have discovered the page towards the end of the book which contained the final reference to the case of Patience Spall, who was arraigned and convicted at the Bury St Edmund's assizes on the last day of August 1656 and burned in the village of Blaxhall the following morning.

She found it now, and this is what she read.

There seems to have been little local sympathy for Patience, described in one contemporary account as 'a sallow, skelly-boned maid', ill-favoured, and as having a face like wormwood. For her victim and his young widow, by contrast, there was widespread compassion, heightened by the tragic circumstance that Daniell Parmenter should have died on the very night of his wedding to Katherine.

It may be that Patience was indeed responsible for the fire, or perhaps the villagers were primed to attest against her, for the prosecution case did not rest solely upon the usual supernatural signs which so many witches were convicted – the milk which curdled at her touch, the noontime flight of a nightjar – but upon the testimony of two separate witnesses who both claimed to have seen her out abroad that night in the proximity of the Parmenters' barn.

If Patience was truly at the barn; if she saw Daniell go inside; if she did light the flame which set the place alight, and, if so, why – the answers can only be a matter for conjecture. Why would a young girl burn to death a bridegroom on his wedding night? To the modern psychoanalytic mind, some explanations may of course suggest themselves. Had Patience, perhaps, a morbid hatred of the sexual act – some say, as a result of incestuous abuse at the hand of her father? Or might she have had an obsessive sexual fixation on Katherine Parmenter which, frustrated, impelled her to kill the new-wed husband in a jealous rage? Whatever the truth of it, we shall never know, for Patience Spall took the secret with her to her unconsecrated grave.

By now it was nearly seven o'clock, and inside the house, at the French windows, the morning sun slid between the curtains which last night they had never stopped to close. There it warmed the single pair of naked feet which were flung uncovered from beneath the quilt – but the exhausted Nick never stirred. The sun burned strongly for such an early hour, its brilliance unfiltered by the heat haze that would build up later on; it was going to be another blazing day. A minute more, and its rays crept round to fall across the witch bottle, which still lay on its

215

side where Kathy had left it, on the rug beside the base of the chimney breast. Sunlight glinted on the smooth, pellucid glass, palely tinged with green.

In the garden, heavy with outdoor morning scents and the lassitude of the night's expended energies, Kathy's mind turned round and round in slow, soporific circles, while the print drifted in and out of focus before her eyes.

...the tragic circumstance that Daniell Parmenter should have died on the very night... the tragic circumstance... the newly-wed husband... the very night of his wedding to Katherine...

There must have been a crack in the bottle: the merest whisker – no doubt the result of Nick's invading spade – snaking its filigree path through the ancient glass. It was only a hair's breadth, but sufficient to let in oxygen. The sun seared through the glass and on to the twisted cloth inside which, desiccated by the centuries, was cracking and crisped to tinder, impregnated with its long-dried sulphurous cocktail; it scorched the knot of fabric through the glittering glass, bringing to a simmer the anhydrous witch's brew. *In the cauldron boil and bake.* The curve of the bottle's flank served to focus and intensify the light, concentrating the rays on a single point, a pinprick, deep in the blood-dark folds of cloth.

A soft, plosive pop, inaudible beyond the confines of the bottle, released the first gauzy wisp of smoke and with it a smouldering, acrid odour. *Fire burn, and cauldron bubble.* Then came the flame. Bluish and tentative at first, it began to lap along a ridge of fabric, but quickly grew bolder, darkening to purple and rich red, then leapt, hungry and orange, to lick the inside of the glass. Finally, it found the crack, the way to the outside air and

216

life-giving oxygen – where, invigorated, it bucked and swayed its wild banshee dance, until it met the threads of Persian wool.

Fire burn...

It was the scent which jerked Kathy to wakefulness. It caught unmistakably at her throat – the sour, dry, abrasive rasp of fresh smoke. The book fell and, blindly, barefoot, she was running across the dew-wet grass, running towards the smoke which scrolled from French windows, towards Parmenters, and Nick.

CURLEW CALL

This is such a brilliant place, Mum. I'm going to love it here, I know I am, even though I'm stuck out on my Larry lonesome with just an old lady for company and everybody thinks I'm crazy. I can actually see the salt marshes from my bedroom window if I lean out a bit and look eastwards towards the estuary. Well, not the mudflats when the tide is out, but the reed beds, anyway – the feathery tops of the reeds. And at high tide you can see the water, too, when the sun's on it, shining through in little silvery strips. Now I'm lying here in bed sending this before I go to sleep and all I can hear is curlews. Imagine – actually dozing off to the sound of curlews! Night night. Love you.

Sorry about the short and rather incoherent message last night. Honestly though, Mum, I was so knackered by the time I'd got here. Crossing the Underground took for ever with my massive rucksack, up and down all the escalators bashing people and having to apologise, and I missed the train from Liverpool Street that I was supposed to get and that meant a longer wait at Ipswich for the connection to get up here, and it stopped at every bush and cow shed all the way and there wasn't a buffet car or even one of those trolleys to get a Twix or something. But I had just enough battery left to ring Miss Keble, who says to call her Agnes, and she said not to worry at all, my dear – she always says 'my dear' – and the last bus wouldn't have gone yet and she'd wait the tea. That was how she said it, 'I'll wait the tea', which I think is brilliant, like something out of *Miss Marple* or *Downton Abbey*.

She gets about the house like a demon in her wheelchair – the ground floor at least. She's had all the old wooden steps between the rooms levelled off, even though she says she had to keep quiet about having it done because the house was built in the reign of Henry VIII and she'd have needed listed buildings consent. Her bedroom is downstairs and a shower and loo and this little room that she calls her studio, which actually when I caught a glimpse looks full of books, but then so is the sitting room which she says we're to share. There's a telly that looks as if it ought to be in black and white and have newsreaders on it in bow ties who talk like the Queen and say 'This is London'. So I hope it works OK and gets all the Freeview stuff at least so I can see *Autumnwatch*, and Agnes doesn't insist on us sitting down together to the *Antiques Roadshow* or *Songs of Praise* or something dreadful. But anyway, she seems nice, and she's a good cook as well. We had smoked haddock for this tea that she'd 'waited', two huge fillets each with parsley sauce plus a poached egg on top and proper bread from a loaf, not the pre-sliced plastic kind. Granary – always my favourite, as you know. And it really was tea in the old-fashioned sense, because she made us a pot of Earl Grey with it, which was a bit weird – I mean, Earl Grey with fish! – but not as bad as you'd think, and better than just tap water.

219

When I find out where the shop is I'm going to lay in some Diet Cokes.

Agnes says I can take the day off today – which feels a bit funny when I've only just arrived and not actually done anything yet – but she says she doesn't paint every day, or at least she doesn't need to be taken out to paint, because she often brings her canvases back and finishes them off at home in the studio. From memory, she said. And then she said something about getting older and falling back on memories more and more, and I had no idea what to say to that. It was a bit embarrassing. But she didn't seem to mind, or maybe even not to notice. That's a nice thing about Agnes, I've decided – she doesn't seem to get embarrassed about stuff at all, or be bothered if you can't think of the right thing to say. Except that... well, it's also maybe that she's a bit distant, as if she's lost somewhere off inside her own head and not really here with me at all, which could be unnerving if I let it get to me. Probably comes with her living here so long in all this isolation. But she says I should have today to myself, to settle in, or go and explore without her getting in the way. 'Make your own acquaintance with the marshes' is how she put it, which I thought was an odd thing to say, as if she thinks they're alive and she goes out and communes with the mud or something, but it was also rather poetic. And it means a whole glorious day out on the estuary – just me and my binoculars and, hopefully, twenty or thirty species of waders and wildfowl.

Meanwhile I can hear the curlews again, calling out across the reed beds. It seems to be the regular soundtrack of the marshes at this time of the evening, in the hour or two after the sun's gone down. You wonder what they're doing out there in the dark, sleepless and crying like that. And if you lie still and listen – really listen – there's something so pitiful about the sound, it could nearly break your heart, like someone whistling hopelessly over and over for a dog that's lost.

I saw the avocets! I knew they might be here, and did hope autumn would be a good time to see them. Their nesting grounds are mostly nearer the sea – Havergate Island or the reserve at Minsmere – but they disperse inland up the estuaries post-breeding and before they fly off south, fattening up on the rich pickings in the mud here. There might even be a few overwintering here – I do hope so, because they're so beautiful.

You know I've never been just a twitcher, Mum, one of those anoraks only interested because they're rare or to tick them off on a list, like train numbers or something. It's them – themselves, the birds. You look at the pictures of the avocet in the field guides and you think, what is going on with that bonkers beak? I mean, pointing up at the end like that, like they've flown into a brick wall. But it all makes sense when you see them in the flesh, actually down on the mudflats doing their thing. They use it to do a sort of sideways sweepy movement, scooping along just below the surface of the water where it's shallow over the mud, like skimming cream off the top of the milk, or the fat off the roasting tin before you made the gravy, like you used to when you did Sunday dinners for me and Dad. And it's absolutely the opposite of the curlews with their downwards-pointing bills, who look all solemn like short-sighted maiden aunts, as if they ought to have one of those lorgnette things perched on the top, and they move along really slowly, peering down into the water and looking for just the right place before they dig. Then they do it ever so delicately, like a surgeon doing some tricky operation with a pair of long-nosed forceps. The little sandpipers and dunlins are different again; they have those shorter beaks, straight and sharp like sewing machine needles, and they go along stabbing them in and out as if they're hemming a pair of curtains, absolutely metronomic, with their tails bobbing up and down at the other end in counterpoint. I could have watched them all day.

In fact, I more or less did, and totally missed lunch, which Agnes said she always has at half past twelve, but she didn't seem to mind and said it was 'only cold cuts, my dear' which seemed to mean some leftovers of what I'm guessing was her Sunday roast. She told me to help myself from the fridge so I made a sandwich with some more of the nice granary and a bit of pickle and she made us a pot of Earl Grey again, which she seems to live off, and sat with me while I ate. And I said – just to make conversation – did she often cook a joint when it was just her? After I'd said it I wondered if it sounded rude, as if I was accusing her of being lonely and a bit sad, but she didn't take it that way, I don't think. She just said, 'Mother always did, every Sunday.' She didn't say it wistfully or anything but she did go rather quiet on me, the way she does, so I wittered on about how you didn't bother much with big dinners these days, since it was just you and me and no brothers or sisters, and she frowned and repeated, 'No sister?' but in a vague sort of way as if her mind was still on something else. So then, because we were talking about Sunday roasts I told her about the avocets scooping the fat off the gravy and she frowned for a bit longer, and finally blinked a couple of times and nodded slowly and said she knew exactly what I meant.

Dad Skyped me from work at lunchtime (his lunchtime, I mean – Chicago lunchtime, not ours here) but it was pretty hopeless. He'd get three words out and then it

222

would freeze up and just sit there buffering. Agnes does have broadband, supposedly, but it's dead slow – even YouTube is a struggle for it and I can't watch iPlayer at all. So we gave up and Dad emailed instead. Not that he had anything much to say. He was just taking the mickey the way he always does, going on about how quaint he thinks it is, me spending my gap year in the country as a lady's companion as if I'm in an Edwardian novel. It's the painting thing, too – Dad reckons carrying Agnes's easel for her is going to be all E. M. Forster. I think he imagines I'll have to read aloud to her in the afternoons, and she's reclining on a rattan chaise longue rather than stuck in a motorised wheelchair. He was on about how she ought to be taking me to the Riviera to stay at the Hotel Splendide and not just out for tea in Aldeburgh, and if some bloke called Maximilian turns up in a fancy sports car I should check he hasn't been married before. Honestly, he thinks he's so funny. And anyway, that's Daphne du Maurier, isn't it, not Forster? We did it at school.

I told him, though. It's not the job so much – though it can't be as bad as au pairing for some pack of screechy, spoilt kids – it's where I get to be. I can hardly think of anywhere in the whole country that's got such an amazing mix of wetland habitats all plonked in together along one little stretch of estuary: reed beds, intertidal mudflats, salt marsh, saline lagoons with sandbanks, grazed marshland and floodable water meadows, and even the strip of vegetated shingle out at Orford Ness. In ten minutes' walk you can be in native woodland, or cultivated pine forest, or open heath, or farmland bounded by ancient hedgerows. It's like God designed a heaven especially for birdwatchers and dropped me in it. Give me this over Monte Carlo any day.

Dad can joke about what larks I must have here with

Agnes, sipping sherry and playing bezique, and I can tell him, that's not the point, the point is the birds. But actually I am glad to have Agnes here, or *someone* here – because I'm not sure even heaven's a place I'd like to be completely on my own in, the way Agnes has been in this creaking old house.

I've done my first day's work, and it wasn't exactly arduous. It was one of those misty late September mornings, all pale and gleaming, which tells you it's going to be hottish later on, and Agnes wanted to make an early start. 'To catch the light,' she said, as if there wasn't about twelve hours of the stuff in front of us, but I suppose she meant the angle of the sun or the particular glow at that time of day. Painters always go on about the quality of the light, don't they? And you could see what she meant, because once the mist lifted there was a sort of crispness to the edges of everything as if it was all newly outlined in fine black ink. I can see why it might make you want to sketch or paint, if I could manage to draw anything that looked remotely recognisable or you could even tell which way up the picture was meant to be.

Today I'd have painted the dunlins. Once I'd helped Agnes to where she wanted to be on the riverbank and got her all set up with her easel at the right height and comfortable in her chair with the brake on and her blanket tucked in, and unpacked her tubes and palettes from her satchel and her brushes and knives so they were all within reach, I was free to wander off and daydream, provided I stayed within hailing distance in case she needed anything. I had my binoculars but there wasn't much about except the dunlins, and I didn't need the bins to spot those. A great flock of them swooped in as the tide started to go out and leave the mud exposed, all freshly pockmarked with air bubbles where the little crustaceans and things were hastily burying themselves, which to the dunlins meant an all-you-can-eat buffet breakfast. They're so funny when they're in a group like that. They run along together in a pack, more like little brown mice than birds, because they sort of hunch their heads down on their shoulders and when they're knee-deep in the sludge they're all foreshortened and you don't see their long legs. There'll be a line of them along the edge of the water and they're all scurrying in the same direction and then for no apparent reason they all turn in unison and go heading off back the way they came, just as if one of them has given a secret signal or it's choreographed. Or it's like the sea on the shingle, with the flecky brown lip of a wave coming rolling in one way and then breaking and rolling out again. I sat there on a patch of sedgy grass with my eyes half shut and the sun on my back and watched them until they were just moving patterns and I could have gone to sleep if I hadn't had prickly stalks of reed sticking in my legs and the damp slowly soaking through my jeans and making my bum wet.

About midday Agnes said her hands were starting to feel cold, although to me it seemed pretty warm there in the sun. She gets arthritis in her fingers, and it's different holding a brush, I suppose, from just sitting about like I was with my hands in my pockets. And she's got a bit of a cough coming on. 'Besides, you're young,' she said, 'so you don't feel it the same.' Which I think may be rubbish, actually, because last winter when I went to Chicago to see Dad I was wearing about four pairs of socks, and woolly tights under my jeans, and was still so freezing I thought I'd need thawing out with a blowtorch, but Dad just laughed and Vanessa was only wearing one jumper and a jacket – but then she's Illinoisan born and bred, so

225

she's used to it. I wondered if she'd mind my seeing her painting – Agnes, that is – but she didn't seem bothered whether I did or not. I mean, she didn't rush to cover it up or make excuses about its not being finished yet like I'd have done, but neither did she exactly show it to me or want to talk about it or explain what she was trying to do. It was just there and I could take a look if I felt like it.

It wasn't the usual sort of thing you expect of an East Anglian landscape, with a low horizon and piles of cloudy sky. In fact, it was quite the opposite, almost all foreground, with the reeds forming a sort of fringe at the top and most of the canvas taken up with the mudflats themselves. She hadn't even drawn the dunlins – maybe she'll add them in later. It really was just the mud. She'd picked out all the swirls and squiggles which the tide had left as it trickled out. And the colours! You think that mud is only grey and brown but when you look properly, the way Agnes had, you can see that she's right, and that it's also the blackest black, and pure white, and it holds glints of red and gold and ochry yellow, and reflected blues and greens, and deep, imperial purple. I think she must have used more or less every tube in her satchel just to paint that mud.

Then I had to pack everything up again for her and help her back along the bank to the road, because after that she can get along OK without a push, but she still needs me to carry the easel even though the rest of the stuff stows quite well under the chair. After lunch she said she thought she'd work at home in the afternoon so we didn't go out again but she asked me to go to the shop at Snape and get a few things and suggested that I 'take the bicycle', which got me all excited because I was thinking, brilliant, I'll be able to borrow it when I'm off-duty and cycle over to the coast to look at seabirds, or over to Rendlesham Forest or even up to Minsmere. Until I opened the shed and saw it. Talk about a boneshaker! It must have been in there since about 1940 if the spiders' webs were anything to go by and when I hauled it out it weighed a ton, as if it were made of reinforced steel. I can just imagine Agnes as a teenager in a peaked cap and big khaki shorts: the Suffolk Girls' Heavy-armoured Bicycle Corps. Who needs tanks? This bike would have seen off Hitler, all right. To be fair, the tyres were pumped up and it was fine once I got going, even if it had no gears and the chain made an alarming grating noise. I think when she sends me to the supermarket at Saxmundham I'll wait for the bus. And maybe get some WD40 while I'm there.

The curlews are at it tonight, as usual. I went out for a walk upstream along the river just as it was getting dark, and was rewarded by a short-eared owl – my first one ever. It's true it's called the marsh owl, but I reckon it was lucky to see one this early in the year, because you mainly think of them as winter refugees from Scandinavia, but perhaps this one had actually summered and bred here. It looked pale underneath like a barn owl, but its wings were dark at the tips, and it was behaving all wrong for a barn owl, too, cross-hatching the water meadows methodically at a height of just a metre or so, a few slow wingbeats and then a glide, more wingbeats and another glide. I don't know what it was finding – maybe water voles or frogs. But it was hunting in absolutely silent concentration, and nothing much else was stirring at all, apart from when a ragged V of geese came over making that rhythmic honking noise of theirs, heading inland to roost for the night.

That, and the curlews. It felt as if they were following me all the way home, but I suppose their cries just carry a long way, especially on a still evening. It was completely

227

dark on the way back except for a few early stars, and I suppose it was with being on my own, too, because they started to sound weird and spooky, almost human – like a human child, wailing in the darkness, or calling out for help. But I told myself to get a grip, and by the time I'd got in and switched on all the lights in the kitchen and called through to Agnes, who was still in her studio, to ask her if she wanted any toast, and had put the kettle on for the inevitable Earl Grey, and then stuck my head outside the door again while I was putting away my wellies, they were back to sounding like normal, plain old birds.

Did I say that Agnes has given me her old room? Her old, old room it must be, I mean, from when she was a kid, because it's got all her old kiddy things in it. She gave me lovely guest towels and soap the night I arrived, like in a hotel, but of course she hadn't been able to take them upstairs and lay them on the bed or anything, so when I got up there I had to move two moth-eaten teddy bears and one of those old cloth dolls with yellow wool for hair to get at the pillows, and there was a rather misshapen sort of shawl thing laid across the foot of the bed, made up of different coloured knitted squares all sewn together, which must have been done by a child. And there are some child's drawings on the wall, pinned up to the beams – she could obviously really draw, even when she was a girl. There are two or three of the river or the garden here at the house, and several of a little black dog with a red collar, one of those spaniels with its tongue lolling out that looks as if it's laughing. Photos, too, in frames on top of the big chest of drawers, of Agnes in various summer frocks with dark hair in pigtails, aged seven or eight or nine but still very much with Agnes's features.

It all made me wonder when she moved downstairs

– how long she's been in the wheelchair. I suppose I'd just assumed it was some recent thing – well, somehow with elderly people a wheelchair doesn't seem that surprising and you put it down to some problem of being old – but perhaps she's actually been disabled a long time, since she was young. Or even since she was a child – some accident, maybe? Wouldn't that be so horribly sad? Maybe the little girl with the pigtails never grew up to ride the bulletproof bicycle at all. Maybe all she got was a wheelchair. You don't like to ask, though, do you, and she's never said. But why else would there be a room with everything left in it like this – almost frozen in time, like a museum, or a shrine to Agnes's childhood? If she'd just carried on living in the room she'd have chucked out the scroggy old shawl and rag doll and there'd be her more recent sketches instead of her old kiddy ones of the dog and maybe some teenage things lying about, and the bookshelf would have Jane Austen on it or Georgette Heyer or whatever she was into and not be stuck at *The Swiss Family Robinson*.

I mentioned it to her at breakfast. 'It's nice of you to let me have that room' is how I began, and I wasn't sure she'd know what I meant but I couldn't think what else to say that didn't sound as if I'd been prying – well, not poking through her stuff or anything but at least thinking prying thoughts – so I left it at that. Agnes looked hard at me for a really long time, except that she didn't seem to be looking actually *at* me. In fact, I almost wondered if she'd forgotten I was there, but she can't have because finally after an absolute age she said, 'I thought you'd like to be able to see the marshes, my dear.'

Agnes's cough is worse today so she took herself back to bed after breakfast. I wondered if I ought to stick around in case she needed anything but she said, 'No, you go out and enjoy yourself,' which I thought was funny because it made it sound as if I was about twelve and was going to go and play in the garden. But it was a glorious bright day, with everything looking all freshly washed after a high wind and battering rain in the night, and it also occurred to me that there might have been some migrants driven inshore, taking shelter from the storm. So I decided to risk life, limb and terminal exhaustion by riding the two-ton rattletrap of a bicycle out to Iken to see what I could see.

I had been hoping for spoonbills or a little egret or maybe even a razorbill – a stray one of which, according to a local birding website, turned up after strong winds this time last year. Instead I got totally distracted by sitting and watching some little penguin-suited oystercatchers feeding on a spit of mud that was jutting out into the estuary. They're crazy-looking things, with a staring red eye that makes them look mildly deranged, and those scarlet beaks, too, which always seem a couple of sizes too big. Their name is just right for them, although I think it was mainly mussels they were getting rather than oysters. What's amazing is all the different techniques they use. Some of them wedge the shell against something and then use their beak to prise it open, and some seem to look carefully for the sweet spot and then give it a sharp stab, while others abandon all pretence at subtlety and just stand there hammering away until the thing smashes open. I was trying to decide if there was some pattern to it – like maybe the males were hammerers and the females were prisers or something like that – but in the end I decided it was just random.

Because it was low tide there were loads of these bars and spits of mud, and even banks of it islanded out in the water – and almost all of them patrolled by waders or at least a few teal or wigeon. I was watching this old guy in a boat – just a little wooden thing with a puttery engine on the back – who I think was heading out fishing, and it was quite a business, picking his way along the estuary avoiding the mudbanks. There are a lot of willow branches sticking out of the water all the way along and he was steering a zigzag course between them. I thought at first they were actually growing there because they look a bit like spindly saplings that have got themselves surrounded in a flood, but then I saw him stop and pull one out and replant it a little way further over, and I realised they must be put there for navigation, to help anyone in a boat to get about without running aground or being mired in the mud. I guess that after the storm last night the channels and banks have all shifted about. It's the same even up near Agnes's in our own little patch of river: the mud is all hollows and ridges and runnels, with wet bits and drier bits, which are left in slightly different places every time the tide runs out. It's got to be pretty treacherous, however well you know it. No wonder you never see fishermen in waders, actually out on the flats; they seem to stick to boats. Don't worry, Mum – before you ask, I'm not about to get sucked in and drown. I'm staying firmly on the bank with my binoculars.

Poor old Agnes doesn't seem great at all tonight. The fits of coughing really rack her and leave her shaken and exhausted-looking, all sort of hunched and hollow-shouldered. I can hear her hacking away down there now, doing a duet with the curlews outside. I wonder if I ought to get her to the doctor tomorrow.

Sorry I haven't emailed for a while, only we've had a bit of a drama here. Agnes has had to go into hospital.

I took her to the GP like I said, and she listened to her chest and did a lot of frowning and prescribed her some penicillin, but after a day or two it was clear they weren't really knocking it on the head, and the cough was worse and she was complaining of chest pain, too, and off her food and looking deathly pale, so the doc said she ought to go to A&E, and because she has no car and it would have meant me taking her in on the bus they actually got her an ambulance – though it was just one of those sitting-down ones they use as an outpatients' minibus, no blue flashing light on top or anything.

At Emergency they poked her about and did a lot more listening and frowning, and took blood samples, and then whisked her out of her own chair and into an NHS one and off into the bowels of the hospital, and left me to get the bus home. I went back again in the evening during visiting hours, which was all quite an undertaking because the bus to Ipswich takes an absolute age and then you have to wait for a different one to get you up to the hospital, and really I might as well have hung around the café all afternoon or taken myself for a walk instead of trailing home and back. Anyway, it turns out Agnes has pneumonia. They've got her rigged up to a drip, which is apparently partly because they're concerned she might be dehydrated but also to get some hard core intravenous antibiotics inside her. She was completely out of it. I talked to her for a while but I couldn't tell if she was even properly aware I was there – I suspect she must be on some pretty zonking painkillers, too – so I just sat there a bit longer and then set off for the bus stop and the long trip home again.

That was last Thursday. She's off the drip now but still very weak, so they're doing some more tests, she says, and keeping her in for observation. It's going to be at least another week, they reckon, depending on how she does. And I'm left to fend for myself, with nothing but a lot of empty rooms and the curlews outside to keep me company.

So sorry, Mum – another long gap since I last communicated, and this time there's no excuse because I've not exactly been short of time on my hands. Agnes is still in hospital. The pneumonia is turning out to be a bit stubborn, and they say she's got pleurisy as well which might mean something viral going on, not bacterial like the pneumonia, which is why the antibiotics haven't sorted her out. Something like that, anyway – this is all gleaned from what Agnes says because I'm never there when the doctors come round, and she's been in and out of consciousness and not always completely on the ball. Even further off inside her head than usual. I'm not convinced she's eating anything either. I bought some Earl Grey teabags, because she only has loose leaf at home, and took them up there, because I thought, well at least she must be drinking and she can't survive without her tea. I asked the nurse about it but she said she didn't think there was anything they could do because they just make it in the one big urn, which is a bit depressing but I suppose is bound to be how it is. Agnes looks all sort of diminished, propped up on the hinged metal bedhead thing and her regulation pillows – older, when you look at her face, though that might be the harsh strip lighting showing up the lines, but also oddly childlike at the same time, as if she's receding back into being the little girl in those photographs. It's probably the way they organise you and you just have to lie there and not make any decisions about anything. I left the teabags anyway, just on the off chance.

So now I've got nothing to do, no job left – not that it ever seemed like a proper job as such, but even less to do than before, I mean. I wondered about coming home for a week or two until she's discharged. Agnes said, 'Take care of the house for me,' but there's honestly nothing to do, beyond sticking a quick hoover round now and then and remembering whether it's the grey bin or the blue bin to go out on a Tuesday. It's not that – it's her, it's Agnes. I go up there every day, and I'm thinking, who would she have to visit her if I cleared off home?

It's made me realise, too: I don't think she's had any friends drop round to the house the whole time I've been here, and she doesn't seem to chat to anyone on the phone or want taking to the pub, or wherever it is that people like her get together with their mates – I don't know, fundraising coffee mornings or an art group or something, or even church on Sundays. And being on my own in that echoey old house, all by itself on the edge of the salt marsh, has had me thinking a lot about what it must be like being Agnes. Not that she seems to mind in the least; she seems to like being away in her own thoughts. It's as if she's not only tied to the place but actually part of it – connected by her childhood, and the pull of the past. But I seriously couldn't hack it for long. It's been grey and foggy this week – not just early river mist that burns off by mid-morning but proper full-on November fog that lurks around all day until you've forgotten what the sky looks like. It's the sort that seeps into everything until it's dripping. Apart from my daily trek to the hospital and back I've barely been outside the house. All this time to myself, but I've not even been out birding – it's so gloomy and miserable and you wouldn't see anything until you were practically treading on it anyway. Plus also... well, it might sound a bit pathetic but things look different in the fog, all distorted and with the shapes and distances messed up, and I'm a bit scared I'll somehow lose the path, even though I know it pretty well by now, and end up blundering off into the marshes and getting lost or cut off by the tide or something.

Even indoors, it feels as if the fog has crept in behind you – or at least, you can sense it out there all the time, pressing in at the windows. Stupid, I know. Maybe it's just because of the way it blots out the view. It blots the sound, too, but only partially. Everything sounds dampened down and fuzzy round the edges but weirdly amplified at the same time, if that makes any sense, so you can't tell whether a noise is close by or off in the distance somewhere. A car on the Snape road can sound a million miles away and then the curlews, at night, can seem like they are right outside my window, when I know they are really way out in the reeds.

No – I couldn't last by myself here for a fortnight, never mind months and years like Agnes. It would drive me nuts. When I thought about it, it occurred to me that I've hardly ever gone to sleep on my own – really alone, I mean, with no one else in the house – because there was always you and Dad along the landing, and after he left there was you, and if you went away or were even out late there'd be a babysitter downstairs or Grandma came over and slept in the spare room, and when I went on sleepovers or school trips there were always other people, usually snoring away in the next bed, and even that night on holiday in the New Forest when I was going to camp out and listen for nightjars I only lasted until about 2 am before I came creeping back to the cottage. I know it's weedy of me, and I know lots of people are single and live on their own, and I'll be on my own at uni next year, but that's different, because that'll be in a hall of

235

residence with other students all round me, not by myself in a whole big empty house in the middle of nowhere. Even the reign-of-Henry-VIII thing, which in the daytime I think is great, and the old beams and low ceilings and funny dark corners and the great gaping fireplace are quite fun, at night just sets me thinking about all the people who've lived there and conjuring up ghosts. I wondered if Jess fancied coming down for a few days, because she's got reading week at Keele, but apparently there are some parties she doesn't want to miss and, really, you can hardly blame her, because who'd want to come out here and stay where there's nothing for miles around except a lot of mud and she's not even a birdwatcher?

I plucked up courage to talk to Agnes about it this afternoon. I thought, she's always so matter-of-fact and never takes offence, so I'll just ask. Aren't you ever lonely, I said, living by yourself in the house? She gave it some thought, in that far-off way she has, and then said no. And then she added something I thought was strange to start with, but kind of made sense afterwards when I puzzled over it on the bus home. She said, 'Not as lonely as I'd be if I were somewhere else.' And I decided what she must mean was, at least in the house she's got her memories around her whereas anywhere else she'd have nothing at all. I picture them as physical things, her memories – real and tangible. Except in sepia, like antique photographs.

It's twenty years, she says, since her parents died, and I gather she's been on her own there all that time, pretty much. I asked her if she had any brothers or sisters, but I don't think she heard me. She'd drifted off again, so I just left her clean pants and nightie on the stand by the bed and crept out quietly.

When I got home it was dark as well as foggy, and I went round switching all the lights on, even in rooms

I'm not going in, and the television, too, just for the companionship. Rubbish soaps and a no-brain game show – but at least it was human voices. I might even Skype Dad tonight, crappy broadband or not. Sleep tight, Mum. Love you.

Yesterday it rained absolute buckets, hardly stopped all morning, though at least it cleared the fog and I actually got outdoors and along the estuary for a quick walk after lunch. The dunlins and sandpipers seemed as relieved as I was to be out and about, blinking in surprise at the sunshine and shaking out gleaming if slightly battered-looking feathers. But then this morning the fog was back with a vengeance, and I haven't been outside all day, beyond standing at murky bus stops. It's just been house, bus, hospital, bus, and house again.

Even up on the ward I didn't get to talk to anyone, except to say hi to the ward sister. Agnes was asleep, but pretty restive and sounding distressed; I heard her mutter something about drowning. The sister said it was probably the opiates she's on, but it's no surprise if she dreams she's drowning, poor thing, with all that fluid clogging up her lungs.

Back here, I had a look at Agnes's paintings. I didn't mean to – I really wasn't snooping or anything. It's just that I was wondering what she might like me to take up to the hospital for her, like maybe one or two of her books or even a sketchpad and pencils, so I went in the studio to see what I could find, and her canvases were all in there, stacked against the back wall. There are dozens of them. And here's what's peculiar, Mum – they are all of the mud. I don't just mean she only paints pictures of the mudflats. That would be fair enough, since it's what's out there. But they're not of the marshes or the reed beds or the sky or the wildlife; there are none with a boat on, or a fisherman, or the trees in the distance, or the Maltings. All she does is paint the mud itself, over and over and over again. Maybe she likes the colours and the endlessly changing patterns. Maybe she wants to focus on one thing until she's got it completely mastered – as if you could ever master that untamable, shifting mud. But I don't know... there's something about it that feels a bit disturbing, a bit obsessional. I must admit it gave me the creeps; I had to go and make myself a sandwich.

More fog today – and no sign of the doctors being any closer to letting Agnes out of hospital. I'm starting to go stir-crazy, rattling around all alone in this house. I spent half the morning pacing the bedroom. I've tried reading but I can't settle to anything, and there's never anything on telly in the daytime.

I found myself looking again at all her stuff – Agnes's old stuff from when she was a kid, that is: the cloth doll and her drawings and the snaps of her as a small girl. And she is small, in all of them – every one. It hadn't exactly struck me before. Like I mentioned, she's no older than eight or nine in any of the pictures in the bedroom. And, OK, so maybe that's when it happened, the accident or illness or whatever it was that put her in her chair, so she had to move to her bedroom downstairs. That's what I decided before. But there are no photos at all anywhere else in the house – just a framed one in the studio, I noticed, which looks like it's of her mum and dad. Did they stop wanting pictures of her, after it happened, do you think? If so, it seems so dreadfully sad. It's just as if Agnes stopped dead in her tracks, right there and then; as if she'd stayed eight years old forever, or simply ceased to be.

There are other things, too. On the dressing table there's one of those old sets with a jewellery box and hand mirror and hairbrush, with the lid and backs all matching in pink mock mother-of-pearl, the way a little girl would love. I bet they were Agnes's prize possession. And there are hairs still trapped in the bristles of the brush: dark hair like in the photographs, like she must have had before she went grey. I picked it up and turned it over and over, and honestly, Mum, there was something about those trapped child's hairs that made my own stand on end.

It's partly that it's so personal, I suppose, touching the hairs from someone's head, such an immediate, physical connection, even across all those years. As if I could turn round and Agnes would be there at my elbow, except in a pinafore dress and pigtails. But it's also creepy because it makes no sense. Why would she leave behind her cute pink vanity set? Why wouldn't she take her hairbrush with her when she moved rooms?

I'm going to go bonkers out in this place by myself, I know I am. I've got the bedroom window opened wide now, as wide as it will go, even though it's freezing. I wanted to let in some air that doesn't feel stale and lifeless, as if it's been locked in here for decades. But all it's done is invite the mist to come inside, creeping round the frame and over the sill, damp and colourless and cloying. And I can hear the curlews more sharply than ever, keeping up their everlasting anguished lament.

I had this really vivid dream. There was a child and a dog, and both of them were lost out there on the mudflats. Lost or trapped, and calling out for help. No surprise, I suppose, since I'd been looking at photos of a child and drawings of a dog, and listening to the curlews when I turned out the light. But it was so real – so absolutely vivid. I woke up with my mouth dry and my throat tender and swollen, the way they feel when you've cried yourself to sleep. I dragged myself out of bed and closed the window. It was drizzling outside and the cold seemed to have soaked through the whole room during the night, leaving the air grey and heavy. Even with a jumper on under my dressing gown I felt chilled to the bone.

I needed to look at the drawings again, at Agnes's childhood sketches of the dog, the same small black spaniel who was lost in my dream. She's signed them all at the bottom right hand corner, in lumpy childish handwriting. 'A. Keble', she's put, or just her initials, 'A. K.' But on one of them she's written her whole name: Agnes Keble. Yet when I looked closely, there was something funny about the 'g' in Agnes, which didn't loop down below the line the way it should. I think I'd vaguely assumed, when I glanced before, that she'd stuck a capital 'G' in among the other, lower case letters. But that would be an odd thing for a child of eight or so to do, it occurred to me now, especially in her own name. And the 's' at the end wasn't quite right either, hardly there at all. The more I stared at the name the more it looked less and less like 'Agnes', and more and more like 'Anne'.

Suddenly I was whirling round the room in a fever, pulling out drawers, dragging down suitcases from the top of the wardrobe, opening boxes. I couldn't help it – I had to know. In fact, with a horrible, crawling certainty, I thought I already did. So many children's things: the little dresses and shoes and knickers and woollen mittens that shouldn't be here. Things that Agnes would surely have moved downstairs with her – if they had been hers.

Finally, at the bottom of a shoebox, beneath a layer of desiccated tissue paper, I found what I was looking for. The red leather dog collar, still with the lead attached, and the tarnished metal tag. A quartered sheet of yellowed newsprint, which I didn't need to open to guess the tragedy that was folded away inside it. And the photographs – the bundle of missing photographs, tied together with string.

Only the one on top was visible, but that was enough. It showed a dark-haired girl of eight or nine in a dress of checked gingham, her pigtails caught up in loops like big gypsy earrings and holding a laughing spaniel on its lead. The child from the photos on the chest of drawers, the child whose room I'm in. And beside her, in matching checks, half a head taller and maybe two years older, a matching, dark-haired child. Her big sister. Agnes.

I've opened the window again; I don't care any longer about the cold. It's coming down now in earnest, but I can't tell the wet outside from the drench of tears. Out on the salt marshes everything is silent, apart from the *pock-pock* of the rain as it stipples the mud and in the distance a single curlew, crying out its loneliness through the sheets of grey.

MACKEREL

The first slice is under the gills, angled in slightly towards the head. You don't push the knife right through to the board, but let it stop as it meets the resistance of the backbone. Then you spin the fish around and chop off the tail – the dark, spiny, deeply forked tail – before scraping it away sideways onto the worktop with the flat of the knife. Next you flip the fish onto its other side and repeat the cut at the gills, this time pressing down more firmly and sawing slightly to and fro to sever the spinal cord and remove the head, which slides to join the tail on the blue-and-white tiles. Last comes the tricky part. I must have done it a thousand times, but no two mackerel ever fillet quite alike. The tip of the blade goes in at the dorsal line, just above the backbone and a quarter-inch behind the place where the head used to be. You slide it one way and then the other, parting flesh from bone. Then the same thing below, at the centre line of the belly, scooping out and discarding the guts. Turn the fish again and, grasping firmly by the tail end, insert the knife across its width and draw the blade smoothly towards you, lifting the sweet tawny flesh, working more by feel than by eye and prising gently as you go, until the fillet comes springing clear of the pale, elastic bones.

I've got a pair of mackerel tonight, because my Harriet is coming. I know you shouldn't have favourites, but that's what Hattie is: my first and favourite grandchild. Long and dearly awaited, she was, and then late arriving when she came, almost two weeks after the due date. 'Starting the way she meant to go on' – that's what Carole always says, with a mother's rough, dismissive fondness. But Hattie is a considerate girl and never late for her grandma, not even nowadays, and doesn't assume like some folks that the old have nothing to do all day and won't mind waiting.

The knife was Billy's – not Bill's, my husband's, but Billy's that drowned. Billy the Kid, we used to call him. It was his knife, that he gutted the fish with as they landed them. We found it, later; it had stayed in the boat with the catch when he went over. He had it for his fifteenth birthday, from his dad, but he never reached his sixteenth, and now it's my filleting knife. The knife has got to be sharp, that's the key; no use trying to fillet a fish with a blunt edge. I know there are folks who swear by a steel, and there's other contrivances they'll sell you these days, with whirligig grinders that turn like corkscrews, but to my mind there's nothing like a good old-fashioned whetstone. Two or three good swipes along each side before I make a start, and that knife of Billy's is as keen as the day it was made.

A quick swab down of the chopping board and I replace them side by side, the four plump, glistening fillets. There's nothing so fine in all the sea as a mackerel's skin: the silver-white tinged almost to pink below while up above the silver-green is striped and squiggled with bold black lines, like seaweed snaking in the shallows, or sand patterns left by the ebbing tide.

I use another knife for descaling: stouter, with a flatter

243

blade. Rasped backwards against the lie of the skin, it sets the scales upright and bristling, and they come away easily, collecting against its edge like slivers of ice when you run your glove along the gate top on a frosty morning. A tool for every task, my own mum used to say, and each one fit for purpose. To snip off the fins, it's the smaller of the kitchen scissors. To pluck away the last of the tiny, threadlike bones, it's tweezers – bought as eyebrow tweezers, from Boots the Chemists, but they live in the kitchen drawer with the wooden spoons and the potato peeler.

She's a good girl, is Hattie, and she loves her mackerel, though it's a rare treat now to find one landed on this stretch of coast. When Carole and Billy were small they were the staple catch from May to November, for my Bill and the other men fishing out of Aldeburgh. A mainstay, a livelihood. The water at times was so thick with them, Bill said, it was like looking down into a vat of churning, molten silver. He almost felt as if he might be snagged and run aground in them: more fish than ocean. And of course you think it will last for ever, when the sea offers you riches in such store. So you take the gift and, like a greedy child, you take too much. But they didn't know, Bill and the others – how could they know, back then, when we'd never heard the word 'sustainability'? – that they were fishing the mackerel to near extinction in this part of the North Sea. So now it's mainly the flat fish – dab and sole, plaice and skate – plus sea bass, when they're running. Sea bass are popular now; they're where the money is. Any mackerel on the slab is mostly from the Atlantic now, the fisheries in the north and west – except for these two, line-caught up in Lowestoft, a special tea for my little Hattie. I'm doing them the old way, the way she always likes them, dipped top to tail in seasoned oatmeal and fried in a pan of best butter, nicely foaming as they go in but not allowed to brown.

* * *

What can I tell you about her, my grandmother? How to encapsulate, how to cut down and trim and fillet for the pan, the weeks and days of her eighty-nine years, lived out within a span of six short miles of the Suffolk sea, but each one filled to the full?

I could tell you, first, that we all call her Ganny, from when I was tiny and couldn't say my 'r's. I could tell you that the skin of Ganny's hands is rough and raw from handling crates of fish in winter; I could say she's as quick and handy with the knife as any backstreet cut-throat, but her touch was soft as a whisper when she used to comb and plait my hair. I could say she's a quiet subversive, a gentle setter, then breaker, of rules: a licker of fingers dipped in the cake bowl, a dispenser of jam from the jar with a spoon. I could say she knows the words of fifty songs, the old songs, of rope and sail and fishing net, of fishermen and sailor boys and maidens waiting on the shore, of storms and shipwrecks, and a light kept lit upon the harbour wall for a boat that's never coming home. I'd say she knows the words of every verse, but cannot hold a tune.

* * *

The young get about so much more than we ever had the chance to do. We women, I suppose is what I mean, though the menfolk never ventured far afield either, unless you count the fishing grounds of Denmark or Norway, or the war. Hattie's just back from Italy: picking olives, if you please. You never saw an olive when I was first married to Bill, or olive oil either, except in the chemist's. I had a little bottle for the stretch marks, I remember, after Carole was born. Now it's in every village shop, and it does give a nice flavour when you're frying fish, though to my mind there's still nothing quite like butter.

Eight months, it is, since Hattie was last here and sitting at my kitchen table – just newly out of college then, a Bachelor of Arts – and now she'll be back full of stories to tell, and brown as if she'd been at sea. I wonder if she remembers that her first granddad died in Italy? Though why she'd think of it, I don't know, when he wasn't really her granddad at all. Captured by the Italians in the Peloponnese in '41, Frank was shipped to Italy and set to work on a farm there. Not much more than a smallholding, he said in his letters, with some scrubby vines and a few olive trees. I kept the letters, even later, after I met Bill; one a week, he wrote me, for almost three years. He was killed joining up with the Allied invaders in the winter of '44. Funny how things work out. If it hadn't been for the times, that rush to wed before a tomorrow that might not come, it could have been an Italian farm girl he'd left on her own and pregnant instead of me.

That was in the mountains in a place they call Abruzzo and fifty miles from the sea, but Hattie's been up near Genoa, almost on the coast. I found it in the atlas. They'll have fishing there, but it won't be mackerel. It will be all the Mediterranean fare: sardines and anchovies and squid, most likely, or setting traps for lobster and prawn. My Bill never laid lobster pots but he always came home with a smile if he happened to snag one in the nets. You get a very good price for a lobster.

Funny how things work out, as I say. It seemed the end of everything when Frank's baby died, arrived before he had the strength for it, poor mite, and bundled off in an old sheet so as not to upset me, the way they did in those days. I never held him, nor even heard him cry; he hadn't the lungs. But perhaps the fates knew best. I was barely seventeen, a chit of a thing myself, and no man on hand to provide.

Marine ecology, that's what Harriet was studying, what she took for her final exams. What, I wonder, would Bill have made of it – his little Hattie, with an honours degree in the life of the sea? I was asking her mum what she thinks she'll do with all this learning, after she's shaken the itch to travel from out of her feet. Carole says she thinks maybe she'll try for the Ministry – our Hattie, allocating quotas, deciding what fish the men can land! Or maybe she'll go back to university and study some more. Her own research project, a PhD. A doctor in the family, no less.

It wouldn't be mackerel she'd be researching, though, I don't suppose. They've never been what you'd call a fashionable fish. Back in the day, when they were plentiful, we took them for granted. An everyday fish, a working man's supper, brought home for the family table because it could always be spared. It never had the glamour of white fish. Bill always said that mackerel were the greediest of feeders; take any bait, they would, he said – as easy to net as fallen fruit. And maybe that's how they gained their reputation as scavengers, with their muddy flesh, somehow unclean, like rats of the sea. Some used to say they fed on the corpses of dead sailors. There were old fishermen's tales of slitting open a mackerel's belly and finding sixpence, a gold ring, a human tooth. Bill would laugh and said he'd never found any treasure – only ever, once when gutting them on the deck, a tiny crab, entire and perfect in every limb as a still-born child.

247

More went for smoking even then than for eating fresh, as if the smoke might be a purifier, as well as masking their muscular flavour. And Tom Peckitt certainly smoked them a treat, back when the men still landed them aplenty. Me and Bill, though, always loved our mackerel fresh – and Hattie, too, though Carole might turn up her nose and call it unrefined. For me, it's an honest taste, an outdoor taste, of the beach when the tide goes out, of wet rope, sea wrack and tarpaulin.

Then there's all those bones. Bill and me, we enjoyed a mackerel cooked whole just as well as filleted, but there's plenty of folks nowadays won't be troubled picking out fish bones on their plate. Nor do they lift away cleanly, not in the way a trout comes off the bone, or a bass or bream; there's always some fiddle-faddle to a mackerel. But cooked on the bone it keeps its full robustness, for those of us as likes it. I gut the fish and trim off head and tail and fins, then slide some bits and pieces in the cavity for flavour – an onion, sliced fine as you like, and a couple of fresh bay leaves, or a handful of fennel stalks, or rosemary or thyme. Then I lay it on a sheet of greaseproof and sprinkle it with liquid – a squeeze of lemon, or a splash of cider, it used to be, when Bill was alive and I always kept some in the house. Fold up the paper to a nice tight parcel and lay it on a baking tray; thirty minutes in a hot oven and you've got yourself a perfect feast. When you take it from the oven, the greaseproof is puffed up high with steam. There's nothing quite like the moment when you open the parcel and let out the vapour, piping hot and savoury, better than the fug from the chip shop door on a cold winter's evening. It's worth the scalded fingers every time.

* * *

I must have made this journey seventy times: three times a year, at least, for my twenty-three years. First as a baby, I suppose, in a car seat or Moses basket, and then as a toddler learning to chant the litany of names. Four stops from Ipswich to where Gampa would be waiting in his old brown Humber estate – Westerfield, Woodbridge, Melton, Wickham Market – and then the uncharted territory beyond, known only ever by the beats of its poetic metre: Saxmundham, Darsham, Halesworth, Brampton, Beccles, Oulton Broad South and Lowestoft. The recitation was as familiar to me at six or seven as the one we listened to in reverent silence while Gampa sat close to the old, mesh-fronted radiogram: Shannon-Rockall-Malin-Hebrides, and Forth-Tyne-Dogger-Fisher-German Bight. Both were part of the secret rhythm of those years, the pat-a-cake, dig-and-delve rhythm, hopped on the pavement in chalk or rapped out with a stick on iron railings, words with no need of meaning but also steeped in it.

The smell of the carriage is different now, without its foreground foetor of stale ash, but the background notes remain as they always were: the shared, overheated air, the plush grimed smooth, and something metallically mechanical. Even before you get off the train there's a sense round here of being out of time, of slipping back into old paths previously trodden, that doesn't exist in London, or is perhaps so deeply buried we no longer feel its tug. At Woodbridge, as soon as the compartment doors hiss open, the air that bursts in is saline and holds the snap of ozone; it carries with it like flotsam the smells of the boatyard and the beach, those Gampa smells of oilcloth, tarred rope and creosote. And fish – of course, of fish.

My visits here could be the pages in a book of recipes:

Ganny's many ways for cooking fish, each one shiny bright and treasured, threading through my childhood like a necklace of shells. Sundays were a day apart from all the rest, back when Gampa was alive: the one day a week when no boats went out, making Sunday morning special. Breakfast would be a kipper, salt as driftwood and leathery brown, with a knob of butter to melt in its hollows and thick brown bread on the side, or else smoked haddock poached in milk and perched on a mound of spinach, the fishy milk thickened with flour and coating the spinach to a creamy, gloss pea-green. It was Gampa's favourite, but my brothers hated it – spinach, and at breakfast time! Down at the tideline, while Gampa checked his floats, greased bearings or tinkered with the pumps, Jonah would pick up laver and gutweed by the handful and toss it at Sam, while they chanted in delighted horror: *spinnage spinnage spinnage*. It made me imagine a great underwater spider, crouched beneath a rock to spin out patiently its web of sleek green seaweed.

A Friday teatime treat was Ganny's fish pie, made with the scraps from the end of the catch: heads and tails and handfuls of brown shrimp, dabs and sprats too small to weigh and sell. She always let me mash the potatoes to go on top; standing on a stool to see over the edge of the bowl, it took both my hands to press down with the masher and squeeze the lumpy mixture up through the mesh of tiny, diamond holes until it curled and toppled like lugworm casts in the sand. I could shell the peas, too, sending them popping from the pod to rattle and jump in the enamel basin. I even sliced the slippery, eye-streaming onions with the little vegetable knife, but I wasn't allowed to touch Ganny's filleting knife – 'your Uncle Billy's knife', though he died before I was born and was never as old as I am now. Billy the Kid is what Ganny and Gampa used to call him, and it suited him better than Uncle. That's what he stayed, after all – forever a kid of fifteen.

Billy's loss was the first to line her face – still a young face in the photographs before his death, abruptly aged in those taken after. The first loss: but its mark was criss-crossed over with many more. There was Gampa, of course – a long, drawn-out departure, first in the bedroom they shared and then in the little back parlour when they moved him downstairs. Hushed and curtained, it felt like church when they nudged me in at the doorway, the figure in the bed less Gampa than a plaster saint. It was a tumour in the colon, releasing and reseizing him, cruel as a cat; they must surely have wished he could follow his son down swiftly underwater, and never come up for air. Cancer played games, too, with Ganny's friend Rebecca; hers was in the kidney and looked to be beaten, Ganny told us, before it came back everywhere at once and took her quickly in the end. With Harry Housego next door, who'd survived the war and German prison camp with nothing worse than the shade of a limp, it was, finally, his heart; his friend Philip Root had fought in the Battle of Britain but died in his armchair at the nursing home in front of *Bargain Hunt*. Then there was old Rose Wilderspin who nursed her Albert for five whole years before outliving him by less than one, succumbing to septicaemia after she fell among the raspberry canes on her allotment. 'It'll soon be only me left,' Ganny likes to say, with as much determined pride as sadness.

Mackerel was always my favourite. Sometimes she fetched smoked ones from Mr Peckitt's smokehouse, which was just a shed with a stovepipe chimney. She'd bring them home in a packet of greaseproof paper, folded in at the corners as neat as a hospital bed. Old

Tom Peckitt, according to Ganny, had been in the Post Office and before that the army, and must have learnt those corners in one or the other. The skin takes on a coppery sheen in the smoke, one colour overlaying another like the foil and cellophane on a Quality Street. I used to beg Ganny to let me peel it off, as satisfying as easing the scab from new pink skin. We'd eat it just as it came, squashing the flesh onto triangles of toast that were cut so thin they'd curled up their corners to the grill and dried to a clean snap. Real smoked mackerel – Mr Peckitt's smoked mackerel – is a world away from the sad little fillets you buy in Sainsbury's, with the colour of burnt toffee and a texture to match. It's the colour of creamy *café au lait* and so soft you'd think it had been whipped, and there'd be just the fish and the toast and a jar of Ganny's cucumber pickle.

Best of all, though, I liked them straight from the catch, silver and black, so gleaming fresh you'd think they'd flip and flop away from Ganny's surgeon fingers and Uncle Billy's knife. I loved to watch her at work. In no time at all there'd be two perfect fillets, jacketed in oatmeal and sizzling in the pan.

* * *

It was years before Mother even told me he was a boy, Frank's baby. Yet I still felt his absence like the loss of a limb. That's what you hear people say, isn't it, but it's not quite right. He was dragged from inside me before his time, a bloody bundle – 'flesh of my flesh' as the Bible says. It wasn't like an arm or a leg torn off with the splinter of bone but something more slippery, something inside, and it left me emptied out, a gutted fish on the slab. It floored me far worse than the news, when it came, about Frank, whose face and voice by then had faded in my mind until he felt as if I'd made him up, with no real existence of his own outside the weekly storybook of his letters.

If Frank's boy had lived he'd have been thirteen when I married Bill, and very soon another man to help out on the boat. If he'd lived, then maybe our Billy would have stayed at home that day, stayed safe at home until he was grown. There are fewer drownings on the boats these days; you never seem to hear of them, at least. The ship-to-shore is better now, for if they run into trouble – digital, like everything else. And the forecasting, too: they always seem to know when storms are on the way. Although, of course, when Billy went it wasn't in a storm – just an averagely heavy swell, as Bill told the coroner. He was reaching to release a tangle in the nets and he slipped and went over, got himself trapped beneath the hull. *Death by misadventure* is what they called it. Just one of those things.

Frank was a farmer before he was a soldier, though the good Lord spared him few years for either. But Bill was always a fisherman. It was in his blood, and through him in our Billy's, too. It was Bill who was the Aldeburgh boy: the boat had been his father's, and his grandfather's before. Me, I've lived here all my life: in this village, in this cottage. I was born in the big iron bed upstairs which still feels empty without Bill beside me. My marriage to Frank was restricted to his leaves so we never had a chance to set up house; when he left me expecting, I was glad to be at home with Mother. After the war there were no jobs for women, and Father, then Mother needed looking after. By the time they were gone... well, by then I was courting Bill. I look at little Hattie with the world at her feet: her olives in Italy, her

PhD. But in those days things were different. It really never crossed my mind to leave.

* * *

Eighty-nine years, and all in one place, is impossible to imagine. I've lived for less than a quarter of that, but I've combed beaches on three continents; I've snorkelled among corals, and looked through a microscope at xenophyophores from three thousand metres down on the deep seabed. I've visited half the capitals of Europe and lived in one of them, while Ganny's never even been on the Tube.

The boat was Gampa's but the cottage was Ganny's, left to her in the fifties when her parents died. She was getting on for thirty when Gampa married her and moved in, but she still looks skinny, a mere child, in their only wedding photograph, clutching the arm of a stocky, weather-beaten man of twenty-two. It seems odd to think she'd been married before. *A widow*. The word seems all wrong for the girl back then who's half as wide as Gampa and squinting against the sun, though she grew into it much later in her second widowhood.

Grew into the cottage, too: although it's only her now, she still seems to fill it. But when I think back it was maybe always that way, inside the house. Down at the beach and on his boat, Gampa felt like a giant to me, with his broad jaw and arms like knotted cables, and his great, square hands in constant motion. Indoors, though, he was a very different man: still, quiescent, he hardly seemed to fill the space he stood up in. *A big fish*, they say, don't they, *in a small pond*. And Ganny was always mistress of hers, while Gampa came and went like the shoals he followed, out in his boat to the fishing grounds but back every evening to his chair by the fire. Rather like the fish themselves, in fact. I read how North Sea mackerel in the same way as salmon run each spring and autumn between feeding grounds and spawning grounds a thousand miles apart, drawn by who knows what deep patterning of under-water currents or ancestral memory or DNA, and always to the same square mile of sea.

And here am I, too, swimming back home in the familiar channel. Woodbridge, Melton, Wickham Market. Funny how, in all those years of incanting the names, it never struck me as strange that the station known as Wickham Market should actually be at Campsea Ashe. There's been no car to meet us here since Gampa died. There was no persuading Ganny behind the wheel, and the old Humber rusted under the apple tree for years before it finally disappeared, whether sold or gone for scrap I never knew. There's a taxi firm in Wickham that we normally use but today I can't resist the lure of the lush June lanes, dripping with late afternoon insects and the musk of elderflower. I'll walk.

* * *

Bill was the Aldeburgh boy – have I already said? He was the one with brine in his veins while I am the landlubber, born and raised six miles inland. Most of the Aldeburgh fishermen live in the town, but Bill's family were only the tenants of their two-up two-down in the little flint terrace, one row in from the beach. He had the boat but I had the house, so Blaxhall was where we made our home. It has the feel of seafarer's country, even this far from the coast. From November to March every dip in the lanes seems to fill with water but in summer it's sand that gathers in the hollows.

This is a land of sand. The earth hereabouts is nothing but; it's a wonder anything grows in it at all. On the common it's a pale powder grey, soft as ash and lifted by the slightest breeze, but on the roads it's as golden yellow as any treasure island beach. Every May or June it starts its creeping invasion, sending fingers across the tarmac from right and left. Baked to dust by the sun, it shakes out from around the feet of the bracken and cow parsley, the campion and cuckooflowers which swell the verges. You could almost fancy it the work of strange, secret tides which rise in the night to cover the fields and lanes, then slip away before daylight to leave new spits and sandbars like a signature on the landscape. A land with the imprint of the sea.

The house is never free of it either, however often you sweep. It blows in on the draft through doors and windows, sneaks in on feet and clothes disguised as mud but dries to fall as sand and settle in the cracks and creases of the furniture, and form small dunes, if you'd let it, behind doors and in corners. Once I found a miniature cockleshell, finer than the finest bone china, just lying on the kitchen floor. I'll never know how it came to be there.

* * *

Ganny found a seashell, one time, inside the cottage. She revealed it to me like a secret. She'd kept it safe in her old tartan shortbread tin on the top shelf of the dresser, with her hoard of hag stones and the change for the paper boy on Fridays. Letters, too, tatty and yellowed, bound up in a bundle with string. From her first husband, she said, who died in the war – Frank, his name was – but she never offered to untie them. The shell was perfect and pearly white, as tiny and translucent as a newborn baby's fingernail.

256

Some of the hag stones were ours – Sam's and Jonah's and mine – that we'd found with Ganny down on the beach while Gampa plucked snags of weed from his nets. Don't get your feet wet, she'd say, and end by standing with you, holding hands, with the foam washing over your shoe-tops. The stones only have power to ward off ill luck if the sea has worn right through them. Some have a hole so big they're like a pebble amulet, but others you have to hold up to the light, or against the back of your hand and blow to check if you can feel your breath. The larger ones Ganny strung outside by the cottage door, but the smaller ones went in the shortbread tin. What with her hag stones and her herbs and infusions – willow bark for sprains, clove for toothache, sage for throats, green mint for chests – they might have thought her a witch in the old days. But fishing folk are a superstitious lot, and wouldn't think twice about it. I've seen some of the men loop a hag stone on a string around their neck when they put the boat out. Maybe Billy the Kid should have worn one.

The sun is still like a three-bar fire on the back of my neck although it's nearly six o'clock and the skylarks, from an invisible altitude, are babbling their salute to what's been a blazing day. From unbroken blue three hours ago in London the sky has acquired, arcing in from the west, that high fan vault of rippled cloud that Ganny taught us to call a mackerel sky. It came as a surprise, years later, to discover that it wasn't just her name for it.

Sometimes, scouring the shingle banks for the elusive hag stones, I'd pick up shells. They always held a fascination for me. The budding marine ecologist, Mum would say, even at four years old. Most precious were the helix univalves – the whelks and sea snails – which spiralled round like mini helter-skelters. But I liked the bivalves, too, especially mussels: the many colours of them, green and mauve and indigo like a starling's wing. And the textures: brittle and flaky without, or chalky and calcified, but always liquid smooth within.

Seashells, I learned much later, are not composed of cells as bone is, but are one part protein to ninety-nine parts calcium carbonate: more mineral, in effect, than animal. The way they grow from year to year has a special magic to it: new material is added asymmetrically at one edge only of the shell, in such a way that the newly enlarged structure is always an exact scale model of its younger, smaller self. Auto-similarity, the mathematical biologists term it. And, miraculously, almost every different seashell type can be represented by a three-dimensional model generated from a single, simple equation: compliant, like so many forms found in nature, with the essential rules of geometry.

I told Ganny some of this, a year or two ago, one day when we were cleaning cockles together at the sink. How the pattern was mapped three centuries ago and more by Christopher Wren.

She nodded slowly. 'The man who built St Paul's cathedral?'

'That's right.'

I wondered how much she really understood, but when the cockles were all rinsed she wiped her hands, stood back and nodded again, and said, 'I like to hear you talk, child.'

Ganny had her own theory – and I've never seen it contradicted anywhere – that the layers you see through an oyster shell mark out the years of its life. You could count them, she said, like the rings through a tree trunk. 'If you had a microscope,' I said with a grin, but Ganny wasn't laughing when she said, 'You do.'

Mum's coming back tomorrow, and bringing Sam; Jonah will be arriving, too, tomorrow or the next day, driving down from Aberdeen. But just for tonight it's only me – only me and Ganny.

If a shellfish secretes a fresh mineral layer around itself each year, then the shell that you see, the shell that you touch when you pick it up, is new, but it's still the same creature. It's like the bluebell wood on the track to Farnham Hall, which has been there since the Domesday Book and – who knows? – perhaps for centuries longer. I remember reading that bluebell bulbs have been found which date back to Roman times. Putting up fresh shoots every year for two millennia: different flowers but the same bluebells.

The sand lies deep along here below the tall, banked verges; it kicks up, sun-warm, between my sandaled toes. There's St Peter's, across the field at the foot of Silly Hill. Gampa was never a churchgoer, nor Mum either, but Ganny rarely missed. I used to go with her sometimes for the joy of hearing her sing the hymns – vigorous, word-perfect and completely out of tune. There's a young female rector there now who meets with Ganny's approval. She's the one Mum's been speaking to this week, on the phone.

And now finally here's the cottage: I can see the roof and one gable end, half obscured by the big ash tree. There's no spool of smoke now above the chimney as there would be in the winter. The lane turns; here's the gate. I have Mum's door key with me, but out of habit I stop and call out from the threshold. 'Ganny! It's me.'

I catch the sizzle of the frying pan, the smell of foaming butter, of mackerel and cracked pepper. But instead of the kitchen I make for the stairs.

The bedroom door stands ajar, and through it I see her standing by the window with a tea towel in her hand,

259

wearing the dove-grey cardigan she had on the last time I saw her. She turns towards me, but slowly and not as if I've startled her, and a smile breaks over her face.

Then she is gone, like a fish that catches the sunlight through the water for an instant before it twists away. And there is only spiralling dust, and the room stripped bare, and the piled-up cardboard boxes.